WAR GAMES:
KILL
ZONE
VICKI HINZE

Medallion Press, Inc.
Printed in USA

DEDICATION:

To my Beloved Angels: Kaylin, Alyssa, Logan, Madeleine, Wyatt, and Addie. You are my heart, my sun, my rainbow, you hung my moon and stars. I'll love you forever and ever—and that's a promise. Don't forget. Gran.

Published 2009 by Medallion Press, Inc.

The MEDALLION PRESS LOGO
is a registered trademark of Medallion Press, Inc.

Printed in the United States of America
Typeset in Adobe Garamond Pro

ISBN# 9781934755617
10 9 8 7 6 5 4 3 2 1
First Edition

ACKNOWLEDGMENTS:

As always, there are many to thank for a completed work, and only me to blame for any challenges anyone finds with it. I'm especially grateful for the contributions of:

My husband and hero, Lt. Col. Lloyd Hinze (Ret.).

Brainstorming partners and friends: Debra Webb, Elizabeth Sinclair, and Kathy Carmichael. Thanks for keeping me on track, guys.

Sandie Scarpa, my assistant and master research whiz, who doubles as my resident guardian angel. I don't always slow down enough to show you the appreciation and gratitude you deserve, Sandie, but it is always there in my heart.

My children, who know my every flaw and somehow manage to love me anyway.

It would be impossible for me to write the books I do without the noble men and women of the Armed Forces. You inspire me. Thank you for taking the risks and making the sacrifices necessary for the rest of us to live the lives we do. You're the stuff of heroes in the truest sense of the word, and I thank you from the bottom of my heart--for me, my children, and the future of my grandchildren. God bless and protect each of you-and those home waiting for your safe return!

My humble appreciation to the Medallion Press team for all their effort and energy. You're a blessing!

this mission and not executing their orders were too high, and only unsuspecting innocents would pay them. Who could live with that?

Tiring, her muscles burning, Morgan did her best to stay in position near the yacht. Lightning streaked jagged bolts across the distant inky sky. The storm was definitely rolling in, and when one did, waterspouts typically rode heavy on the outer feeder bands. That could be problematic—though not nearly as much so as the fact that they were getting too close to the outer perimeter of the kill zone. They'd crossed her personal comfort threshold about a click ago. No one in her right mind wanted to be caught in a tornado over water under any circumstances, but while on this mission? And even those not in their right mind wanted no part of anything that could be construed as violating the kill zone. It'd bring out the worst of bureaucracy and political posturing and keep them all tangled in relentless red tape for the duration.

That possibility had Morgan extra nervous. Fighting the target was going to be bad enough. But fighting it and a merciless Mother Nature simultaneously? *Not good; not good at all.*

Finally Taylor whispered, "Move out, Guardian One. Go. Go. Go!"

Silently, Morgan sliced through the rolling waves, narrowing the distance between her and the target's yacht. With a little luck, she would be out of the water and the team would complete the mission and be back on shore before Tropical Storm Lil blew in full-force.

Once the target was hit, it wouldn't take long. *If* the target was hit . . .

Not allowing herself to focus on that possibility, Morgan whispered into her lip mic, "Verify coordinates. Exact positioning mandatory."

Taylor Lee answered. "Twelve-point-two-two-one miles."

Anything beyond twelve miles was legally considered international waters. "We're cutting it pretty close, Home Base." Morgan would have felt better with a little more of a pad. Even half a nautical mile would have helped remove the inevitable skepticism. Two-tenths of a mile was a sliver that left them wide open to criticism. Some bastard would definitely exploit it and take exception, too. And not necessarily a bastard from the enemy's side of the fence.

Politics was always an issue. It shouldn't be, but it was. If Morgan ever doubted it, which she hadn't, she would only need to look at the S.A.S.S. headquarters to prove it. A political pissing contest between Commander Drake and the Providence base commander was exactly how the S.A.S.S. ended up plunked into a shack in the middle of no man's land when there was plenty of terrific office space for its headquarters available on base at Providence. That one Commander Drake clearly lost, but she did win the command, which is what had ticked off the base commander in the first place. He wanted the job; she got the job. Political.

"I know we're close, but it can't be helped," Jazie responded.

Taylor agreed. "We've got what we've got, and that's two-tenths."

Morgan waited for Commander Drake to agree. Without that half-mile pad, team consensus just wasn't good enough. Morgan wanted command support.

"It is what it is, Guardian One," Drake said.

That was good enough. The commander didn't like it any more than Morgan did, but she'd accepted it. Higher headquarters had deemed this a high-priority mission, and while that designation gave the commander and Morgan and her team extra latitude to be lax on some of the regulations, all bets were off on them breaching the kill zone.

Experience proved all bets were off, too, on any high-priority mission going down according to plan. *Anything* could happen. And on this specific high-priority mission, it was almost a certain bet something unanticipated *would* happen.

Morgan's S.A.T.—Special Abilities Team—wasn't performing a routine mission.

It wasn't going up against an ordinary adversary.

And it wasn't tasked with neutralizing an ordinary target.

"He's topside," Taylor Lee whispered. Tension elevated her tone a full octave. "Target is on deck. Repeat. Target is on deck."

"Take him out, Guardian One," the commander said, her voice hard, anxious, and urgent. "Do it now."

That urgency, too, Morgan understood. The longer the delay, the greater the odds the target would pick up on the S.A.T. team being on site, and if he did, the odds were astronomically favorable that he'd successfully turn the mission into a bloodbath. He wasn't a rookie. His instincts were professionally honed; he was an expert in neutralization missions. And Morgan and her team were functioning in a capacity that fell far outside their normal area of expertise. That was a huge disadvantage for them to absorb generally, but against a professional of his caliber, it translated specifically to *deadly*.

Unfortunately, tackling this mission had been officially deemed essential and critical. The honchos up the chain of command had determined that the S.A.T. team's participation couldn't be avoided. The mission, they felt, could not be accomplished without the team's special abilities. Unfortunately, the president agreed.

Morgan understood that. She didn't like it, but she understood it. Still, she was a psychologist, an intuitive one, a civilian subject-matter expert who acted as a consultant to the S.A.S.S. and Commander Sally Drake. Morgan was not a typical S.A.S.S. operative assigned to interventions or to terrorist-response missions. The same was true of her team members, Jazie and Taylor Lee, who also had special cognitive skills.

They were all three good at what they did. Damn good—or Commander Drake wouldn't tolerate them, much less welcome them as one of her units. But, while the team members had trained for hand-to-hand combat, it wasn't among the skills at which they excelled or even ones they used frequently in their routine consults. Yet their special ability skills were what made activating them on this particular mission necessary, and the bean counters had projected their success by a reasonable margin, provided they acted alone and avoided hand-to-hand combat.

Morgan couldn't take offense to the caveat; facts were facts, and she agreed with the bean counters. The bigger the team, the greater the odds the target would spot them before they could accomplish the mission and, if reduced to hand-to-hand combat, her team would be pretty well screwed.

Actually, with just three-to-one odds against this specific target, they were also apt to end up pretty well dead.

Fear shimmied up her spine and turned the taste in her mouth sour. She swallowed hard, shook the splashing water from her face. Holding back a salt-induced sneeze, she took aim and sighted the target through her scope. *Don't miss, Morgan. Whatever you do, don't miss . . .*

The live version of the photographed man she'd seen during the mission briefing stood on deck, half-facing her. The photos of him had been good—strong angular face, black hair, gray eyes, about six-two and put together like fantasy personified—but compared to the real thing the photos paled. Animated, the man was drop-dead gorgeous.

Damn shame. Morgan leveled him in her crosshairs.

The first guy she'd seen in a year that snagged her attention, and she had to shoot him. *Didn't it just figure?*

She rolled with a wave, steadied her aim, and then fired.

He crumpled to the deck.

"He's down," Taylor Lee responded before Morgan could, relaying to the Apache and Home Base. "Target is down."

Morgan released her tension, letting a shuddered breath escape through her teeth. Relief swelled and expanded inside her until the knots in her stomach loosened their clench. "Confirmed," she reported. "The target is down."

Thank God.

CHAPTER 1

"Is everyone all right?" Colonel Drake asked.

Morgan looked back at Taylor Lee, sliding fully behind the steering wheel in the boat. She shot Morgan a thumbs-up, and she relayed to Home Base. "We're fine, Commander."

Sally Drake had been as nervous as the rest of them about the S.A.T. team penetrating to pull an interception, but when orders to activate the S.A.T. had come down from Secretary of Defense Reynolds himself and he'd explained the urgency and stakes, she'd had no choice but to execute them. Neither had Morgan.

"Good," Commander Drake said, clearly relieved, and then addressed Jazie in the Apache. "Position note, twelve-point-one miles," she said, and then reeled off the GPS coordinates, making them a part of the official record.

"Zone compliance is verified. Move in, 248. Guardian Two, position and prepare to board the vessel."

Morgan closed the gap between her and the *Sunrise,* then hauled herself out of the water and up the stern's metal ladder, primed to fire on any opposition. Intel had reported the target as traveling solo. Word he'd left behind was that he'd been storing it for his brother, Bruce, while Bruce had been serving in Iraq. Now Bruce was back in Magnolia Beach, Florida. Time to return the boat. The story checked out, so far as it went, but mistakes happened in the shadowy intelligence realm, and Morgan wasn't ready to assume the traveling-solo report was also accurate and land herself and her team on some killed-in-action statistics list.

The target lay face down, sprawled on the deck. His arms were extended, his face turned toward her. The tranquilizer was potent and should have taken effect within seconds after he had been hit, but drop-dead gorgeous was also drop-dead deadly. Extreme caution was not only warranted, but to ensure her team's survival, it was required. Her finger on the trigger, Morgan hung back out of reach for a long moment and watched him intently for any signs of movement. Seeing none, she inched closer . . .

Lightning flashed. He sprang to his feet and lunged at her.

Adrenaline shoved through her veins. Her heart pounded in her ears. She feinted left, dropped and rolled, swung her gun up, and looked into his eyes. *Ice-cold.*

Riddled with rage. Instinctively, she recoiled, squeezed the trigger, and fired again.

Caught full in the chest, he flew backward off his feet. His head clipped the steering console, and he crashed hard, hitting the deck with a dull thud.

The impact shouldn't have been significant enough to take him off his feet. Morgan glanced down; he must have slipped on the wet deck.

Regardless, this time, he was lights out and staying down.

Rattled, Morgan blew out a held breath, settled down enough to get her heart back into her chest where it belonged, and then transmitted her report. "Target was faking it, Home Base," she said, trying to keep the tremor out of her voice. "But he's down now."

Taylor Lee hit the throttle and sped across the water in their boat, quickly closing the distance between her and the yacht. She tied off on the *Sunrise* and then climbed aboard and joined Morgan on deck. Confirming with a quick look that the man was down and out cold, Taylor grunted. "Missed him the first time, eh?"

"You think?" Morgan glared at her. He'd come close to knocking her on her ass, and while she was decent at defending herself, she wasn't foolish enough to believe for a second she could take him one-on-one. He wasn't using it in his current job, but he'd had the same training she'd had plus a lot more, and he had size, reach, weight, and strength on his side. He'd have pulverized her within seconds. Yet none of that bothered her as much as not getting the job done with her first shot.

She would have sworn she had caught the man in the neck. She'd have bet her life on it, in fact, and being wrong right now, when she already felt under-qualified for the mission and on shaky ground, played hell with her confidence. Could she trust her judgment at identifying the target by intuition when she couldn't trust that same intuition on a simple shot she had fired at the man?

Taylor squatted beside him and patted him down. "No weapons."

"Means nothing." He either hadn't expected trouble or wanted to appear as though he hadn't.

She looked over and up at Morgan. "You searched the vessel yet?"

"Not yet." Hell, she had barely recovered from the near miss, and she wasn't at all sure that if she tried to move now her legs would hold her. As far as she was concerned, the regular S.A.S.S. operatives could keep their jobs and the anxiety that came with them. *Too intense.* Morgan was quite happy with her tamer psych consults. Her team rarely worked directly with individual opponents, just offered profiles or insights usually. And exposure wasn't nearly so dramatic or stressful when the subjects were on your side.

The clopping sounds of the Apache's props grew louder. Stirred up, the balmy wind tugged at her eyelids and skin and, in short order, the aircraft hovered overhead. Morgan cupped her hand at her brow to shield her eyes, and glanced up. Jazie dropped a line from the chopper's open door to the *Sunrise's* deck and then took it down.

She landed lightly on the deck, motioned in a wide circle above her head for the Apache to give them some space, and then turned to Morgan. "I can't believe it." Her tone turned incredulous, and her eyes stretched wide. "You *missed* him with your first shot?"

"So it seems," Morgan said through clenched teeth, definitely prickly. They'd give her hell about this for a solid month.

Sighing inside, she spoke into her lip mic, "Give us half a click, 248." She couldn't yet release the chopper, but she did need to take precautionary measures to preserve any evidence onboard, should the target prove to belong to their adversary, Thomas Kunz.

Now that the target was down, she could breathe again, but it was no sin to admit that she'd been scared stiff. Seasoned operatives had quaked at going toe-to-toe with Kunz. He held the undisputed votes of the Department of Defense, Homeland Security, and the S.A.S.S. as public enemy number one. Anyone with sense had a healthy fear of the ruthless killer.

The chopper pulled away, cut a wide arc, and waited. Its sounds weakened to a dull roar in the night. The wind direction had shifted. Tropical Storm Lil was definitely on the move. Morgan watched the lightning in the distance.

In the last half hour, the outermost feeder band had moved substantially closer; their timeline had shrunk by at least half.

"Yeah, she missed," Taylor Lee piped in, refusing to let it go. Shooting Morgan a smarmy look, she added a sing-song lilt to her voice. "I'm seeing lots of time at the firing range in your immediate future."

Morgan took the heat without comment, which wasn't easy, and let go of the opportunity to remind Taylor Lee that she was already the better shot. That's why she'd been in the water. "Just check the vessel."

"Why?" Taylor placed her palm flat on the back of the target's head. "Jazie's taking her in. She should do it."

Tucking her long blond hair inside her shirt, Jazie tugged her collar up and her black stocking cap down on her ears, ignoring Taylor and telling Morgan, "If you don't mind, I would rather do it myself. If I'm taking her to port on my own, I want to know no one else is here."

"Jazie Craig." Fiery and outspoken, Taylor Lee slid Jazie a blistering glare that should have dropped her as cold as the target. "Are you saying you don't trust me to search this vessel?"

Oh, boy. Here it came. Morgan ground her teeth and prepared to pull rank to restore peace and get them back on point. Fortunately, Jazie read her mind and handled it on her own.

"Of course not." Ever diplomatic, she effortlessly blew off Taylor's heated question and toned down the tension with a smile. "I'm saying I'd rather bet my life on a check I've run myself than on one anyone else has run."

Getting the message but still taking exception, Taylor turned to Morgan. "Are you going to let her talk to me like that? We're a team here. What good is a team without trust? You're our fearless leader—and my damn maid of honor. Defend me, Morgan."

Damn it. Did they have to go through this nonsense now? "We have trust, but Jazie also has a point. It's her neck on the line." Morgan held off completely speaking her mind and shrugged, electing instead to shift the topic and get back to business. "You have been pretty preoccupied since this latest engagement to . . ." Morgan blanked out. "What's his name again?"

"Rick," Taylor said from between her teeth, clearly agitated. "I'm marrying this one, okay? So knock off pretending you can't remember who he is."

"Sorry," Morgan said and meant it. But her forgetting the new guy's name wasn't a pretense *or* as horrific—even for a maid of honor—as it might seem. Actually, it was ridiculously easy to understand, and even Taylor would see that if it were happening to anyone else's fiancé.

In the three years they had been a team, Taylor Lee had been engaged at least half a dozen times. But while she loved engagements, she wasn't so hot on actual marriage, and so she'd yet to make it to the altar. Now some would consider that odd, but when you have special skills, you also have special challenges. No one understood that like someone else with special skills and special challenges. So while the three of them had started out as professional associates, they also had become true friends. And in situations like Taylor's frequent engagements, true friends bit their tongues and swallowed any skepticism or sarcasm they might ordinarily express. This was a matter of the heart, and one never does anything but fully support true friends on matters of the heart—even when doing so comes at inopportune times and minds should be on other matters, like now, with the target sprawled on the deck. Regarding Taylor's fiancés, Morgan and Jazie had been true friends. They'd kept their mouths shut and had taken turns at being Taylor's maid of honor. She switched men; they switched positions. No problem.

So far, the job had been pretty painless for them both. Taylor tired of fiancés pretty quickly, before the duties got too deep.

"Vessel's secure," Jazie said, emerging from the cabin.

"Great." Morgan looked at Taylor Lee, whose hand was still on the target's back. "You done yet?"

"Yeah." She pulled away and stood up, then backed up a few steps.

Jazie looked over, silently asking whether she should wait or go next. "Go ahead." Morgan nodded at the target, delaying her own examination as long as possible. The unbridled rage in his eyes when he'd lunged at her had been powerful, and she still felt the remnants of it sizzling on her skin. He'd intended to kill her, and if he'd reached her before she'd shot him, he damn well might have. Knowing it still had her shaking inside. She needed to get grounded before scanning him to work past the fear. Otherwise, she would just be wasting her time.

Jazie didn't say anything, but she'd picked up on Morgan's struggle. "Go on, Jaz," she repeated, eager to have it done without discussion. The sooner the mission was put to bed, the happier she'd be.

Silently, Jazie bent down, let her hand hover just above his spine, and swept down his torso to his waist. She paused, and then reversed, brushing up his back to his head. Surprise flickered across her face, the corner of her mouth tilted up, and she glanced at Morgan. A knowing light burning in her eyes, she stood up and then backed away.

"What?" Taylor Lee asked her. "Why the grin? Did I miss something?"

"Wait." Biting her lower lip to downplay her megawatt smile, Jazie gave Taylor Lee a negative nod and lifted her hand. "Go ahead, Morgan."

Intuiting why Jazie was amused, Morgan pulled out her flashlight and stooped down beside the target. She clicked on the light for a millisecond—just long enough to see his neck. The telltale evidence presented itself: a droplet of blood.

"Damn it." That from Taylor Lee. "You *didn't* miss

him with your first shot."

"No, I didn't." Somewhat relieved, Morgan shoved her flashlight back into place at her hip and then scraped her fingertips over his angular face.

Stubble. Lean flesh and bone. Toned, relaxed muscle . . . Nice. Far too nice . . . She backed off, dusted her palms, then tried again, reminding herself he wanted her dead and when he awakened he would want to kill her all over again. That should have provided all the influence necessary, but it didn't, so she reminded herself who he could be: *Thomas Kunz, the most feared terrorist on the planet—or one of his lethal body doubles.*

That sobered her right up, put her mind solely back on business. Opening her mind, she cut her senses loose, giving them free rein. She sank deep, then deeper, beneath and beyond the physical, and then deeper still until she tumbled fully into the nebulous realm of pure sensation . . .

Anger.

Surprise.

Outrage.

She let the feelings flow through her and then slowed down and carefully examined the area just inside his hairline, under his jaw, looking for thin ridges of scars that would signal he'd had plastic surgery. But she found none there, none at his ears or inside the tip of his nose, all of which confirmed her intuitive reaction to him.

"Unbelievable." Obviously impressed, Taylor grunted from beside Jazie. "I can't freaking believe it. It honestly took two tranqs to knock him out?" Admiration tinged her tone, admiration and a little interest that was purely female and purely sexual. "The guy must have the stamina of a bull."

Morgan blanched. If the woman pulled one of her sex-kitten purrs, Morgan might just tranq her.

Jazie tilted her head. A long blond curl escaped her hood and hung down over her shoulder. From around it, she studied his face. "I know you didn't expect a lightweight—not after seeing his photos."

"I'm engaged." Taylor Lee snapped off a couple of photographs of him and the deck for the records, then clamped the camera back to a loop at her waist. "I wasn't . . . noticing assets, only relevant specifics."

"Right." Taylor Lee was full of it. She *always* noticed assets. But being honest—if only with herself—Morgan had noticed, too. And she hadn't expected a lightweight. Still, a two-tranq knockout was a rare thing, especially with a neck shot. She glanced at Taylor Lee. "Noticing or not, it did take two to drop him." Positioning her fingertips at his throat, she checked his pulse and stilled. Strong and surprisingly steady, considering the dosage he had absorbed. An odd tingle started in her fingertips, coursed through her hand and up her arm to her chest. Certainty filled her. Surprisingly breathless and distracted, she ran a quick second scan to double check, dragging only her index fingertips over his face and neck and then through his soft, thick hair.

The sensations were powerful, strong, almost . . . erotic.

Stunned, she drew in a sharp breath and rocked back on her haunches. "Damn it." *Erotic?* Where had that come from? *Who cared?* She blew past it, not wanting any part of it. She'd never reacted personally to a patient in her practice or to a subject in her S.A.S.S. consults, and she wasn't going to start now.

"Damn it, what?" Jaz asked.

Morgan didn't dare answer. But with the risks, she had to confirm, and again tested her impressions. Blessing or curse, they didn't change.

"Two scans?" Taylor asked, lifting both hands, palms up. "What the hell is going on here? Is something wrong with you, Morgan?"

"The water was cold," she lied, grabbing the first plausible excuse that came into her head. If she admitted that erotic stirrings from a target might have interfered with her input and she'd had to scan twice to confirm her own findings, she would never know another moment's peace. Taylor Lee *and* Jazie would see to it, and they well might report it to Colonel Drake, which would be a hundred times worse. As it was, it'd haunt her. She didn't need insult added to injury from anyone else, and doubt was not a welcome thing in an S.A.T. team leader.

"We need to move," she told them. "When he wakes up, we're going to have two hundred pounds of Special Ops-trained, pissed-off man on our hands. I'd prefer it if, when that happens, we have plenty of backup around to deal with him."

"So is he, or isn't he?" Jazie propped her hands on her hips. "Inquiring minds want to know."

"He's the real Captain Jackson Stern." Morgan nodded and looked from him up at Jazie. "If Thomas Kunz tried to substitute himself or someone else as a body double for Stern, he failed."

"You're sure?" Taylor Lee narrowed her eyes. They glistened dark against the smooth rubber cupping her head. "No doubt?"

"I'm positive," Morgan said, as certain of it as she had been that she'd hit him with the first tranquilizer dart. She stood up.

"As positive as you can be without DNA backup," Taylor Lee said.

Morgan nodded, giving her that one, and then swiveled her gaze to Jazie. "What did you get?"

"Not a peep." She shrugged. "Sorry. But I'm not surprised," she said, tilting her head. "The man is unconscious."

No internal dialogue going on for Jazie to tap into and overhear. Logical. Disappointing and expected, but logical. "He is that." Morgan nodded, shifting her focus to Taylor Lee.

"I didn't see a thing." She crossed her arms over her chest. "Like Jazie said, right now he's too drugged out to be seeing any mental images I can pick up. Wish it didn't, but I'm afraid that puts all the weight on you."

It did. Morgan would have liked confirmation from at least one of them, but she wasn't going to get it. Disappointment shot through her, and she gave herself a full second to feel it and then moved on. "It was an outside shot," she reminded them. "We go with what we've got." Morgan nodded at Jazie. "Cut the Apache loose."

"Just a second," Taylor Lee said, a little apology in her tone. "Not that I'm doubting you, but we are just a tenth of a mile inside the zone," Taylor reminded Morgan, shifting her weight foot to foot. "I'd feel a lot better about this if one of us could verify your findings before we lose the option to retreat and recover."

"So would I." Morgan agreed. If further examination proved Jackson Stern was a body double and he was in the U.S., then all kinds of problems would rain down on their heads, which is why the honchos had insisted the S.A.T. team interdict him and verify his identity using their special skills while he was still in international waters. "But that's not happening, so we have no choice but to act on what we've got—"

"What you've got," Taylor Lee corrected her.

"Exactly," Morgan said, a bite seeping into her voice. "And what I've got is that he's the real Jackson Stern."

The only way to prove his identity beyond any doubt was for Dr. Joan Foster to test him with drug therapy, and being pregnant and in her last trimester, she couldn't very well come out here into international waters to intercept the man and administer those tests. He had to be S.A.T. verified and then brought to her. And Morgan had to pray like hell that she was right about him, because if she was wrong . . . Oh, man, she couldn't be wrong.

Jazie signaled, and the Apache peeled off and sped away. The night again grew empty of sound except for the waves crashing against the *Sunrise's* hull and the dull rumble of wind and thunder rolling off in the distance.

"Just so we're clear." Taylor Lee frowned at Morgan. "It's the risks of being wrong I'm doubting, Morgan, not your intuitive abilities."

"Hell, I don't know why you're not doubting my abilities," Morgan said. "I doubt them all the time."

Jazie stepped around an anchor and chain. "Could it be because over three years they've been bulls-eye accurate about 80 percent of the time?"

"Eighty-seven percent," Morgan corrected her, "but it's *which* 13 percent of the time I'm wrong that keeps me doubtful all the time." And scared to death, especially when the costs of being wrong carried consequences this stiff.

"So humble," Taylor Lee said, and then stood up. "That's just as well, I guess. You'd be a pain in the ass with a big head."

"Taylor Lee!" Jazie sighed. "No offense, but you really do need to learn that some things that float through your head are better left floating and not said."

"Why? Truth is truth, isn't it?" Taylor Lee looked

back at Morgan. "So okay. We'll all feel better when Dr. Foster verifies Jackson Stern is really Jackson Stern. Fine. At this point, we can't risk doing anything other than what we're doing."

"Now, I'll agree with that," Jazie chimed in. "Especially not when we're up against Thomas Kunz and G.R.I.D."

None of them were likely to forget this adversary. Kunz was the head of Group Resources for Individual Development, the biggest black-market intelligence broker of U.S. resources, assets, and personnel in the world, and both Thomas Kunz and his organization had committed atrocities so horrendous that no one in the intelligence community could forget them, much less the S.A.S.S. Special Abilities Team tasked with determining the truth.

S.A.S.S. units didn't exist on paper, and the operatives assigned to them were buried in the Department of Defense's Office of Personnel Management, like many covert or paramilitary operatives. The S.A.T.—Special Abilities Team, namely Morgan, Taylor Lee, and Jazie— were buried even deeper. They were civilian consultants and, while everyone in the chain of command had an occasional need for their subject-matter-expert services, not one person in that same chain of command wanted anyone else in or outside the chain to know it, or to even know the S.A.S.S.'s S.A.T. team existed. So Morgan and her team were assigned to Commander Sally Drake because, for reasons of national security, darn few knew the S.A.S.S.

units existed either, and that was that. S.A.T. was official and buried deep, yet accessible to those in the highest circles with security clearances exceeding top secret.

But no matter how deeply they were buried, neither Morgan nor Taylor Lee nor Jazie had a single illusion about Thomas Kunz or G.R.I.D. He knew the S.A.T. existed. And with or without their special skills, he and his multinational, greedy G.R.I.D. henchmen were more than capable of killing every member of the team, or worse, of capturing them and keeping them alive to torture.

Kunz was a master at torture, and the twisted, sick bastard liked it.

Having viewed what was left of some of his victims still curdled Morgan's blood.

Jazie moved beside them. "Well, let's don't linger at getting Captain Stern to Dr. Foster. If it took two shots to drop him, odds are good that he won't stay out the full four hours and, like you said, Morgan, when he wakes up, he's going to be one pissed-off puppy."

Not exactly what Morgan had said, but close enough, and the sooner she got Stern delivered to Dr. Joan Foster, and the farther Morgan got away from him, the better she'd feel. Joan, however, wouldn't exactly relish receiving the Kunz bait.

Once, Kunz had held Joan captive. After he'd killed her parents and grandparents, he'd abducted her husband and son and had threatened to kill them too unless Joan performed behavioral modifications and memory implants as well as other psychological warfare therapies on both Kunz's body doubles and on those in sensitive military and other intelligence-rich positions that Kunz held captive.

Nearly two years ago, an S.A.S.S. unit led by Captain Amanda West had rescued Joan, her husband, and their son. She had been working under Commander Drake ever since, trying to help bring Thomas Kunz and G.R.I.D. to justice. Joan was the first woman alive with the knowledge and expertise needed to successfully deprogram one of Kunz's body doubles. For a long time, she alone could tell the difference between the doubles and the originals. Now she had trained two other doctors, which helped Commander Drake sleep a little easier at night. But the sooner Joan verified that this man was the real Captain Jackson Stern, the better Morgan would feel about her decision to bring him in.

"Going live." She warned Taylor Lee and Jazie she was opening up communications to Home Base again, then stepped back, tilted her lip mic into position, and turned it on, brushing her jaw with the backs of her fingers. "Home Base?"

"Go ahead, Guardian One," Commander Drake said.

"No scarring or other visible signs of plastic surgery noted on the target." By sight or feel, either of which could be inaccurate, they were operating in near blackout conditions. A flashlight-enhanced visual on more than his neck would have made Morgan more secure in her intuitive findings, but prolonged or frequent light was too dangerous; they could be spotted and destroy an opportunity to bring down those ashore who were purportedly waiting in the harbor for Stern's arrival. One shot of light could be attributed to lightning. Any more than that was simply too risky. "I believe it's him."

"That's enough for me," the commander said, then delicately warned Morgan to take no unnecessary risks. "We've already got one corpse, and another individual who could be facing the needle. I don't want any more complications."

Facing the needle? Morgan frowned, confused. "But there is no death penalty." At least there wasn't in the military. The worst penalty that could be inflicted in this case was life in prison.

"If the victim was murdered off-base, then we're out of it. The locals have jurisdiction, and they can—and probably will—put the death penalty on the table."

"But we have possession—"

"For the moment, yes. We do," Drake said. "The locals are being cooperative until we know for a fact where the actual murder occurred. Fortunately, we have a history of good relations there, and we're both cooperating in a joint investigation," she explained but stopped short of sounding convinced that the cooperation would continue indefinitely. "Get the target to the base for further determination. Transport is waiting," she said, then added the coordinates.

"Yes, ma'am." Morgan shoved the lip mic away from

her face. "You heard her." She grabbed Stern under the shoulders. "Catch his feet, Taylor Lee."

Jazie took the *Sunrise's* wheel, and Taylor and Morgan hauled Stern into their little boat then settled in, with Stern prone, Morgan beside him, and Taylor Lee driving. Lightning sizzled, striking eerily close. The smell of it filling her nose, Morgan looked back to the wheel. "Be careful, Jaz." Plenty of reinforcements waited for her, but if for some unforeseen reason Kunz's assassins were there too, anything could happen. He didn't tolerate anything but the best from his associates, and that wasn't good news for anyone up against them.

Jazie smiled and nodded. "No problem."

Praying she was right, Morgan gave the signal. Jazie and Taylor Lee took off in their respective boats, cutting across the rough waves in parallel directions.

"Quit worrying. She'll be fine," Taylor Lee said, speed plastering her skin and pulling at her eyes.

"Of course, she will." Thomas Kunz's assassins expected Stern to be on the *Sunrise* and arriving later at Magnolia Beach's harbor, but Jazie would take the yacht to the bay, dock it, and then turn it over to a forensics team from Providence. They'd do their thing and a joint forces team would take the boat on to the harbor.

Jazie wouldn't be with them. After docking the boat, she would meet the team at the Providence Air Force Base hospital, where Joan Foster would be waiting for Morgan and Taylor to arrive with Captain Jackson Stern. If, as expected, the G.R.I.D. assassins should be waiting for Stern at Magnolia Beach's harbor, members of Task Force 248 would greet them, and they were just itching to do battle. The guys on the task force had as many reasons as the S.A.S.S. to hate G.R.I.D. and Thomas Kunz, and their anger had been building up a head of steam for a long time. Morgan almost felt sorry for the assassins.

Almost.

Thomas Kunz and G.R.I.D. had been responsible for the deaths of too many operatives and too many Americans for Morgan to feel genuine sympathy and not fear. Kunz was stunningly clever, a genius by anyone's standards, and he'd proven it repeatedly in their clashes.

Capturing the would-be assassins would benefit the S.A.S.S. more than killing the lowlifes, but history had repeatedly proven that Thomas Kunz compartmentalized his G.R.I.D. operations and only he and his senior operations manager, Moss, aka Beefy, knew details beyond any individual's operational segment. Not even Kunz's second in command, Marcus Sandross, was privy to all phases of any operation. Unfortunately, neither Kunz nor Moss ever got within striking distance of anyone else to risk being intercepted, though S.A.S.S. once thought it had Kunz safely incarcerated in Leavenworth (it turned out to be one of his body doubles).

Two S.A.S.S. operatives had experienced close encounters.

Captain Amanda West had broken the operation's manager's nose once, and Katherine Kane had gut-wounded him in a G.R.I.D. compound cave in the Middle East. They had dubbed him Beefy and, unfortunately, he had survived the gut wound. Amanda had gone toe-to-toe with Kunz and barely lived.

At least these reports summarized prevailing belief. Kunz was as bad as or worse than Saddam Hussein with his dozen known body doubles. Who knew if any of the S.A.S.S. operatives had ever encountered the real Kunz? That is, besides Amanda, of course, who had originally discovered Kunz was using body doubles to infiltrate high-powered, sensitive government positions. She'd been abducted by Kunz and brought to one of his Middle Eastern compounds, where she ran into her own double in a mock apartment that matched her own home down to the minutest detail.

The shock of that discovery had rocked foreign governments, Homeland Security, the Department of Defense, all the intelligence agencies in the world, and the psychologist in Morgan. Even now it roiled through her, and she cringed against it and all it implied.

Morgan knew Kunz was involved in this mission and in the case that had spurred it and prompted the honchos at higher headquarters to assign the S.A.T. to it. His involvement blanketed her bones with fear and sent her flesh crawling, warning her that a horrific experience such as the one Amanda West had endured could happen again—this time, to her.

Morgan glanced down at Jackson Stern, bouncing against the deck with each wave and roll and pitch of the boat. Or was her intuition wrong? Was Stern really Stern and not a body double? Or had Kunz already successfully struck his first blow and won the battle in their ongoing war?

Either way, one thing still didn't make sense, and it was significant. Why had Thomas Kunz gotten himself and G.R.I.D. involved in a domestic dispute that ended in homicide? No matter the angle, it just didn't compute. Not to foreign or domestic intelligence agencies. Not to the honchos in D.C. Not to Commander Drake. And not to Morgan.

There had to be more to this than murder.

Knowing Kunz, much more. But what?

"Signal." Taylor Lee pointed to a light on the shore.

"ETA?" Morgan shifted focus to the shoreline and guessed their estimated time of arrival to be in about three minutes.

"Three forty-five," she said, honing the time.

Morgan shot a millisecond beam on the light and then double-checked the coordinates Commander Drake had given her on her wrist monitor. They matched; it was their ride. She pulled her lip mic into place. "Got you, Guardian Four," Morgan said, acknowledging the waiting chopper's signal. It would fly them to Providence. "ETA 3:45."

"Roger that, Guardian One."

Recognizing the voice as Captain Amanda West's,

Morgan stiffened. Another chill slithered up her back-bone. Though others were involved, she headed the actual S.A.S.S. team assigned to bringing Kunz and G.R.I.D. down—the team Morgan previously had been brought in on multiple times as a consultant profiler. And the tense pitch in Amanda's tone had Morgan's intuition receiving rapid-fire warnings.

Fear.

Danger.

Death.

Amanda had good reason to fear Kunz, considering the man had held her captive for three months and sub-jected her to horrific torture. He had even buried her alive, and no doubt she couldn't shake knowing that the only rea-son she had escaped with her life was that he had wanted her to escape.

She knew the specifics on the S.A.T. team. She knew their experience, their credentials. She knew Morgan tested off the charts as an intuitive, that Taylor Lee was similarly classified as a psychic who saw things, and that Jazie Craig heard things few other humans could hear; often, mere thoughts, and yet Amanda still feared Kunz would succeed at whatever terrorist activity he was attempting to launch against them through Jackson Stern.

Amanda feared he would outwit them and win—and if he did, then thousands, if not millions, would die.

Unfortunately, Morgan feared the same.

And if he did win, then that opened three questions in her mind.

What would his success cost the U.S.?

How many people would forfeit their lives?

And when the attack was over, how many in the S.A.S.S. and in the S.A.T. would lie among the dead?

CHAPTER 2

Amanda secured clearance and then landed the helicopter on the concrete pad adjacent to the hospital. Double doors on the ground floor of the nearby five-story gray-brick building opened wide, and two burly men dressed in hospital whites rushed out, pushing a gurney. A very pregnant Joan Foster followed them, hair pulled back in a bun, lab coat flapping in the wind stirred by the props.

In short order, the men had Jackson Stern out of the chopper and strapped to the gurney. They each grabbed a side and rolled him through an opening in the roped off area surrounding the pad, across the wide walkway to the building, then on inside using the same doors they'd exited. Joan escorted them down a long, wide hallway, and Morgan and Taylor Lee brought up the rear until the others disappeared with Stern behind broad wooden doors that marked the boundary of Joan Foster's private domain. No one entered it without her express invitation, and that included Taylor Lee and Morgan.

"What we do now?" Taylor Lee asked, coming to a halt.

Morgan stopped beside her and, staring at the wood grain in the solid doors, offered a silent prayer that her intuition had been accurate and the man on the gurney was Jackson Stern. The closer they had gotten to Providence, the tighter the knots had wound in her stomach and the more she had doubted herself. It was fear. Pure and simple, unadorned fear, and the only cure rested in Joan. She would reveal the truth. *God, please don't let me be wrong. Please . . .* A trickle of sweat slid down between Morgan's breasts, and she felt clammy all over. "We do the only thing we can do." She slid Taylor Lee a level look. "We wait."

"Wearing this?" Taylor Lee motioned to her wet suit. "I don't think so. It doesn't breathe."

It didn't. "Borrow a pair of scrubs—a couple pair." Morgan was eager to get out of her wet suit, too. In the water, it was great. Outside it, the suit was hot and itchy. "You know where the linen closet is—around that corner, on the right." Morgan pointed down the hallway. "I'll meet you in the waiting room."

"Works for me." Taylor Lee took off down the hall.

About 2:15 A.M., Commander Drake phoned. "Any word yet from Joan?"

"Not yet." Wearing green scrubs and footies, Morgan hauled herself out of the hard blue chair without complaint. The scrubs and socks beat the wet suit and fins. She walked down the row of chairs toward the door, ignoring the weather report on the TV. Taylor Lee had muted the sound and then promptly dozed off. She'd slept soundly until Morgan's cell phone rang. Now she sat straight up in her chair and stretched like a cat, working the kinks out of her shoulders. "Shouldn't be too much longer."

"No, it shouldn't," the commander said, then added, more to herself than Morgan, "unless she's run into something unusual."

That comment put more knots in Morgan's stomach. In the hallway, she leaned back against the drab wall. A coat of paint wouldn't hurt. Something bright and cheerful would be welcome though, being the ass he was, the base commander, Colonel Gray, would spit nails before making anything on base cheerful or welcoming. "I did have to shoot him twice," Morgan reminded her. "Could be taking longer because of the drugs."

"Could be," the commander agreed. "If Joan had run into anything odd, she would have stopped and called. She has in the past, anyway."

That disclosure had Morgan feeling a bit better. She pushed away from the wall and peeked back into the waiting room. Taylor forked her fingers through her long black hair. Typically sleek and smooth, it was rumpled and no doubt her head itched too, after being confined in the wet suit. They'd both be more comfortable after a shower.

"Jazie there yet?"

Morgan glanced around the edge of the door to a small table in the corner next to the TV. Taylor moved over to it, then slid onto a chair on one side. "Okay. I'm ready."

Jazie sat down across from her on the other. Keeping an eye on the tropical update on Lil, Jazie dealt from a deck of cards and they began their umpteenth game of spades. "She got in about two hours ago. We're together in the waiting room."

"I know you're all exhausted, Morgan, but I have to ask you to hang around until we hear from Joan. We're on hold on our next move until we do."

"No problem." Morgan rubbed her neck, trying to sound as if she meant it. Fighting the wave action in the gulf had her more than exhausted; she was positively bone weary. "After we hear from Joan, we should take a look at the body."

"That can wait," she said.

"Maybe, but we don't know that." Morgan hedged. "We could lose control of the body."

"True." The commander hesitated. "But that's not the reason. Tell me why you wouldn't rather get some rest first and then examine the body. The *real* reason."

Leave it to Drake. Gift or experience, she was too astute by half. "Frankly, since I knew the victim, I would rather not have to examine the body at all." Her mouth went dry. She licked at her lips then added, "It makes doing my job more difficult." Morgan bounced back against the wall, knowing that the commander's concern stemmed from a different source. She thought being tired would diminish their special abilities—and it might. Better to address that before being called out for holding back again. The commander had a notoriously short fuse. "We could have to scan twice," Morgan admitted, rubbing the back of her neck with the palm of her hand.

"Which doesn't do a damn thing toward explaining why you want to do it now, then," the commander countered.

"No." Morgan stared at a brown water spot on the tile ceiling. "I guess it doesn't."

"Don't make me ask for the complete truth a third time, Dr. Cabot."

"No, Commander."

"Why examine the body now?" she asked, sounding more curious than angry. "Why not just wait?"

Whether or not Colonel Drake would understand was anyone's guess, but in her three years as commander of the

S.A.T. team, when Drake had doubts, she generally kept them to herself. Morgan suspected doing that took a great deal of restraint, and she respected her for making the effort, so Morgan decided to at least attempt to explain her rationale. "I wasn't attempting to deceive you. I was just trying to give you something true and easy to accept."

"Spare me," Drake retorted. "I'm more pliant than I look."

Tough as nails came to mind. Giving in, Morgan went to the bottom line. "When someone dies suddenly and it's a violent death, they often leave a strong . . . imprint, if you will. It fades over time to just a trace that's hard to detect. Kind of like a footprint in the sand. At first, it's clear. Then it's disturbed, and finally it disappears."

"I see," Commander Drake said, her voice devoid of judgment. "So your best odds of picking up anything— impressions, sounds, images—are by scanning the victim as soon after death as possible."

Total grasp. The woman never ceased to amaze Morgan. "Right. When the imprint is strongest."

"Mmm. It's a bit of a trade-off, then," she said more to herself than Morgan, reasoning through it. "When you're tired, you pick up the least sensory input, but now is when the victim's body is sending the strongest signals you can pick up."

"Yes, that's right."

"So it's a crapshoot, then, on which way it goes."

"Exactly." Morgan cleared her throat. "We won't know which proves strongest, the S.A.T. team's abilities or the victim's imprint, until we actually examine the body."

"I understand, Morgan," she said. "For the record, that's not lip service. This is similar to gut instinct. You never know if and when it's going to work—only that when it has, it has."

Relieved, Morgan agreed. "Yes."

"And if it doesn't work now, then nothing prohibits you from trying later, right?"

"That could be the case, but often subsequent impressions are weaker than the initial one. I don't know why."

"Hmm, could be like first impressions for the rest of us. If it's good, it takes a lot to change it—and if it's a bad one, it's nearly impossible to alter."

"A lot like that, yes." Morgan smiled. It was positively refreshing to not be asked to help and then have doubts about you or your assertions tossed in your face at every turn. If her parents had been able to harness half of Sally Drake's insight, Morgan would have lived an entirely different life. But to do that, they had to at least start with open minds, a trait neither of them possessed.

Of course, if they had been open-minded, Morgan likely wouldn't be a psychologist today. She had entered the field to better understand herself and her gift because she'd grown up without a single person in her sphere of influence willing to even try to understand. While she was on her path to self-discovery, she had earned a couple of degrees and had decided to use them. Maybe, she'd thought, she could give someone else with a gift the support she had lacked. Especially as a child, her gift had been frightening and confusing. Then 9/11 had happened and she'd been called on to help many more people by defending them and her country, and that was that. The die had been cast, and her course had been set.

"If the man is Captain Stern," Sally Drake said, "he's going to be resistant to giving us any information unless he is made aware of the full circumstances and personally authenticates them."

"Highly likely." Especially considering that Morgan had given him a double shot of tranquilizers. Only an idiot or an idealist would expect him to endure that and then be in an accommodating mood. More than likely he'd go straight to Secretary Reynolds and work his way down the chain of command to Drake.

"Effective on Joan's verification, I'm pulling him into the need-to-know loop on G.R.I.D.," the commander said. "Excluding Darcy and, of course, me, the captain carries a current security clearance that's higher than anyone else's in the S.A.S.S. or on the S.A.T, so full disclosure to him on whatever we've got on this isn't an issue."

That shocked Morgan. Darcy Clark was the intelligence officer for all of the S.A.S.S. units and the S.A.T. She had direct ties all the way up the chain to the president, just like Commander Drake. But why was Jackson Stern's clearance that high? "I wouldn't have suspected his clearance to be at that level," Morgan said, speaking frankly. "If memory serves me, he's not even active duty—he's a reservist now." Highly unusual. Ordinarily, his security clearance would be reduced to match the needs of his current position.

"You know as well as I do that things in our world are seldom as they appear." Commander Drake permitted herself a little sigh. "The fact is, two years ago Secretary of Defense Reynolds issued a personal directive on Stern. I don't know why." She paused and chose her words with care. "I can't say I'm comfortable not knowing why, but I've just spent forty minutes on the phone with the secretary and another twenty minutes on this with General Shaw," she said, naming her immediate boss at the Pentagon. "They're not filling in any blanks for me, but they are in agreement on Stern. If he's the real McCoy, he's authorized for full disclosure."

"Maybe it's because of his brother and his current situation," Morgan suggested, thinking aloud. The honchos could be taking all possible steps to avoid any five o'clock news mudslinging at the military.

"Could be. But, frankly, they didn't say and I didn't ask. They issued the orders, and I'm following them. They want full disclosure to Stern and his direct involvement in resolving this situation."

"Direct involvement? Don't you find that odd, considering the relationship issue? Seems they'd be concerned about accusations of conflict of interest, and order the exact opposite."

"I find many things odd. From our perspective, one would think they would," she agreed with a grunt, as if stretching for something. "But their perspective is different. There could be a thousand reasons they've taken this position—we are dealing with Thomas Kunz—but whatever their reasons, it's their call. Their rationale isn't germane to my orders."

"Which makes it not germane to my orders," Morgan said, extending the directive down to her level. "All right, Commander." This should be an experience to remember. Considering the circumstances, the man would make her life a living hell. "I'll do my part, but I wouldn't expect him to be enthused about working with me."

"Hell, Morgan, of course he won't. You did shoot him. Twice."

She wrapped her arm around her body, flattened it against her abdomen. "Exactly."

The commander grunted, clearly amused. "My gut says he'll get over that quickly enough. The man is a professional."

"No doubt." The question was, a professional *what*? It sure as hell wasn't anything reported in his dossier. Not with his security clearance and a directive directly from the

Secretary of Defense. Way too much clout for a junior captain. Way too much.

"Darcy did say to warn you . . ."

Another warning? Morgan was almost afraid to ask. "About what?"

"Captain Stern," Drake said. "Expect more than the usual upset in your initial briefing. Apparently, he has always been extra protective of his brother."

Terrific. Morgan shoots him twice, kidnaps him, subjects him to medical testing he doesn't understand, and when he's done with all that, then she gets stuck giving him the initial briefing and breaking more bad news to him. The worst kind of bad news. And then she gets to work with him.

The man would make her life a living hell *and* hate her guts forever.

And she couldn't blame him. Shoes reversed, so would she. Naturally, she'd had to muck things up even more. He would be the one to snag her attention and bring on freaking erotic sensations. *Perfect. Bloody damn pathetically perfect.* "Okay, Commander," Morgan said. There was nothing she could do about any of this, so the quicker she accepted it and pressed on, the less energy she'd waste on something she couldn't change. "Thanks."

Jazie and Taylor Lee had stopped playing cards and sat staring at her. Feeling anything but okay, she signaled them a thumbs-up, and they returned to their game.

"I'll be down there in about ninety minutes," the commander said. "I'll meet all of you downstairs."

In the morgue. It was the only thing downstairs. "Yes, ma'am."

The line went dead. Morgan closed her cell phone and then dropped it into her pocket. "Commander's on her way in." She lived north of the Regret outpost, so her ninety-minute estimate meant she wasn't ready to walk out the door.

Jazie shuffled the cards. "Do we all have to be here?"

Morgan nodded. "I'm afraid so."

Taylor Lee groaned and slumped over the table, her long black hair spilling over her shoulder. "Damn it, I want a bed."

"Complaining won't help, Taylor Lee." Jazie plunked down the ten of spades. She grumbled something unintelligible, then added, "So we're parked here until further notice."

Morgan returned to her seat. "For a while longer, anyway."

That while longer spent cooling their heels in the waiting room turned out to be until 4:30 A.M., when a very weary Joan Foster waddled into the waiting room. Rumpled and totally wrung out, she touched Morgan's shoulder, awakening her from a light doze.

Morgan stiffened on the hard chair, blinked, and then screwed up her courage to ask Joan the question she most wanted answered. "Well? Is he who I think he is?"

Joan nodded. "He is Jackson Stern," she said, stifling

a yawn. "And he has no idea of anything currently going on with G.R.I.D., though he does of course know G.R.I.D. exists."

How did he get into the need-to-know loop on G.R.I.D.? And why didn't Commander Drake know it? She knew everything about the U.S.'s interactions with Thomas Kunz and G.R.I.D . . . or so they both had believed until now. "Where is he?"

"Getting dressed." Joan sat down on a chair beside Morgan and rubbed her cracking knees. "Don't worry. Dr. Vargus and two orderlies are with him. Jackson Stern isn't going anywhere, but I have to tell you, the man is not in a kindly mood."

"Can't blame him there."

"No, we can't," Joan agreed. "But under the circumstances, we didn't have a lot of choice. Still, I wouldn't bet on that bringing him around."

They really hadn't had any choice. They had to know the true identity of whom they were dealing with on this. Morgan stilled. "Why does he know about G.R.I.D.?"

Joan tried but failed to suppress a shiver. "I have no idea." She gazed at Taylor Lee, sleeping on chairs close to the T.V. and then dropped her voice so only Morgan could hear. "Even under drug therapy, he refused to disclose that. He automatically reverted to a verbal loop of his name, rank, and social, and nothing I tried broke it." A twinkle of fascination lighted her eyes. "I've never seen anything like it."

Morgan gave that a moment's thought. "Deep-seated programming?"

"That'd be my guess, but I can't be sure." She frowned. "I have access, I thought, to everything used in psych-ops. But this is new to me."

Alarmed by that, Morgan asked, "Are you sure it's ours?"

"Ninety-nine percent." She swept her short hair back from her face. "I know Kunz had nothing like it when I was there, and he hasn't had time to develop something this significant in the time I've been gone."

"It's been two years, Joan," Morgan reminded her.

"True," she said, "but I would have run into some precursor of it on other operatives the S.A.S.S. has brought in, and I haven't. No program retains final form from the onset. There are always glitches or security leaks that require adjustments."

"Of course."

"One thing I know for a fact is that this is not a precursor. If it were, I'd have found a way to break the loop. I tried, and didn't."

So it had to be theirs and not G.R.I.D.'s programming, which was good news, and apparently the technology's floor was at security levels above top secret. "Did you talk to Colonel Drake about it?"

"I phoned her just before I came in here," Joan said,

half-collapsing into the chair beside Morgan. "She wasn't surprised." Joan rubbed at her ankle. It was swollen to double its normal size. "I took that as good news."

"So do I." Colonel Drake knew what this loop programming was about then. It wasn't unknown to her. "You need to get checked for that swelling. Has all the signs of pitting edema."

"It does." She sighed, propped her hands over her extended stomach. "Being on my feet for sixteen hours straight is not a pleasing thing in my condition."

"That's rough in any condition," Morgan said. "Better watch it or you'll end up on bed rest these last few weeks."

"Oh, a woman can dream . . ." She smiled. "Where's Jazie? I assumed she'd be here with you."

"She is," Morgan said. "Her low-fuel light was on, so she ran down to the cafeteria to scrounge up some food."

Joan smiled. "That one is always hungry."

She was.

Morgan let her gaze slide over to Taylor Lee. A few seats down, she slumped sideways, feigning sleep, but she flinched. Morgan pretended not to notice that movement, though she herself felt plenty surprised that Jackson Stern knew about G.R.I.D. Odd, when fewer than two hundred people in the entire U.S. government were aware of it.

"And that one never eats." Morgan looked back at Joan. "I can't wrap my mind around why a reservist Hurricane Hunter is in the need-to-know loop on G.R.I.D. Or why his security clearance is out in the stratosphere." Morgan lifted a shoulder. "It makes no sense."

Joan leaned toward Morgan and again dropped her voice. "You know he was active duty before going to Keesler as a reservist."

Keesler Air Force Base was in Biloxi, Mississippi. Home of the Hurricane Hunters. Morgan nodded. "I read that in the mission briefing profile."

"Then you know when he was active-duty he was assigned to Tactical?"

Again, Morgan nodded. That much she'd been told in the pre-mission briefing. Not what he'd done in Tactical, but that he'd been assigned to it.

Joan sent Morgan a steady look. "He worked for Nathan for a while."

"Nathan Forrester?" Morgan knew Nathan. He had been dating Kate—Captain Katherine Kane—for a good while now. Theirs was one of the few long-distance relationships Morgan had encountered that actually seemed to work.

Joan nodded, sharing a knowing look.

He and his unit had had direct contact with G.R.I.D. operatives in a couple of their foreign compounds, mainly in the Middle East. Morgan had worked profiles for them. "So does Kate know Jackson, then?" She was a senior S.A.S.S. operative on Amanda's team who specialized in explosives and biological and chemical warfare weapons systems. Kate was very competent, very thorough, and very short-tempered. But if she knew Jackson Stern, then why hadn't the commander assigned her to the post-interdiction mission? Stern wouldn't be nearly as snarly with Kate—and if he was . . . well, Kate could out-snarl anyone Morgan knew.

It seemed as if every new bit of information brought more questions than answers, and that made the already tense Morgan very uneasy.

"I doubt she knows him. Stern left Tactical about two months before Kate went over to Nathan's unit to assist on the G.R.I.D. mission where she met Nathan."

"Too bad." It was, but at least it made sense. "Stern has to be doing more than hunting hurricanes, Joan."

Again she nodded. "Common sense says so, but what exactly he is doing, I have no idea." That clearly irritated her.

It shouldn't. In their jobs, often what you didn't know outweighed what you did. Yet when your life was in another's hands, it was nice to be able to gauge how competent and capable those hands were. But with Secretary Reynolds and General Shaw being closed-mouthed about Stern, she likely never would know and that just had to be accepted. Ironic. Their jobs required them to question everything and in many areas to simultaneously trust implicitly on nothing more than faith. "Whatever he does can't be significant to our situation, or the honchos would have briefed us."

"One can but hope. But I wouldn't bet the bank on it." Shifting her weight, Joan gained her feet with a little groan and rubbed her lower back. "I'd better get in there. He should be through dressing by now."

"Is he stable?"

"Very. Bitter, and as secretive as one would expect considering his past positions, but there's more, too," Joan said. "Whatever it is, it didn't fall within the perimeters of our professional discussion, so all I can tell you is that it's personal in nature and he's beyond reluctant to discuss anything that even touches his private life."

His private life. The very part Morgan would have to address in her briefing with him. Morgan frowned. If he'd been reluctant before, he would be militant after he heard what she had to say. Her stomach flipped. "Great."

"Sorry." Joan shrugged.

"Me, too." Morgan had always been lousy at conveying bad news. A medical school colleague once told her she had to ignore how news would impact others; had to keep their reactions from becoming personal. So far Morgan had failed at doing that, though she'd tried. The problem was in not knowing whether to hope one day she could do it, or to fear one day she would. *A compassionate wreck or a cold bitch. Which should she choose?* Frankly, neither sounded healthy.

"Your duties on this really suck." Joan clasped Morgan's upper arm. "I know you hate being the one to tell him. If it helps, I hate giving out bad news, too."

Morgan met Joan's gaze, saw the dark circles beneath

her eyes, and recognized the shared dread burned in them. "It never gets easier."

"No, it doesn't." Joan resented that, too. "I'm not sure which is worse. Telling someone they're dying, or telling someone that somebody they loved has died. Both leave me a total wreck for a week."

"I'm down to three days," Morgan confessed. "*If* I work really hard to tell someone who is going to live. If not, it drags on." She took in a deep breath, then let it out slowly. "This one is going to be bad."

"It's a double whammy," Joan agreed. "You shot him."

"Twice."

Joan flinched. "Ouch."

"Yeah."

"Sucks," Joan said again. "But you'll get through it."

"One minute at a time." Morgan repeated an old med school saying. The students were run ragged, and when it got unbearable, they'd stop thinking in shifts and start thinking in hours. Getting through the next hour. And when that seemed too hard, they'd drop back to one minute. Just get through one minute. And then the next. And then the next. Everyone in her class had used the method more often than any of them would like to remember, much less admit.

"Or if that's too long, one second," Joan said.

"Yeah." Morgan swallowed hard, and shifted the

topic. "You look exhausted."

"I'm pretty wrung out," Joan confessed. "These sessions can get rough, and right now I just don't have the stamina I need to do them."

Jazie walked in, carrying chips and sodas, in time to hear that remark. "No salty chips for you," she told Joan. "If your ankles swell much more, we're going to have to call them thighs."

"Nasty thing to say to a woman in this delicate state." Joan smiled and looked down, pivoted her foot side to side. "True, however. They are enormous."

Morgan couldn't disagree. "When is the baby due?"

"Three weeks." Joan let out a little groan and parked her forearm on her stomach. "I am *so* ready."

"I'll bet." Pregnancy was rough in winter, but going through that last trimester in the summer with the heat and humidity running at record highs had to be sheer hell. "Get off your feet for a while."

"I'm on my way home now. Dr. Vargus will type up our report. If I'm lucky, I'll get to see Jeremy before he goes to day camp."

Jeremy was Joan's seven-year-old son. Very bright and very serious, thanks to a couple of years of living as a hostage in a G.R.I.D. compound. "Tell him hello for me."

"I will." Joan walked back toward the double doors. Her hand resting on the metal plate, she stopped and looked back at Morgan, winked, then spoke to Taylor Lee. "You can wake up now, Taylor Lee."

"Who's sleeping?" Taylor said, taking a brazen tact on her eavesdropping. "I've been awake the entire time."

"Yes, I know," Joan said, a weary smile tugging at her lips. She glanced at Morgan. "He'll be out in a few minutes. Feel free to use my office, if you want privacy to talk."

"Thanks." Jackson Stern would need that privacy. What she had to say was going to put him in a world of hurt.

Jackson Stern walked through the double doors and into the waiting room looking more angry than Tropical Storm Lil footage. His gray shorts and once-white shirt had dried stiff from the salt spray. His black hair was wind-tussled, clinging to his broad forehead and ears, and sheer fury flashed in the depths of his flinty gray eyes. "Well." He paused, clenched his jaw, and glared at each of them. "Which one of you assassins is going to explain what the hell is going on here?" His gaze landed on Morgan, and recognition lit. "You." He jutted his jaw and hiked his chin. "Start talking."

He knew she had shot him, all right, and his tone rivaled the wind howling outside the bank of windows on the waiting room's far wall. Wouldn't that just do wonders for their discussion? *Crowning glory.* Morgan glanced at

Taylor Lee and Jazie. "Please go meet the commander downstairs," she said in her best formal tone, hoping he'd remember sooner rather than later that he was a professional. "Captain Stern and I will be with you shortly."

Jazie looked worried about leaving Morgan with him. Taylor Lee had that curl in her lips proving she was jealous as hell that she had to leave and miss the fireworks. But both women walked out silently, Jazie giving Stern a friendly nod that he returned with a frosty glare.

Morgan watched them head down the hallway and waited until they turned the corner and their footfalls faded to be sure they were out of earshot. "We need to go where we can speak privately, Captain Stern. If you'll follow me, please . . ."

He didn't budge. "I realize you're a little blurry on details. Otherwise, you'd know who is on your side and you wouldn't have dropped me with a tranq, much less popped me with two of them," he said in a voice dripping sarcasm. He paused, gave the waiting room an exaggerated scan that set her teeth on edge, and then frowned at her. "But has it escaped your notice that there's no one else here, um . . . just who the hell are you?"

"Dr. Cabot," she said, tolerating his smart-ass comments and using her title to put professional distance between them. "You're right, of course. At least, in part."

"Still blurry, I see." He folded his arms over his chest. "Which part?"

Again, she took his tone in stride, but if the jerk swaggered and threw her another barb, she was going to let him have it. Even she was only willing to go so far in this situation. If he didn't have to look hell in the eyes, and if she weren't the one about to put it there, she would have verbally smacked him down already. "We are alone here, but this waiting room isn't private." When she told him what she had to say, he would want that privacy, even if he didn't yet realize it and, when he did realize it, he still wouldn't be grateful to her for it. He'd be too preoccupied with other emotions. Darker, meaner, more relentless emotions.

Dread seized her stomach and compassion slid through her chest, tightening it.

Damn it. Don't feel, Morgan. Don't dare feel . . .

"I see."

He couldn't register anything, except maybe the red haze of anger in his eyes. But she couldn't expect him to feel gratitude toward her now or, for that matter, ever. She had shot him. Twice. And now she was going to deliver a blow that would change his life forever. That, summed up, gave them an unpleasant history. Few in their line of work ever got past unpleasant histories.

He'll remember you forever.

He'd hate her forever. *Damn it, don't care, Morgan. Would you wise up? Don't care. He's just an associate. Get through the mission, finish the case, and close the book.*

Calmer, more in control, she hiked her chin. "As I

said, if you'll follow me . . ."

"Fine." He moved toward the door. "Somewhere private *and* close, Dr. Cabot. I'm typically not a patient man," he said rubbing his neck, where the trickle of blood from her tranq dart still stained his skin. "At the moment, I find I'm even less patient than usual."

"I understand," she said, answering honestly, then walked out ahead of him. Joan's office was close and empty, if small. Someplace where she could put more distance between them, like her own office, would be better. He could react to the news violently, and a little spare room to dodge him could come in handy. But Morgan's office was back on the coast; she didn't maintain an office on base at Providence. The entire S.A.T. team used her private practice's office in Magnolia Beach. Jazie and Taylor ran her office and acted as her assistants, and when not otherwise occupied on missions, Morgan counseled military members who carried top secret or higher security clearances. On occasion, she also counseled members of their families, which was how she had first met the victim who tied her to this case. "This way, Captain." She tensed her shoulders against the daggers he glared into her back.

He fell into step behind Morgan and they moved on down to the first corridor, turned left, continued to the second door on the right, and then entered Joan's office.

Morgan clicked on the light. It was small but, by military standards, it ranked relatively large. There was no window. A worn green leather sofa, chairs, a gray metal desk, filing cabinet—locked, of course—summed up the majority of furnishings. *Generic.* The office could have belonged to anyone, except for the tons of personal items littering the walls and desktop. All files had been secured—a requirement one didn't dare to violate under any circumstances; not in this litigious society—and her blotter was bare except for spiral doodles. "Can I get you a cup of coffee?" Morgan asked.

He frowned at her and didn't bother to try to hide it. "I think I already have enough foreign substances, not to mention adrenaline, in my body—don't you?"

Guilt flushed heat in her chest that swept up her neck. She shouldn't feel it. In her position, he would have done the same thing: his job. But she did feel it. It angered her, and it irritated her. She let the anger flow through her and released it. The irritation, she squelched. Even if he didn't know the pain coming his way, she did, and that bought him a moment of grace. "I expect you do," she said, conceding the point.

Lifting a hand, she motioned to the small leather sofa and then to the two well-worn chairs on the visitor's side of Joan's desk. "Please, have a seat." Morgan walked around and sat down behind the desk, then clicked on the green banker's light. A soft glow spilled over the blotter and warmed the room.

Wary and tense, Stern opted for a visitor's chair and

lowered himself into it.

Rather than using Joan's chair, Morgan sat in the visitor's chair beside him. "I suppose you have a lot of questions."

"Damn right." A muscle in his cheek twitched. "Wouldn't you?"

"Yes, I would," she admitted. "Fortunately, I've been given the necessary authorization to answer them." She swept wisps of her shoulder-length blond hair back from her face. Tons had escaped the topknot she'd twisted into place over twenty-four hours ago. "But for the sake of clarity, perhaps it would be best if I just explained."

He curled his fingers around the padded chair arms as if only his will was keeping them from going for her throat. "By all means," he said, sounding far more controlled than his body language or her intuition signaled. "Brief and succinct," he warned her. "Please."

Morgan nodded. "Have you heard of the S.A.S.S., Captain Stern?"

He didn't answer. His eyes and expression were poker-face blank with no outward signs of recognition, but she intuited his knowledge and his uncertainty beamed through, loud and clear. He wasn't certain of her security clearance.

They could hesitate and trip over ambiguity for hours, or she could make an adjustment. "Let me back up a little," she said, taking a different tack. "I'm a psychologist," she said. "With your security clearance, you know that it can be challenging at times to not be able to speak freely about your experiences. Well, it's my job to listen to those things and more—classified things." She got more explicit. "And to help those having difficulty working through the challenges that come with jobs in our . . . realm . . . constructively."

She paused, but he still showed no reaction. It cost him to bury the questions he burned to ask, so she spared him and went on. "I also assist family members of people in, shall we say, delicate positions. Often they have issues with their spouses' or sponsors' jobs that they need to work through, too."

Again, no reaction—and apparently no clue yet where this was leading or how it tied into his abduction in the gulf.

"I have other duties, as well," Morgan said. "Ones for the S.A.S.S."

Finally, he responded with a noncommittal, "I see."

"No, you really don't." Unable to delay the inevitable any longer, she worried her lip with her teeth. After this next disclosure, he'd probably look at her as if she were out of her mind. Most people she told were skeptical, and even more assumed she was delusional. It normally irked her, but she'd become fairly adept at forcing their less-than-generous opinions to roll off her back. However, he'd snagged her attention. Touching him had given her erotic tingles. It'd been a long time since she'd felt a spark of interest in a man—a bad experience can do that to you. Now, having remembered the pleasantness of it—even if it had come at the worst possible time—she wasn't eager to replace those memories with new ones of him calling her crazy. "I'm sorry I had to shoot you, Captain."

He grunted.

"I had to verify that you were who we believed you were before you could be brought ashore and to the hospital here to verify it."

Lowering his lids, he hooded his eyes. "Who were you afraid I might be?"

"Someone from G.R.I.D." If he knew about the S.A.S.S., he knew about G.R.I.D. Regardless, Kunz's organization definitely had come up during his debriefing with Joan. And, from what Morgan was picking up from him now, he'd made some deductions of his own about the intervention and abduction. "Yes, we feared you could be connected to G.R.I.D."

"As a spy?"

Wily as a fox. "No, Captain." She tilted her chin and looked him right in the eye. "As a body double."

Uncertainty swam across his face. Surprise followed it. "Why?"

"Because Intel couldn't be certain either way. They intercepted communiqués between Thomas Kunz and two of his G.R.I.D. associates, Merk and Stick. Both of those men are new to the S.A.S.S. list of known Kunz associates, but Intel had previously pegged them both."

"So these communiqués claimed I was a body double?"

"No." She laced her hands in her lap. "They warned

that you or your G.R.I.D. double would be returning your brother's boat to Magnolia Beach and that three G.R.I.D. assassins would be waiting for you at the harbor."

"Three?" He looked less angry, but far more troubled.

Understanding why, she nodded. Who wouldn't be troubled at learning they'd showed up on Thomas Kunz's radar?

"Merk and Stick are the would-be assassins?" he asked.

Quick grip on the situation. Impressive. "Yes," she verified. "The third man is new to the S.A.S.S. and to Intel, though he's apparently an established G.R.I.D. operative. Mason is his name."

"Never heard of him," Stern said. His forehead wrinkled, and he frowned. "So am I me, or a body double?"

The question was reasonable. Joan had deprogrammed many operatives who were doubles and had no idea. "You are not a body double."

Relief washed through him. But before he absorbed it, he tensed again. "Why is Kunz after me now? These days, I just fly into hurricanes. I'm no threat to him or his cut-throat organization." Stern rubbed his nape, confused. "If I were still in Tactical, I could better understand this."

The dreaded time was at hand. Morgan paused, gathered her strength, steeled herself to block out her emotions, and then looked him in the eye. "Jackson, we believe the reason Kunz wants you dead is related to your brother," she said softly, addressing him by his given name. News like this was horrific and hard to swallow at the best of times, but it was nearly unbearable when delivered by a stranger. The illusion of an attachment between herself and Stern was better than nothing, and it was the best she could offer.

Puzzled, he stilled. "This is about Bruce?"

Bruce Stern was also a military captain; a biological warfare expert who, less than three months ago, had returned home from an extended assignment in the Middle East. "Yes, it's about Bruce," she said, then added, "and, regrettably, it's about his wife, Laura, too."

"What?" Jackson's puzzlement gave way to shock. "How does Laura fit into this?"

Feeling his concern, both for his brother and his sister-in-law, Morgan battled herself and lost. To hell with the proper reactions. He was terrified down to the marrow of his bones, and what she had to tell him would only make him feel worse. She reached over, clasped his hands in hers, and held on tight. "Jackson, I wish there were an easy way to say this, but there isn't." His pain seeped through her, and she bore its heavy weight.

His eyes dulled. "It's bad."

"The worst," she said, helping him brace. "I'm afraid that Laura has been murdered."

His face bleached white. "Laura? Murdered?" He gasped, blew out a forceful breath. "No. No, that's impossible. No one could ever want to hurt Laura. She's . . .

she's . . . No, that's not possible. I . . . I just talked to her on Sunday."

"She's dead, Jackson," Morgan said firmly. "The ME says she died between midnight and 2:00 A.M. Monday morning."

"Hours." He stared up at the ceiling, seeing far beyond it. "Just hours after we talked."

The truth hadn't yet fully settled in. He was still in shock. "When on Sunday did you talk to her?"

"It was after dark, probably around nine o'clock." He nodded. "Oh, God." He stared at the pool of light spilling onto the desk, and the truth rolled over him in unrelenting waves. For a long moment, he just sat there. Didn't move. Didn't utter a sound. Didn't blink.

Morgan waited. Giving him time to come to terms. Aching for him. Nothing was as bad as this. Losing someone you loved was harder than learning you were dying. She'd seen and sensed that far too many times to doubt it.

Finally, he cleared his throat. His voice had deepened. Grown reed thin from the unshed tears clogging his throat, burning the back of his nose and his shiny eyes. "What happened to her?"

He loved Laura, as a brother loves his sister. The pain of losing her was crippling him—tightening his chest, making his heart race, his pulse throb—and Morgan was feeling the brunt of it right along with him. She didn't want to tell him the rest. Didn't want to be explicit and make Laura's death even more devastating. Would he let her avoid it? Could she?

Morgan, don't you dare be a coward. Don't you dare. He deserves better. He deserves the truth.

But he's in so much pain!

Coward, her conscience insisted. *Tell him the truth!*

Remorse swam through her stomach, coupled with the grief, and she met his eyes. Tears blurred her own, and she blinked hard. "I'm so . . . sorry."

"Bruce." Jackson swallowed hard, clearly reeling. His Adam's apple bobbed in his throat, and he sucked in a sharp breath. "Where is my brother? Is he all right?"

She stared at him.

"Good God, I can't believe I even asked that." Jackson jumped to his feet. "What a stupid question." He shoved his hands through his hair, gripped his skull as if to keep it from exploding. "Laura is dead. How the hell can he be all right?" Jackson blinked hard, fast, and furious. "How will he be all right ever again?"

Morgan wanted to comfort Jackson, but there were no words that could comfort. Nothing she could do would make any of this easier to take, so she simply sat there, waiting for him to absorb the initial shock and to indicate he was ready to hear more.

Soon, he stilled and looked down at Morgan. "You aren't answering me." A muscle in his jaw ticked. "Where's my brother? He needs me. I . . . I have to get to him, be there for him."

Morgan rose to her feet slowly and clasped his arm. "You can't go to him right now, Jackson," she said, compassion softening her voice. Her eyes stung, and her throat threatened to choke closed to avoid the words she had to say next. "I'm afraid Bruce can't see or be with anyone right now."

Jackson's face bleached white. "Is he . . ." His voice failed; he couldn't make himself ask the question.

He didn't have to; that much she could spare him. "Bruce is alive," she hastily assured him, sensing he was too raw and wounded to bear much more. "But, well . . ."

"Damn it, woman." He gripped her upper arms and squeezed. "Stop this agony and just tell me."

"I'm so sorry, Jackson." Morgan looked up at him, tears sliding down her cheeks. "Bruce has been arrested for Laura's murder."

CHAPTER 3

Under the pretense of getting Jackson some water, Morgan excused herself and lingered outside the office to give him a few minutes alone to absorb the double shock that had him reeling.

She walked down to the employee's lounge and then snagged two bottles of water from the fridge and a tissue from a box on the counter to dry her face. Strong emotions were hell on her, and there couldn't have been any stronger grief than over a loved one being accused of committing the murder of another loved one. That had to be positively the worst. Nothing in her experience rivaled Stern's pained response, and she wondered if he was so traumatized by the double whammy of two loved ones involved or by the depth of his love for them. How the hell Jackson had remained upright during that emotional onslaught, Morgan had no idea. Just the secondary impact of his response had her staggering.

"You okay, Morgan?"

Recognizing Commander Drake's voice, Morgan turned to face the petite redhead with short, spiky hair, and nodded. "I'll be fine."

Compassion lighted her eyes. "Pretty rough going in there, huh?"

Having experienced none rougher, Morgan avoided the commander's eyes and let her gaze drift down her light blue blouse to her dark blue slacks. "Very rough," she admitted and dragged in a shuddery breath. "He loved her."

Surprise flickered through Colonel Drake, and Morgan quickly clarified. "No, not like that. He loved her like a cherished sister. She was good for Bruce. Jackson appreciated that and he, well, he loved her for it."

"Oh, good. That's good." Relief washed over Sally Drake's face, and then a flush of frank honesty. "Sorry, but the last thing we need to add to all this is those kinds of complications."

"I agree." Drained, Morgan slumped back against the countertop.

Drake hitched a hip on the corner of the table. "What about Bruce? Did Stern love him, too, or was there sibling rivalry or something?"

Jackson's emotions about Bruce had been so strong that

Morgan had had to disengage or she would have been flat on the floor. "No, no rivalry. The man definitely loves his brother." His emotions on Bruce were stronger, broader, vast . . . She needed a minute to sort through them all, let them fall into their proper place. Gripping both bottles of water in one hand, she brushed at her forehead, still feeling the blast of heat from the adrenaline surge that had come with Jackson's reaction to the news. "I think he's pretty much felt responsible for Bruce his whole life. I'm not sure why, but I am sure it's more parental than brotherly, and it's extremely protective . . ." She opened her mouth to go on, but a protective urge clamped down on her throat and she instinctively stopped.

"What?" the commander prodded.

Morgan shifted, her back against the counter, and looked down at her foot. The scrubs' footie was scuffed, though she didn't recall doing it.

"Morgan?"

She looked over at Drake from beneath her lashes, not wanting to disclose her other certainty. It had slotted, and she had a full grasp on it; she just didn't want the information shared. But the commander had that look in her eye. She wasn't going to grant quarter.

Resignation slid through Morgan. "He feels guilty," she confessed. "He's absolutely consumed with it." It had come on like a flash flood and swamped him, but nothing came with it to indicate why. She lifted a shoulder. "I don't know why."

"Guilty?" Commander Drake reached around Morgan and retrieved a bottle of water from the fridge, unscrewed the cap, and then drank down a long swallow. "You're going to have to talk to him and find out what that's all about. It could be connected."

"I know." Morgan pursed her lips; felt the chill of the bottles in her hand penetrate deep beneath her skin and into her bones. "I'm just giving him a few minutes to collect himself." She paused, swallowing as his pain revisited her, and then added, "He's had a lot to absorb in a very short period of time, Commander. Me shooting him, twice; the abduction—he has to be experiencing betrayal issues on all that. Then Joan's interrogation—which we both know is brutal all on its own—and then Laura's death and Bruce's arrest for her murder."

"I do realize he's been through the mill, Morgan," the commander said. "Actually, I'm surprised he's not falling apart."

Her voice took on a hollow tone that cued Morgan she needed a minute, so Morgan gave it to her. She didn't mean to intrude, but Drake's emotions were so strong Morgan couldn't shut them out. Sally Drake was remembering the murder of her own husband, Kenneth, and her reaction to it. She'd felt guilty, too. Her guilt ran so deep it still kept her from getting involved with another man. Her spicy personality attracted many who would jump at the chance—but that guilt had her keeping them at arm's length and, gauging by its force, would continue to do so for a long time to come.

A damn shame. Morgan wished for Sally Drake's sake that it could be different, but she totally understood why it couldn't and wouldn't. Kenneth had been killed by mistake. Sally had been the intended target, and the reason had been directly related to her job as S.A.S.S. commander. On the surface she'd coped reasonably well with that survivor's guilt, but it still gnawed at her and she was nowhere near ready to accept it and put it to rest. In truth, it probably never would go away—and unless it did, she'd never allow another man into her life.

The prisons we build . . .

Turning her attention away from the commander and back to the subject didn't bring much relief. "Jackson is falling apart," Morgan said. "Inside."

"Of course, he is." Commander Drake cleared her throat and her mind of thoughts of herself and Kenneth. "Maybe he'll be one of the lucky ones."

Lucky? Confused, Morgan frowned. "What lucky ones?"

Drake met Morgan's eyes. "The ones that see the guilty party brought to justice."

"Would that be lucky?" His brother was the accused, for pity's sake.

"If this leads back to Thomas Kunz and away from Bruce, yes, very lucky."

Following her now, Morgan nodded. "Have you seen Jazie and Taylor Lee?"

Drake nodded. "Jazie is examining Laura's body now. Dr. Vargus is monitoring," she quickly assured Morgan. No exams occurred without oversight personnel in the room. Morgan took every precaution to protect her team's credibility.

"Taylor Lee is waiting her turn in the conference room."

Shoving away from the counter, Morgan nodded. "I'll be down as soon as I'm done with Jackson."

A little frown wrinkled the skin between Sally Drake's eyebrows, and she checked her watch. It caught the overhead light and sparked a glimmer that made Morgan blink. "Bring him down to the morgue with you," she said.

Reluctance fell to revulsion and swept over Morgan. "I don't know if that's a good idea, Commander. He's pretty fragile right now."

"Exactly." Her eyes hardened. "You said that when emotions are most tense, you pick up the most information."

"That's true, but he's very vulnerable right now and I really don't—"

"It's not humane, you're thinking," Drake said. "I understand. I really do. But we can't afford to be gentle here, and Captain Stern wouldn't want us to be. You said so yourself."

Baffled, Morgan crossed the mental minefield. "I said . . . what?"

"He loves his brother," Drake replied. "Listen to me, Morgan. Laura is already dead, and Bruce could die. We're 90 percent sure Laura was killed away from the base. That means the locals will have jurisdiction, and that means—"

"They could seek the death penalty."

"I'd bet on it." The commander nodded. "We need to get as much information and evidence as we can—fast— before we lose jurisdiction and possession of the body."

"All right." Morgan understood the urgency, but she didn't have to like it. "I'll ask him to come downstairs," Morgan said. "But I won't force him to see his sister-in-law if he chooses not to do it. I can't, Commander. It would be a total ethics breach, and I'm not willing to sacrifice him when it isn't absolutely necessary."

"That won't be a problem." Commander Drake sent her a certain look forged by her own experience and memory. "You won't be able to keep him away. He'll want to know everything there is to know firsthand."

"You're probably right," Morgan conceded, then left the lounge and returned to Joan Foster's office.

In the hallway outside, she paused and drew in a breath, hoping courage and stamina came with it, lied to herself that if she weren't exhausted this wouldn't be impacting her as strongly, and then stiffened her shoulders and tapped on the wood.

"Come in, Dr. Cabot."

"I'm sorry, Jackson," she said against the plank. "Can you get the door for me?" She could open the door herself, but she wanted to give him a few seconds more to compose himself. She transferred a water bottle so she held one in each hand.

With an echoing creak, the door opened and she met Jackson's gaze. His eyes were red-rimmed, his face flushed. "You okay?"

Of course, he wasn't. But he did seem to have taken the worst of the shock. If he had, he'd lie. If not, he'd break down again. She watched for signs.

He dropped his gaze. "Yeah, I'm okay."

He lied. *Progress.* She passed over a bottle of water. "I thought you might need a drink."

"Thanks." He took it. The hand that brushed hers shook. "I could use something stronger than water."

Controlled. In enormous pain, but controlled and aware. "It wouldn't help."

"No, it wouldn't." He sighed, rolling his shoulders.

She walked over and sat down on the sofa. "I hoped maybe we could talk for a few more minutes."

"You're a shrink, right?"

She hated the moniker but nodded, cutting him slack.

"Forget the psycho-babble. I don't want or need it. But I do want to talk—actually, to listen. I want you to talk." He stiffened his shoulders, withdrew, and buried his emotions. "What happened to Laura?"

The investigator in him had kicked in. 'He would mourn plenty, and likely for a long time, but he'd do it later. Right now, he wanted answers. And, thankfully, Morgan could tell him all she knew and discuss the situation freely. That wasn't typically an option for her, and it removed a lot of barriers and challenges. She was just weary and afraid enough of Thomas Kunz and G.R.I.D. and this entire mission to be grateful for that. "We honestly don't know much . . . yet. But I'll tell you all I do know."

"Full disclosure?" He sounded more surprised than pleased.

And she suspected that was exactly the case. Full disclosure was rare in her medical field and nearly nonexistent in their shared counterterrorism realm. "Yes." She looked him in the eye. "You have my word on it."

Weighing its worth, Stern flicked the bottle cap with this thumbnail and sat down beside Morgan on the leather sofa. The cushion swooshed under his weight. "You can start with why you shot me on the *Sunrise* rather than just summoning me." Bitterness crept into his voice. "Last I checked, I was still responding to direct orders."

Betrayal. "I know it sucks, okay? And I am sorry, Jackson, but as I explained, we didn't know whether or not you were a G.R.I.D. operative. If we'd summoned you, we would have conceded a crucial advantage." From his blank look, he didn't follow. "The kill zone," she said.

Acknowledgement dawned in his eyes, but the corners of his mouth dipped down and his jaw tightened. "Wait a second," he said, plenty angry but even more perplexed. "On the *Sunrise* you still didn't know who I was, and you didn't find out until after I was brought to Providence and Dr. Foster had done her . . . . whatever you call what she did. It sure as hell wasn't like any debriefing I've ever had."

"We call it deprogramming," Morgan revealed.

The implications sobered him silent. He blinked rapidly. "Yet you breached the kill zone, brought me here, before you knew."

"Yes." Morgan met his gaze without apology.

"I have a feeling I don't want to know why."

"Probably not now," she admitted.

"But I will eventually."

"No doubt or illusions about that." She lifted her shoulders. "And when you do, I'll answer as honestly and accurately as I can."

Satisfied, he changed the subject. "Which brings us back to why you brought me here." His voice dropped a notch, turned wooden. "Do you think I killed my sister-in-law and set my brother up to take the blame for it? Or what?"

"No, Jackson," she assured him. "We know you didn't kill Laura or frame Bruce for her murder." Morgan didn't add that they'd only become certain after Joan had deprogrammed him. Some things were better left unsaid.

"Then what made it imperative to determine my identity before bringing me into the U.S. and, more specifically, to Providence?"

"G.R.I.D. intelligence intercepts."

His eyes narrowed. "On what?" He recognized hedging when he heard it, and he was having none of it. "And I guess I do need to know now how you determined my identity on the *Sunrise*. Otherwise, there's a logic gap in your actions I'm having a hard time working around."

Morgan wasn't sure how to respond honestly and accurately and still come out with any credibility. Never in her life had a man readily accepted her intuition as a valid reason for an action, and there was no reason to suspect that Jackson Stern would be any different.

Oddly, she would normally tell him, since she had authorization, but she didn't want him to look at her as if she'd sprouted two heads. She wanted him to . . . well, to continue to be . . . aware of her, because whether it was good or bad or wise or idiotic, she was definitely aware of him. She had been on the *Sunrise,* and she was now. "I'm not refusing to answer you," she said softly, "but I would rather not be specific about it at this specific point in time. I'm sure you understand," she said, alluding to reasons she knew he'd interpret to be related to operational security measures.

A muscle under his left eye ticked. "Laura."

Morgan took a drink of water and then responded. "I knew Laura, Jackson."

"How?"

Morgan braced for his investigation and offered to open it, hoping he'd see it as a gesture of good faith. "She came to my office for a counseling session about a week ago."

Guilt crashed through him, over to her, and he dropped his gaze to the floor. "I knew I should have come as soon as she called."

"What do you mean? The call on Sunday?"

"No, last week." His voice was filled with self-recrimination and regret. "She was worried about Bruce," he said. "But she always worried about Bruce."

"So you didn't put any weight on her call?"

"No, I did," he told her. "But apparently, not as much as I should have." He forked a hand through his hair, cranked his neck, and glanced up at the ceiling. "It was a bad time. I tried, but I couldn't cut loose before now. Work, you know?"

Morgan nodded. "Then she told you that she and Bruce were having domestic difficulties. Or were you not aware of that?"

"I wouldn't exactly tag what she said as domestic difficulty. She wasn't about to leave him or anything."

"What did she tell you?"

Jackson hesitated, then made his ethics call. "I guess confidentiality doesn't much matter to her anymore, and it could help Bruce."

"It's possible." *Not probable, but possible.*

Jackson leaned forward, propped his elbows on his knees, and looked back down at the floor. The weight of the world rested heavily on his shoulders. "She told me Bruce had become distant before he went to Iraq. She figured he was disturbed about the assignment, but he didn't talk to her about it." Jackson lifted his gaze to meet Morgan's. "She thought he'd be fine once he got the work behind him and got home. But when he came back, things weren't better between them; they were worse."

Getting mixed signals, Morgan shifted on her seat. "It often takes time to readjust."

"No, it wasn't like that." Jackson shook his head, adding weight to his words. "Laura said Bruce had become more remote . . . and he'd done everything he could to force her to leave him."

That surprised Morgan—Laura had said nothing like that during their session—and it surprised Jackson, too. His skepticism radiated in waves. "Are you saying that Bruce wanted a divorce?" she asked.

"That's what Laura said." Jackson straightened up and sat back against the sofa. "But I don't believe it. I never did," he insisted. "Hell, Dr. Cabot, what is your name, anyway? This doctor business is getting old when I'm pouring out my guts to you."

"Morgan," she said.

"Morgan," he repeated, testing the sound of it. Apparently it sounded okay because he turned right back to the subject at hand. "Bruce couldn't really have wanted her to leave him, and there's no way in hell he would ever divorce her."

He felt confident about what he was saying; that was clear enough. The problem was he was as much an outsider as she, and he loved them both, which put him at an even greater disadvantage when trying to discern the truth before his eyes. Love colored everything. It sharpened the positive and softened anything negative. Love and objectivity were never spotted on the same page or through the same eyes. "Things go on in a marriage, Jackson—"

"Yes, they do, and no one knows it better than me." He spoke candidly and easily met her gaze. "I'm sure there were lots of things in their marriage only they knew. It's that way for every couple." He slid around to face her. "But you've got to understand, Morgan. Bruce just doesn't work without Laura. He hasn't since the day they first met."

Morgan's observations agreed with him. "If it's any consolation, Laura didn't work without Bruce, either," Morgan said. "When she came to see me, she made it crystal clear that she didn't want to leave him, Jackson."

"What did she want?" His challenge to her to answer rode in his eyes.

Morgan met it. "To better understand the demands of his job so she could do her part to regain their closeness." Her throat raw and dry, Morgan flipped up the cap of her water bottle and took a sip. "Laura was convinced that was the key to getting their marriage back on track."

"She would know. The woman was so attuned to Bruce that she knew what he was thinking before he knew it." Jackson grunted. "Which makes something about this whole situation feel odd."

Something. That covered a lot of ground. "What?"

"I don't know," he answered honestly. "But I'm kind of surprised that she called me so soon, you know? Bruce hasn't been back from Iraq that long." Jackson looked over at Morgan. "And even if he'd been back forever, I'm downright shocked that Laura went to you for help. I'd have bet against her ever going to anyone outside the family for anything, but especially about anything connected to Bruce's career."

Again, total honesty. Brutal, but honest. Morgan lifted her shoulders. "Many come to me about their relationship challenges. It's what I do."

"No, I don't mean that and . . . don't take this wrong, but . . . what you do is insignificant."

Not take it personally? Sounded damn personal to her. "Excuse me?"

"You're taking it wrong," he warned her, clapping a hand to his bare knee. "What I mean is, Laura would hash things out on her own with Bruce until she was damn near dead from the effort. Her coming to either of us with a problem just doesn't fit. She . . . I don't know. She's strong. She handles things."

"She is strong and clear-minded. But it's been three months since Bruce returned from Iraq," Morgan added.

"When you're living day to day in a hostile situation, three months can seem like three lifetimes."

"Three months?" Jackson stared at her in disbelief. "Where did you get that? Laura?"

"Actually, I remembered it from the briefing."

"Well, either your memory's wrong or your information is," Jackson insisted.

"What are you talking about?"

"Morgan," Jackson said, worry in his eyes. "Bruce got back from Iraq three weeks ago."

Impossible. Surprise streaked through Morgan's chest. "I'm sure I was told three months." There wasn't a doubt in her mind.

"Three weeks," Jackson insisted. "I'm positive of it."

"Positive?" With Thomas Kunz and G.R.I.D. in their lives, it was nearly impossible to be positive of anything.

"Totally positive." Jackson met the challenge in her eyes without wavering.

"How?" She shrugged. "You know Kunz—"

"I was with Bruce in Iraq two days before he returned home."

Morgan absorbed that information, let it soak in. So he wasn't restricted to flying into hurricanes. He was still an operative. A high-level operative, working outside the normal chain of command. "I see," she said, though she didn't really see at all. Yet Secretary of Defense Reynolds and General Shaw's orders regarding Jackson Stern were now making a lot more sense. As was his elevated security clearance.

Morgan had no idea what the man did, but her hunch that he wasn't a reservist or a Hurricane Hunter with the 53rd Weather Reconnaissance Squadron at Keesler in Biloxi, Mississippi, had just been proven. She wasn't certain what to make of that . . . yet. But another thought occurred to her. "You've seen the measures we've taken to prove you were you. How can you be positive that Bruce wasn't a body double?"

"I'm his brother. Do you have a brother or sister?"

She shook her head, not wanting to say aloud that she had no one.

"I know my brother better than he knows himself, and if he were a double, I'd have known that, too."

"Kunz's doubles have fooled the best. Remember Leavenworth?" *Kunz wasn't Kunz.*

"Professional associates, yes. But not family. He hasn't fooled family."

"So far as we know, yet that isn't proof."

That muscle started to tick again. "The man was Bruce."

Jackson wasn't being assertive: he believed it down to his core. Hardly hard evidence, but forceful enough in conviction to warn an intuitive woman not to dismiss the validity of the claim, so she didn't. "Three weeks."

"That's right." He didn't give an inch.

"I don't know what that means in the grand scheme of all this. Not now. But I'll note and remember it." Morgan stood up. "I need to go to the morgue to see Laura. You don't have to accompany me, but if you—"

"Let's go." He was on his feet and at the door waiting for her before Morgan moved, just as Commander Drake had predicted.

Hoping that he'd remain predictable—he had a lot of anger to deal with—Morgan walked out of Joan's office, waited, and when Jackson stepped past her and into the hall, she locked and closed the door.

"On the way," Jackson said, "you can tell me where and how Laura died, and why the authorities think Bruce killed her."

"We don't know where she died yet." Morgan took off walking. "On Bruce, the prevailing thought is he is suffering from PTSD—post-traumatic stress disorder—from whatever he was doing in Iraq." She lifted a warning finger. "Don't bother to ask what he was doing. I'm afraid that information is classified and won't be disclosed to you because I don't have it and can't get it."

"No way," Jackson said flatly. "Post-traumatic stress. Uh-uh."

"Why not?" she asked, then waited for two nurses to pass them in the hallway. When they had, she added, "He's human. He's not immune."

"Of course, he isn't." Jackson surprised her. "But

I didn't see anything that would support that finding in his behavior. Nothing at all, and I would have noticed, Morgan." Jackson worried his lip and then looked at her. "Do you believe he had PTSD?"

"I couldn't diagnose him; I've never met him," she said. "Frankly, I don't know what I believe. Not yet," she said honestly. "I need more time to investigate and a lot more information before I'll be ready to draw any conclusions." Stopping outside the elevator, she pressed the down button and looked at the reflection of Jackson standing beside her. He was a lot taller, dark to her fair, and yet something in the image of them standing together looked . . . right. It felt . . . right.

Erotic.

Heat swept up her face, flushed her cheeks.

"You okay?" Jackson asked, searching her face.

"Um, f—fine," she stammered, embarrassed and grateful he had no clue what was on her mind. The sensation surprised her, coming at her without warning like that. Yet she couldn't shield herself against it. She needed her senses wide open to him to get every possible nuance.

The elevator door opened. She stepped inside, and Jackson followed.

"There is another take on this worth exploring, Morgan." His voice was strained, deeper.

"What?"

Fear and regret filled his eyes. "What if the G.R.I.D.

assassins weren't after me? The *Sunrise* belongs to Bruce. What if G.R.I.D. was after him and they mistook me for him?"

Morgan mulled that over. "It's possible, and the thought has occurred to us. You two do strongly resemble each other." Morgan pushed the button for the basement level.

The elevator door closed. With a lurch, the descent began. Jackson leaned back against the paneled wall and closed his eyes. "Was Laura killed because of me?" Asking the question had cost him, and he was terrified of the answer.

"I don't think so. Nothing about that fits the facts we do have."

He swallowed hard, blinked fast. "I don't think I could live with that, Morgan. I really don't."

He'd used her first name unconsciously rather than deliberately. Initially, he'd been fostering a connection. Likely, an attempt to encourage her to share her insights as well as the facts. Now trust had been established on its own. Not forgiveness but trust. Though it was born in fear and grief, it was genuine and constructive.

Relieved, she nodded. "I know what you mean," she said.

He *could* live with it, of course. Sally Drake lived with it every day. But it did cost her peace to do it. She hoped Jackson was spared that. "Either way, let's not jump to any conclusions."

"No, false conclusions we do not need," he said. "With

Bruce's arrest, enough of those have happened already. At least, I hope they have."

Jackson wasn't convinced that Bruce was guilty—but he wasn't sure he was innocent, either. Laura's talking to Jackson about her and Bruce's challenges so quickly and her coming to Morgan for counseling probably had spawned that doubt. "Let's see what Laura can tell us."

"Laura?" Jackson's eyes stretched wide. "But she's dead."

Morgan flushed, her neck and face fire-hot. "The evidence we can gather from the body, I mean." Again, she'd told him the truth but not the whole truth.

He'll find out in a few minutes on his own.

Her stomach fluttered. He would, and it was probably best that he did. Learning about her special skills, and those of her team, in Commander Drake's presence and with her stamp of approval might help squelch a little of his skepticism.

Not bloody likely.

Maybe not, but maybe it would spare her a confrontation with him over it. And maybe by the time they got around to that confrontation, he wouldn't be as cynical about her abilities.

Wouldn't that be refreshing?

It'd be a miracle.

Jackson cast her a skeptical look but held his thoughts tightly to himself.

Morgan wasn't sure what to make of that, and for the first time since she had been around him, she couldn't intuitively pick up on a thing.

Your luck's holding.

It was—at *rotten*. This was no time for one of those 13 percent non-accuracy challenges to kick in.

A bell chimed, signaling their arrival at basement level, and the door opened. Fatigued and apprehensive, Morgan stepped out and motioned left. "The morgue is this way."

Sally Drake stood in the hallway outside the morgue. Her short red hair standing in spikes suited her face and, even more, her personality. The eagle rank on her shoulder glinted in the bald florescent light shining down from the high ceiling. Morgan and Jackson approached her, and Morgan handled the introductions. "Commander, this is Captain Jackson Stern. Jackson, this is Commander Sally Drake."

She offered him her hand. "My deepest condolences, Captain."

"Thank you," he said, shaking her hand.

She stepped back. "I'm sure Dr. Cabot has made this clear already, but I want to reiterate that your viewing the body isn't essential to the investigation."

"Morgan told me," he said. "But I need to see her. Otherwise, this is, well . . ." He paused a long second, then went on. "I need to see her."

Morgan interpreted. Laura's death was too much to believe without visible proof. Commander Drake would know that, along with the fact that he had to be sure no evidence was missed. There was no need for Morgan to tell her.

Commander Drake slid Morgan a covert glance to gauge whether Stern was sufficiently prepared to go in.

Morgan subtly nodded, indicating he'd be fine. She hoped it was true. Tension stretched him to the limits. From his erratic thoughts, his chest was so tight it was hard for him to draw breath. But instinctively Morgan knew the greater danger to him, and to the rest of them, would be in refusing to let him enter. "Where are Jazie and Taylor Lee?" she asked.

"Conference room." Commander Drake nodded to the right. "They'll wait for us there."

Commander Drake would accompany Morgan and Jackson to preserve the chain of evidence: Laura's body. Especially important since Morgan had known the victim and since Jackson was related to the victim—and the suspect. "Are you ready, Jackson?"

He stiffened and nodded. "As ready as anyone can get."

"Let's go then." Morgan had been preparing herself for

this since she'd first spoken on the phone with Commander Drake and been activated. The morgue was a torture chamber for her. There was no blocking the strong emotional imprints of the victims who had died suddenly and unexpectedly. No blocking the strong emotional imprints of those who had loved the victims and come to the morgue to positively identify them. And, as if that weren't enough, there was also no blocking the flood of strong emotional imprints from those who worked in the morgue, witnessed others in such raw pain, and attempted to bury their own emotional reactions to it. Psychic distance was essential to survival. But in the morgue, psychic distance was as impossible to attain as emotional distance. Consequently, the work force turnover was incredibly high.

Inside her head, Morgan sang to cut down on the volume of sensory input; then she entered the morgue.

Laura lay on a stainless gurney in the center of the room. A white sheet covered her from the shoulders down. The edge of it had been scrunched up over the tip of one foot, so her toe tag was visible.

Jackson cleared his throat and took his lead from Morgan. She walked closer and looked down at Laura's neck, muddied with bruises. She'd been strangled first. Male assailant—large hands. He'd caught her from behind, around the neck, barehanded. Strong.

Absorbing that, Morgan moved the sheet aside enough to free Laura's right arm, and let her gaze drift down it, shoulder to fingertips. More bruises, indicative of having been tightly gripped—but they were on the back of the arm. He was in front of her at the time. Two fingers were broken, and a long gash scraped the top of her knuckle on her ring finger. Where a ring obviously had been, her skin was bare and pale.

"Where's her emerald?" Jackson asked. "Did the ME take it off of her?" He glanced from the body to Morgan.

She didn't answer.

"He had to," Jackson went on. "I'd appreciate it if you'd have him put it back on her as soon as possible. It was her mother's ring. Laura put it on the day her mother died, and she never took it off."

Morgan remembered it from Laura's office visit. "The ME didn't take the ring off of her, Jackson. Apparently, it was forcibly removed during the attack." She paused, then motioned. "See the torn skin and bloody scrape above her knuckle? She was alive when that happened." Morgan glanced over at him, hoping the tremble she felt didn't come through in her voice. "This could be good news for Bruce. Why would he take her mother's ring?"

"He wouldn't."

"Right," Morgan said. "But it isn't uncommon for a professional to take a trophy."

"To track his kills," Jackson spat out with venom. "Bastards."

Plural. He knew there had been more than one attacker. *Insightful.* "You think there were multiple murderers?"

"I'm sure of it. Well, nearly sure. Look at the red prints on her forearms."

Among the bruises, two different forefinger marks dominated the others, and they were definitely not the same size; they had not been left by the same forefinger.

Jackson's voice dropped low and husky. "Did Laura tell you that Bruce had gotten physical with her?"

Morgan slid a wary glance to Commander Drake at the door. She had to be present but wanted to be separate and not interfere with their examination or discussion. She nodded at Morgan, reminding her of the full-disclosure order.

"No," Morgan told Jackson. "She didn't say anything about him getting physical." To be completely honest with him, she had to mention her impressions from her meeting with Laura. "I don't think he was. She would have exhibited some sign: fear or anger. Something."

"You're sure she didn't?" he asked. "Maybe you missed it."

"I didn't miss it." In every case she'd studied, during the first session either fear or anger became evident. Often, both did. "Laura wasn't angry and she didn't fear Bruce, Jackson. Not at all. She was worried *for* him and for their marriage."

Jackson stepped away. "So multiple men grabbed her, and one choked her to death and stole her ring."

"We're not certain yet."

He nodded, glanced at Laura's still face, and then turned away. "I'll, um, be in the hall."

"All right." Morgan watched him go. His strength to

hold it together, when she knew he felt as if his insides had been ripped apart, amazed her.

He walked out, and the door closed behind him.

"Morgan?" Commander Drake claimed Morgan's attention. "He suspects Bruce hit her."

"Yes, he does," Morgan confirmed. "But he isn't certain of it." Still, the thought of it obviously had his stomach tied in knots and pumping acid.

"Looking back with that in mind, could you have missed any sign?"

Damn it. "I didn't, Commander. I was specifically looking for that. I'm sure of it."

"Okay, then." The commander glanced from Laura back to Morgan. "So, do you think G.R.I.D. was involved in the murder, or just in the assassination attempt, which could have been directed at either brother?"

"G.R.I.D. is involved in both," Morgan said, certain of it. "But whether the assassins or Bruce killed Laura, I don't know." A dull throb started behind her eyes, and she rubbed at her temples. "She wasn't raped." The ME would have verified that already, but disclosing it without scrutiny would serve as a checkpoint for Morgan's accuracy. "Typically G.R.I.D. operatives rape women they attack, exerting their authority and control over them."

"True, but not always," Commander Drake countered. "Kunz actually prefers other methods of torture. Pain appeals to him more than degradation."

"Kunz didn't commit the actual murder."

The commander hiked her brows but didn't ask how Morgan knew. Still, Morgan gave her the answer. "He has a different energy. It's very distinct."

"You've never been directly exposed to him."

"No, I haven't," Morgan agreed, sadness creeping through her. "But I have been exposed to Amanda, and she's been directly exposed to him several times. She still carries it with her. Intense emotion lingers, sometimes for a lifetime."

"Which explains why you keep a little physical distance between you and her."

Morgan nodded. "I'd prefer she not know that. She's a good woman, and I wouldn't do anything to—"

"I understand completely, and I agree." Drake glanced back at Laura. "I'm glad Kunz wasn't involved."

He loved torture. The sick bastard took a perverse pleasure in it.

"I didn't say he wasn't involved," Morgan clarified. "Just that he hadn't committed the murder."

"What about Marcus Sandross?" the commander suggested, crossing her chest with her arms. "He loves torture, too."

He did. They'd discovered just how much the man fed on cruelty during Kate's last mission.

"No. He's a strong proponent of rape. Man or woman—it doesn't matter. If he'd killed her, Laura would have been raped."

Historically, Kunz's second-in-command had issued the assassins their orders. Kunz handling that himself was hard for Morgan to imagine. Private and secretive, the man went to amazing lengths to protect himself and his identity. His survival depended on it.

"Morgan, are you saying *Kunz* was with them on this mission?" Commander Drake asked. "Is that what you're thinking?"

"That's what I'm getting so far." Morgan nodded, dragging her teeth along her lower lip. "But something isn't quite right."

"It'll sort out." The commander stared at a nonexistent point above Morgan's head and tossed that disclosure into the mix of evidence, along with their suspicions. Her expression turned sour, and she shifted the topic. "I'm afraid you'll still have to check under the sheet, Morgan." Commander Drake nodded toward Laura on the gurney. "I didn't want to mention it while Captain Stern was with us, but I knew he'd need a moment alone." Regret laced her voice. "It's significant."

"I know." Morgan did know. She had known since shortly after she had entered the morgue. But she lifted the sheet anyway to personally count the thirty-one stab wounds Laura had absorbed in her chest, abdomen, and back.

On feeling the first slide of the knife into flesh, Morgan had made the decision not to lift the sheet in Jackson's presence. Thankfully, she was able to spare him that. Now she examined Laura's left arm, wrist, and hand. Her nails were cracked and broken off at the quick. Every finger on her left hand was broken in at least one place; her forefinger had sustained two breaks, one above and one below the knuckle. Her right hand's pinky had been broken, too, in the scuffle to take her ring, which was after she'd been stabbed over twenty times.

They hadn't wanted death to come easily to her.

Morgan's throat went tight, and her chest hollowed. Laura Stern had fought like hell to live, knowing her murderers would never allow it. She'd prayed for a miracle. And she had died with one thought on her mind:

Help Bruce.

Morgan intuited that clearly. The problem was, how did she interpret it? Did Laura's "help Bruce" mean she had been killed because of him? Or that she was afraid he would be killed next? That she feared he couldn't cope without her?

Or did she mean that Bruce had killed her?

CHAPTER 4

Jackson stood waiting a few steps down the hall, staring sightlessly at something tucked away in the corners of his mind.

Morgan breathed deeply three times, slowly exhaling, to leave her own images of Laura behind and to brace for the onslaught of his. She motioned for Commander Drake to go on to the conference room, and when she did, Morgan walked on to Jackson and stopped beside him. "You holding up?"

He shoved his hands into his pockets, curled his fingers into fists, and pulled himself from his thoughts. Then he looked over at her, grief carving lines of strain in his face. "When can I see Bruce?"

Jackson was okay. Angry. Shocked down to the soles

of his feet. Having to remind himself to breathe, but he was coping.

"Not until about noon, I'm afraid," Morgan answered.

He nodded, gazed off, and his composure cracked. Weary. Beaten. He stiffened, forcing the crack to close, cursing himself as weak. His outward signs of stress deepening, he pleaded, "Are we done here?"

"You are, yes." Morgan spotted movement out of the corner of her eye and glanced over at the conference room door. Taylor Lee stood waiting and sent Morgan a signal in the negative.

Jackson spared Taylor Lee a glance, put her on "ignore," and then turned back to Morgan. "I'll be on the *Sunrise* until noon, if you should need me for anything."

Now she had to cross him again. Poor guy. The hits just kept on pummeling him. "I'm afraid that's not possible, Captain Stern," Commander Drake said from beside Taylor Lee. Clearly she'd overheard his comment, and she was walking back toward them. "Forensics isn't yet finished with the *Sunrise*. They're going to need a few more hours."

"Okay." He sighed. "I'm sure Bruce and Laura's house is off-limits, too . . ."

"Until further notice, yes." She nodded. "I'm afraid so."

He turned his gaze to Morgan. "Where was Laura's body found?"

"On base," Morgan said, hoping he'd leave it there.

The last thing he needed was the specific images the exact location would plant in his mind. Morgan still couldn't shake them.

Commander Drake interceded. "Taylor Lee has contacted the VOQ and booked a room for you."

Morgan winced. Sending the man to the sterile and unfamiliar environment of the visiting officer's quarters seemed harsh and unconscionably cruel. "Commander, no."

Regret washed through Drake. "I know, and I'm sorry. But under the circumstances, what else could we do?"

Morgan didn't have an answer for that.

"It's okay," Jackson said. "I'll be fine there."

He wouldn't. It pounded from his every pore, but he was telling himself otherwise.

"They're expecting you whenever you're ready, Captain Stern," Taylor Lee said from behind him.

"Thanks." He turned to go and realized he didn't have a way to travel. "Could you point me in the right direction? I'm not familiar with Providence."

"A car is waiting out front to take you over," Taylor Lee added.

"Thank you." He nodded to acknowledge her.

"Come on, Jackson." Morgan pressed his arm. "I'll walk you out."

He fell into step beside her, and they silently walked to the elevator, took it up to the main floor, and then walked down the corridor to the outside door.

Morgan had retrieved one of her cards when she'd gone to get the bottles of water, and she scribbled her cell and home phone numbers and her address on its back. "If you need to talk or if I can do anything for you, or whatever, let me know." She passed the card to him. "I'm going to see Bruce at noon, too," she added, dropping her voice. "If you'd like to ride along, I'll be happy to pick you up at the VOQ."

"I would appreciate that, yes. Thank you."

"Of course." Morgan stopped beside the wide glass door that led out of the hospital. "Magnolia Beach is a tourist town, Jackson, which means hotels and rental cars are available most of the time."

He lifted his brows and tilted his head. "Except on holiday weekends."

"Ah, you've been here before."

He sent her a level look. "I wish now I'd driven over far more often."

"I know." His family lay shattered, and now those opportunities to be with them were gone and they would never come again. "With the clarity of hindsight . . ."

"That's it." He swallowed hard, his eyes shining overly bright. "I still can't believe any of this, Morgan." His voice shook. "Laura or Bruce. It's just . . ."

"Give yourself some time. In the last twelve hours, you've had more bad shocks than most people absorb in a lifetime, Jackson. Any one of these things cuts down to the bone."

"Yeah." He closed his eyes for a brief moment. "It's been twelve hours of hell."

She said sincerely, "I'm sorry for my part in it." A tear slipped down her cheek, humiliating her.

He noticed, looked into her eyes, and lifted a fingertip to brush the skin beneath her eye. "I appreciate that." He dragged his fingertip down, following the track of the tear. "I know you're not paying me lip service. This"—he paused to touch the teardrop, then studied her face—"is genuine." Warm breath escaped from between his lips. "It . . . helps."

His feather-light touch captivated her, and she had to make herself think. "Nothing helps right now," she countered, contradicting him. "Not really." But it'd been kind of him to say what he had.

"You're wrong about that." He gave her a slow blink. "I can count on one hand the number of times in my life anyone has shed a tear because I was hurt."

The fisted bands clenching her chest tightened. "That might be the saddest thing I've ever heard."

"I wish I could say it's the saddest thing I could tell you, but I respect you, so I won't." He drew in a ragged breath. "When you put it all together, no matter how bad this has been for me, my brother has suffered more." Jackson's gaze bored into her, seeking her feelings about Bruce in all of this.

She made herself meet and hold his gaze, though

looking at him took effort. He wanted absolution for Bruce, and he wouldn't find it in her; at least, not at this point in the investigation. Still, she suffered pangs of regret that she couldn't give it to him. But ethics were ethics, and a woman couldn't stuff them in a closet and forget them because they had suddenly become inconvenient. She had to choose to wholly embrace or forget them. Honesty demanded it and accepted nothing less.

Morgan had made that call long ago. Yes, there were many times when sticking to her ethics had royally sucked. And, yes, this was another one of them. But she couldn't do anything else, and if Jackson was the man she thought he was, he would be damned disappointed in her if she did— almost as disappointed as she would be in herself. "I expect that Bruce has suffered immensely," she said, speaking truthfully. Whether he was innocent or guilty of murdering Laura, Bruce had suffered. No disputing that.

"I want to believe in him," Jackson said, staring over the car into the parking lot.

"He's your brother. Of course, you do."

He wanted and needed to believe in Bruce, but Jackson had doubts and they were tearing him apart.

She offered him a trembling smile. "If you need to talk or anything, or if you run into trouble or whatever, just call me. I'll do what I can to help you."

"I will." Jackson didn't hesitate to take her up on the offer. "I want to be in on this investigation, Morgan. I realize that's a bit unorthodox, but the classified information Bruce knows and can't disclose to anyone else could bite him in the ass. You know what I mean."

"I do."

He looked relieved to hear it. "I need to know if G.R.I.D. . . ." He paused, then went on. "For Laura."

Jackson's heart demanded it. He was very devoted to both of them and, swimming in guilt already, he wanted to avoid any more.

"I understand, Jackson. You've got the essential clearances. I'm not sure how, but I'll work on the conflict of interest issue and get it resolved. The honchos have cleared you, but that doesn't mean Oversight won't want a reasonable explanation."

"And you don't have one," he said. He had one, but he couldn't disclose it.

"No, I don't." She shrugged. "We'll have to get creative. That's all."

"You're not suggesting we lie . . ."

"Of course not." They both knew she meant it, but he knew the penalties of creativity as well as she did. And the fact that she was willing to endure them for him touched him, which touched her. Her face went warm.

"Thank you. For all the obvious reasons, it means a great deal to me." He offered her his hand.

She clasped it and sensed just how much her care meant to him. His depth of gratitude caused tears to well in her eyes. The impression that he hadn't received much support from others in his life in any form, though he had given tons of it, burned strong. That might just have been the saddest thing she'd ever sensed. She blinked against the wind, wondering what had happened to Tropical Storm Lil. It'd kind of fizzled out.

"My privilege," she said.

He nodded and let go of her hand and then slid into the front passenger's seat of the blue standard-issue Air Force car.

Morgan watched him go. His entire life, Jackson Stern had had to depend only on Jackson Stern. He hadn't been nurtured or protected or supported, even when he'd helped others. It was as if his selfless generosity was expected, perhaps demanded. *Odd.* She'd sensed all that and more. All his life, Jackson had given to Bruce unstintingly, without resentment. Morgan didn't fully understand that yet. Normally, there would be at least some resentment and longing for the same generosity in return. He was aware of the disproportion. He acknowledged it, and even alluded to it in conversation with her. But he didn't resent it. And that baffled Morgan. She couldn't help but wonder why. And she couldn't help but wonder where in hell Jackson and Bruce's parents had been.

Baffled, Morgan expelled a deep breath, steadied herself, and then tapped the door and turned back down the hallway. *Be careful, Morgan. He gets to you, and that makes him dangerous. Especially now, on this mission.*

He doesn't. It's intriguing, and it could be important to the case. That's all.

Liar.

She *was* lying to herself. The man got to her, and she wasn't sure why. Yes, he'd set aside any resentment for her shooting him, and trusted her. He'd openly admitted his vulnerabilities. He'd been devoted to his family in spite of the fact that they had shown him so little devotion. She didn't know which of these traits appealed most to her. She couldn't say—and wouldn't even if she could.

However, her admiration of his character was not a serious concern. It was the inkling of awareness inside her that concerned her immensely. It had already yawned and gained a firm foothold in her heart. From the first moment she'd seen him, Jackson Stern had snagged her attention and held her interest. Now, after all they'd experienced together, he called to her on all levels: physically and emotionally, consciously and subliminally.

To feel this way was not smart, by anyone's measure. But it was the truth and she had to accept it and to decide what to do about it. Something? Nothing? She didn't know. Frustration swamped her, and she mumbled under her breath, questioning herself on all fronts.

Not paying close attention, she stubbed her toe on the edge of a nonskid rug. Pain shot through her foot. "Damn it!" she muttered, doing a little hop to keep from falling.

Why him? Why now? Why during this, when she was up against Kunz?

Taylor Lee met her midway down the corridor. How did she look good in *everything*? Morgan felt like a frump in the scrubs, and Taylor Lee looked fresh, exotic, spectacular, and well rested. *No justice.*

She caught up to Morgan, a pout curving her lips. "He's gorgeous, and you didn't share. I totally hate you." She faked an affronted sniff. "At least tell me you tried to seduce him."

"You're out of your mind, Taylor Lee. And about as compassionate as a stone."

Taylor Lee was crazy . . . but she was right, too. Jackson was gorgeous. He shouldn't be, his face all hard angles and rough-hewn planes, but taken in together, he was amazing to look at. "The poor man is devastated. His family is in tatters, and we've kicked him in the teeth—"

"We haven't kicked him anywhere."

"We doubted him. He feels betrayed, and so would you," Morgan insisted, glaring at her.

Taylor Lee pursed her lips. "You think he wouldn't have done the same thing."

He would have. He wouldn't have had any more choice than they'd had. "That's not the point."

"Well, what is the point?"

Hardheaded. "The point is he has no emotional refuge right now," Morgan said. "When things are bad at work, we cope by focusing on our home lives. When we're in hell at home, we find solace at work."

"That's my point." Taylor Lee lifted a hand. "You could have offered him solace."

Morgan tossed that suggestive comment right back in the form of a glare. "A devastated man with no refuge doesn't need your damn games, okay?"

"Men always need games," she countered. "They love them."

Outrageous. "Why are we having this conversation? It's absurd," Morgan said, too tired to bother hiding her exasperation. "And you're engaged, and you're going to marry . . . this one, remember?" The guy's name had slipped her mind again.

"Rick," Taylor Lee said pointedly, her pout now genuine. "So you're telling me you didn't try to seduce Jackson Stern or even notice his looks?"

Morgan rolled her eyes. She'd noticed. "We were a little preoccupied talking about his dead sister-in-law and his brother being accused of her murder." Morgan took off down the corridor back toward the conference room. "I can't believe you."

"What?" Taylor Lee seemed genuinely clueless and irked by Morgan's objections.

"Don't pull that with me. I know you, remember?"

Taylor Lee shot her a pointed look. "And I know you and what you're thinking. So don't pull that above-it-all crap with me."

"I never claimed to be above anything."

"Good thing." Taylor Lee laughed, warm and husky. "You think he's hot."

"You're hopeless. I swear you are." Morgan lifted a hand. "He's grieving in the bowels of hell, and you're talking about his body and me seducing him? Don't you see? That's sick."

"Like hell it is," Taylor Lee hotly defended herself. "Seduction is a great comfort to someone grieving. It's affirmation that they're alive. I've heard you say that several times."

"Not when you don't know the person. We're strangers, for pity's sake."

"Strangers can comfort."

"They shouldn't. Not with sex." Morgan could smack her. "There's a level of intimacy required to offer comfort that lasts past orgasm—intimacy that doesn't exist between strangers."

"That's absurd. Great sex is great sex," she said with a shrug and a huff. "And I always find great sex comforting."

"Intimacy and sex can be as different as apples and oranges. But you would see them as being the same," Morgan snipped, and then lifted a hand to halt Taylor Lee's comeback. "Listen, just drop it. I'm exhausted, and I'm not in the mood for sparring or nonsense. When it comes to men, you've got a one-track mind."

"That is so not true," Taylor Lee protested, flicking her

hair back over her shoulder. "I'm adept at multitasking."

Raw to the bone, Morgan ignored her, walked into the conference room, and sat down at the table. Commander Drake was already seated in a chair at the head of it. Jazie had changed from green to blue scrubs and had somehow managed to shower; she smelled of soap. Twisting her long blond curls into a ponytail at her nape, she claimed a chair on the commander's left, directly across the table from Morgan. With a healthy yawn, Taylor Lee dropped into the chair beside Morgan.

Steaming cups of coffee had been placed on the stainless conference table. The small room brimmed with the rich smell of it. Morgan glanced down at her watch. Nearly six-thirty. Feeling the weight of pulling an all-nighter, she reached for her mug and then took a steamy sip. Strong and black, the coffee burned her throat going down.

"Jazie?" Commander Drake blew into her white cup, cooling the coffee. "Let's hear your impressions report on the body."

"Only two words came to me, Commander," Jazie said. "Help Bruce."

Frowning, Drake set down her cup. "As in, help him because he had snapped and killed her? Or help him because she sensed danger for him and couldn't do anything about it?"

"I wish I knew, but I don't." Jazie frowned her frustration about that. "All I heard from her were those two words. So there was no context to weigh—"

"Did you hear anything from anyone else?" the commander cut in, picking up on Jazie's pseudo-cagy specificity. Sometimes the key hid in asking the right question.

"I heard plenty," Jazie confessed, blowing it all off. "But that's normal. It's a morgue, Commander."

Drake hooked the handle of her mug. "Did you hear anything else from anyone that's of interest to this case?"

Jazie shook her head. "Just Laura's 'help Bruce,' but the old man they found under the bridge . . ."

The commander nodded. "The John Doe?"

"Yes." Jazie's face flushed, and she laced her fingers atop the table. "He, um, doesn't know he's dead yet."

Drake's eyes stretched wide. Morgan held off a groan, wishing Jazie had kept that to herself. Some things just couldn't be explained to those who hadn't experienced them. "His name is Paul Dodd," Morgan said, at the same time Jazie did, to diffuse focus and then deliberately turned Drake's attention back to Laura. "Help Bruce." The same two words Morgan had intuited. She'd naturally assumed they had been Laura's words, but now Morgan had doubts. Had she intuited them from Laura or from Jazie? Either of them could have left the oral imprint. "Was it Laura's voice, Jaz?"

The question surprised her. "I . . . I don't know. I never heard her voice. I thought so—seemed natural—but I can't say it was for a fact."

Morgan nodded. "Same here."

"So is that it, then?" the commander asked Jazie. When she nodded, the commander turned her gaze. "Taylor Lee?"

"She fought hard, Commander." Taylor Lee set down her cup. It clinked against the metal table. "I picked up on three attackers, all male. Every image I saw was consistent with what I observed at Laura and Bruce's residence." The S.A.T. team had walked through the Stern home before the mission the previous evening.

"Consistent?" the commander asked for clarification. "But not the same."

"I can't say with certainty. What I saw in the morgue was splintered," Taylor Lee added. "That happens a lot in violent deaths. But Bruce did do everything humanly possible to get Laura to leave him. That was clear."

Jotting notes down on a yellow legal pad that would never leave the conference room, the commander paused. "What exactly was splintered?"

"He did get physical with her." Taylor Lee snagged the coffee pot from the counter, then refilled the cups. When she set it back on its warming pad, she went on. "But I think he just grabbed her by the upper arms, like you would if you were trying to get someone to hear *and* listen to you, or if you wanted to force them to understand whatever you were trying to tell them. It was more like that than him trying to hurt her." Taylor Lee paused a long second. A range of emotions chased each other across her face. "I don't believe he actually hit her, and I know he wasn't with the men who killed her. He had nothing to do with . . . No, let me put it this way. He didn't do it."

Morgan stiffened. Taylor Lee had alluded to Bruce being somehow involved or connected, but mindful of Drake's grief over her husband's murder, she was trying to tread lightly, and frankly she didn't have a lot of experience at it. Taylor Lee typically spoke the truth as she saw it and let the chips plunk down wherever they may. Interesting that she felt protective of Commander Drake.

Drake picked up on it, too, but let it pass without comment. "How do you know he didn't commit the murder?" she asked Taylor Lee.

"When the men attacked her, Laura was in bed alone." Her hand at her throat, Taylor Lee gently massaged her skin. Though she didn't sense or feel events like Morgan did, her visuals could be horrific, and of course she reacted emotionally to them. "Bruce wasn't there."

"Wasn't in bed, or the room, or in the house?"

"In the house. I can't explain how I know that, Commander." Taylor Lee shrugged. "I just know he wasn't there."

She noted it on the legal pad. "Anything else you want to add?" A frown settled in, wrinkling the skin between her eyebrows. "Perhaps something in the way of physical evidence we can use to save his ass?"

Taylor Lee looked at Morgan and then back to the

boss, her expression deadpan. "I'm not sure his ass should be saved."

Surprise rippled over Drake's face. "But you just said that he didn't kill her."

"That's right. He wasn't there. The three men she fought murdered her. Well, technically, one of the three did." Taylor leaned forward. "But in the last couple of months Bruce inflicted a lot of pain on Laura. A lot of pain," she repeated for emphasis.

"You said he didn't hit her." Drake's frown deepened, carving lines from nose to mouth along the sides of her face. "You're confusing the hell out of me, Taylor Lee."

"Sorry. I'm tired, and it's showing." She straightened in her chair and chose her words carefully. "Bruce inflicted a lot of emotional pain on Laura," she said, her voice tight with disdain. "You know that can be worse than physical abuse, Commander."

Morgan forced herself not to groan. That comment would go over like a lead balloon.

Drake dropped her voice and sent Taylor Lee a warning look that Morgan prayed the woman didn't ignore. "In the last couple of months," Drake said, "at any time Laura Stern wanted to walk out and leave Bruce Stern, she was free to do so. You said yourself he did everything he could to encourage her to go. She chose to stay, and that, in my humble opinion, makes an inarguable statement about whether or not his ass should be saved. Obviously, Laura considered him worth saving. She hung around. Even now her message to us is to help Bruce. That should carry enormous weight, don't you think?"

"Yes, ma'am, it should." Taylor Lee reached for her coffee cup and wisely kept her judgments and any further opinions of Bruce to herself.

Morgan breathed a little easier and let the tension tightening her muscles seep away. Sally Drake was a dangerous woman to piss off. She wore her power lightly, but if she felt the need to wield it, she did so with a master's ease. And she had a lot of it to wield.

"Is that it?" the commander asked Taylor Lee. "Or is there something else you want to address?"

"No, that's it. But I do have one question." Taylor Lee sat back and thought through what she was about to say, clearly not eager to stomp on another of the commander's hot buttons anytime soon. "Do we know if Kunz's assassins turned up at Magnolia Beach harbor?"

"It's possible, but we can't verify it yet," Sally Drake said with a nip to her inner cheek. "Too many tourists down there, confusing the scene. As of fifteen minutes ago, the marina's still packed with people watching the remnants of the tropical storm."

Magnolia Beach was a small community, but during tourist season, it was a madhouse. Many of the visitors had never experienced a storm or hurricane and were unhealthily curious.

Bad luck for the S.A.S.S., but with the harbor crawling

with strangers, there was no possibility of the task force identifying Kunz's men on the boardwalk or in the marina itself. A lot of vessels would be seeking safe harbor from the storm. So unless the assassins pulled an overt attempt to kill the man standing in for Jackson, odds were they wouldn't be spotted. "The crowds down there work against the assassins just as much as they work against us," Morgan said. "People tend to notice high-powered rifles. It's not something most people see routinely."

"Yes," Drake agreed, then set her pen down and folded an arm over the pad. "Two forty-eight took a lot of photos while the *Sunrise* entered the harbor. Hundreds of them. Darcy is reviewing the digitals now, cross-matching people on site with those on Intel's known and suspected G.R.I.D. operatives' lists."

"Mmm." Jazie sighed. "Huge effort."

Drake disputed it. "It'll take her a couple hours."

"Ah, I forgot," Jazie said. "Having total recall certainly has its perks."

"Yes, it does. The computer is running a cross-match, too, to double check," Drake said. "Frankly, it's redundant. Darcy doesn't miss. If she gets anything significant, she'll fax it to your office, Morgan."

Morgan nodded, waiting to be sure Taylor Lee was done, and then addressed the commander. "Could you clear up a discrepancy for me?"

"I'll try." She motioned for Morgan to go ahead.

An uneasiness crept through her for some unknown reason, and Morgan twisted on her seat. "In the pre-mission briefing, we were told that Bruce had been back home from Iraq for three months. When Laura visited my office, she also said he'd been back home three months."

"That's correct, Morgan," Sally Drake said. "He returned from Iraq in May."

"I'm afraid that our information and Laura's was incorrect," Morgan said, her stomach hollow from all that truth implied. "Jackson was with Bruce in Iraq just two days before he returned stateside—"

"I don't see the conflict." The commander lifted her hand, calling the question. The pen in her hand glinted in the light.

"Jackson says Bruce returned home three weeks ago. They were together in Iraq two days before he returned."

The color leached out of Sally Drake's face. *Body double. Body double. Kunz . . .*

"Oh, man." Taylor Lee groaned. "This sounds really bad."

Jazie held off commenting, but her normally sunny expression sobered.

"Are you thinking what I'm thinking, Commander?" Morgan asked, knowing the answer. Her stomach felt so tight her ribs ached.

Sally Drake's color still hadn't returned. "It's possible we have an active Bruce Stern operative," she said. "G.R.I.D. involvement would explain him seemingly being in two places at once. No one other than Kunz has demonstrated the ability to substitute a man who could fool his wife . . ."

"Maybe he wasn't fooling her," Morgan said, aware that Jazie and Taylor Lee were absorbing everything like sponges and struggling to make sense of the conversation. "Maybe that's why there was such strife between them. Jackson was shocked by that."

"Maybe so." Stiffening, Drake hissed in a breath of air. "According to Joan Foster, we've got over fifty unidentified cases that she worked on while she was Kunz's captive. Unfortunately, she doesn't have total recall. We'd be foolish to deny that it's highly possible Bruce and not Jackson was the victim."

"Of what?" Taylor Lee asked, now out of patience.

"Yes, of what?" Jazie added, just as eager to understand all of it.

Morgan ignored them. She had to; dread and fear had burst inside her and burned her throat. Bruce held a high-level job, worked with biological warfare in sensitive antiterrorism sectors. The ramifications of an active body double working in Bruce's place for an undetermined length of time could be staggering—a dream come true for Kunz and G.R.I.D., but horrific for the U.S. and for Bruce. No one in the chain of command, from the S.A.S.S. to the president, could publicly reveal a thing about body doubles as evidence to clear Bruce of any wrongdoing—even if the

S.A.T. could prove it, which would be next to impossible.

"I realize we've entered a highly classified zone here, but is it possible for us to avoid the cryptic aspect of this discussion?" Taylor Lee let out a sigh of pure frustration and propped an elbow on the table. "The images are senseless and making me crazy," she complained. "It's like I'm stuck in a room where everyone is speaking some lost language known only to ancient wise men or something. What are you two talking about?"

Morgan held the commander's gaze, waiting to see if she would disclose their specific suspicions and unwilling to bet either way.

"Commander, please?" Jazie begged. "What I'm hearing is as confusing for me as what Taylor Lee's seeing is to her. How can we do our jobs if you're not willing to give us what we need to interpret things accurately?"

"That's a fair question, Jazie," Drake said, then glanced from Morgan to each of them. "Kunz uses body doubles, like Saddam Hussein and his sons did. Like many do."

"Okay. Hussein had a dozen or so, didn't he?" Jazie asked.

"We know this, Commander," Taylor Lee said. "Remember, we consulted on the mission with Captains Amanda West and Mark Cross. His double was exposed by eating peanuts. He, unlike Mark, wasn't allergic to them."

"Then you remember that there are other doubles inserted in highly classified, sensitive positions, ones we've yet to identify."

"Joan's doubles, you mentioned earlier . . . Holy cow!" Taylor popped the table. "You think Bruce Stern was doubled?"

"Oh, my goodness." Jazie gasped. "That would make sense of the discrepancy in his return home and of the stress between him and Laura."

"It would," Morgan agreed.

Taylor Lee swiped her hand down her face, taking the possibility in. "So . . . the double wanted Laura to leave him before she noticed all the small details a wife would notice—and Laura realized the man in her home who was supposed to be her husband wasn't Bruce?" Taylor frowned. "Is that what you're saying?"

"I'm considering it possible," Morgan said. She wasn't ready to accept it as fact . . . yet.

"Well, if this is so and Bruce was doubled, then who do we have in the brig?" Jazie asked. "Bruce, or his body double?"

Sally Drake's frown cut the grooves in her face even deeper. Her elbow propped on the table, she cupped her chin in her hand. "That's an excellent question."

"One we'd better answer as soon as possible. We can't know for sure through traditional means, Commander. Kunz has substituted DNA before," Morgan explained to Jazie and Taylor Lee, who hadn't been fully briefed on his tactics during earlier consults.

"Oh, shit." Taylor Lee caught herself too late.

"Yeah," the commander said, letting her off the hook.

Morgan went back to their priority. "If Bruce was doubled—which certainly would explain some of Laura's concerns—then it could be that Kunz switched the double out at some point and reinserted Bruce into his own life." The hair on her neck stood up. "If he did, then the question we really need answered now is when it happened."

"Wait a second." Jazie flipped her hair back over her shoulder. "Wouldn't Bruce know that?"

"Not necessarily," Morgan said. Mark Cross had been doubled and hadn't known it. Amanda West hadn't known it, either, until she'd come face to face with her double. "It's possible he didn't."

"It's happened before?" Jazie said.

Morgan didn't answer. She tilted her head. "If this switch happened, did it happen before or after Laura's murder?" Morgan redirected focus. "Was the double here with Laura while Bruce was in Iraq? Or was Bruce here and the double in Iraq?"

"If the double was in Iraq," Jazie said, "that opens a whole new can of worms."

"Yeah, it does." Taylor Lee agreed, her expression more sober than Morgan ever remembered seeing it. "Can we determine what classified information he accessed during the time in question? He could have passed a storehouse on to G.R.I.D. for Thomas Kunz to black-market."

The truth in that turned everyone somber.

Commander Drake lifted her pen. "I'll pass our concern about that up the chain of command. No choice, considering the powers that be won't reveal to us why Bruce was in Iraq. They've made it clear that our priority is solving Laura's murder and proving Bruce's guilt or innocence—the Bruce we have in custody."

Jazie grunted at the limited scope of their involvement. "Kunz wouldn't let a double sit in jail. He'd want him active, getting intelligence G.R.I.D. could sell. Greed motivates Kunz, right?"

"Greed and causing harm to the U.S.," Commander Drake clarified. "Historically, he has let doubles sit in jail, Jazie. His own double was in Leavenworth for months before we knew he wasn't the real Thomas Kunz."

"Well, yeah, but that's different. While we thought we had him, he was free to do his thing. We wouldn't be watching him because we thought we had him."

Commander Drake arched an eyebrow. "And what's to say he doesn't have a valid reason for doing the same thing with a double for Bruce Stern right now?"

"With Kunz you really can't tell, Jazie." A chilling fact Morgan had learned when profiling the man for earlier missions. He was of German descent and hated his country's dependence on America with such a passion that he'd do anything to destroy it. He had proven his resolve by compiling an international network of the most powerful multinational group of terrorists any nation on the planet had encountered in all of recorded history.

"Never underestimate or second-guess him. You'll end up with egg on your face every time," the commander said. "Or with a bullet in your head."

Shuddering inside, Morgan shifted the conversation to solutions. "So we have a few important questions to answer quickly," she said, and then recapped: "Was Bruce Stern doubled? If so, is he or his double in the brig? Did he or his double kill Laura?"

"He wasn't there," Taylor Lee reminded her. "None of the men resembled Bruce, and I expect a double would."

"Okay, we need evidence to verify that," Morgan conceded. "And we need to know if the killers committed Laura's murder with or without the assistance of the G.R.I.D. assassins. If G.R.I.D. assassins did assist in Laura's murder, are they the same assassins Intel expected to assassinate Jackson at the marina, or are they different assassins?" Her mind continued spinning out questions at a dizzying rate. "Either way, are those assassins here in Magnolia Beach? And were they targeting Jackson or Bruce or, if he exists, Bruce's double?"

Taylor and Jazie nodded in unison, mentally exhausted from the lack of sleep but gearing up to keep pushing for the truth.

"All very good and significant questions," the commander said, looking at Morgan. "See if your team can answer them—the faster, the better, for all the obvious reasons."

With hard evidence. Morgan filled in the blank. The commander had come to respect their special abilities but explaining them and substituting them for hard evidence was not acceptable to her or to the honchos. "Yes, ma'am."

At nine thirty on Tuesday morning, Morgan left Providence and drove the twenty miles back to her home in Magnolia Beach. She used the drive to plan. Before reaching her neighborhood, she had her next actions lined up and ready to execute.

Scooping up the newspaper, she walked inside, tossed her keys on the kitchen counter, dropped her handbag onto a bar stool, and toed off her shoes. Then she phoned Taylor Lee with instructions to rest up and then take a second look at the Stern home, this time seeking physical not psychic evidence that Laura's murder had occurred there—the subtle stuff those without her gift might have missed.

"You got it," Taylor Lee said, then ended the call.

Morgan dialed Jazie, waited for her answer, and then said, "Catch a few hours of sleep, Jaz, then get with Darcy Clark on those G.R.I.D. operative photos taken at the Magnolia Beach harbor. If the marina assassins are in

Magnolia Beach—"

"Jackson Stern has a bulls-eye target drawn in the center of his forehead, regardless of whether they're after him or Bruce or Bruce's double."

"Yes," Morgan agreed, not at all surprised Jazie had gotten a firm grip on it so quickly. She was sharp. Often underestimated by her peers—as many beautiful women, especially blondes, were—but very sharp. "To keep him alive, we all need to know it. That includes him."

"Two hours and I'll be on it."

"Thanks, Jaz." Morgan disconnected, dropped the phone into its cradle, and then hit the shower. She'd been itching for hours from the wet suit and was eager to get the salt water off her skin.

Weary to the bone, she had to make herself get out of the shower before she'd drained the hot water tank. Stepping out, she toweled off and then fell into bed and sank into her pillow, drawing the covers up to her neck. God, she was tired. Her mind whirled, and she tried to force it to shut down. She had to shut down enough to sleep for two hours—the whole S.A.T. team did, or the potential of misinterpreting their impressions doubled. If she had a prayer of determining whether Bruce was Bruce or a double, she needed sleep.

An image of Jackson formed in her mind. Sensations of that attraction, that erotic tingling, came with it. "Not now, damn it." She flipped over onto her side, forced the image out of her head, and remembered to set her alarm, then settled back down on her pillow. *Sleep, Morgan. Sleep . . .*

Her lids grew heavy. She closed her eyes. The images of Jackson popped right back into her mind. Strong, physical images and even more potent intuitive ones.

Gritting her teeth, she tried to shake them off, failed, and, muttering, gave into them to get rid of them. His expressions, the tight leash he kept on his emotions, the childlike vulnerabilities that roused that strong sensation of him facing the world alone. It, more than even her potent physical attraction to him, tugged at her heart and seeped in deep.

Oh, you're in trouble here, woman.

The knowing settled into her mind and took hold. She shunned it, turning back onto her other side, then straightened the tangled covers. *You know what? I don't care.*

Don't care? You don't care? How can you not care? This is your professional credibility you're messing with here.

She punched her pillow and settled back in. *This is my life, and it's more important. I like him, okay? He's the first man in a long time who has attracted me.*

Captivated is more like it.

Whatever. I'm not going to play coward and turn away from it. It's just too damn rare.

You're making a mistake, Morgan. A huge, huge mistake.

Maybe. But maybe not. She yawned, letting out a heartfelt sigh. *If it is a mistake, it won't be my first and I'm sure it won't be my last. Either way, the attraction is. It just is. So deal with—and go to freaking sleep!*

The doorbell rang, and then rang again.

Morgan dragged herself awake, far from ready to get up. Groaning, she glanced at her bedside clock through bleary, burning eyes. "10:15?" *Barely an hour.*

She tossed back the covers, cursing under her breath, then grabbed her robe from its hook inside the closet door. "Oh, man. Of all days . . ."

She slung on the silk robe, which seemed ridiculous considering she wore a wracked out Dallas Cowboys T-shirt she'd slept in since her college days at A&M.

The doorbell rang a third time.

"I'm coming." In bare feet, she hustled to the door and then peeked through the viewfinder, but didn't see anyone outside. *A package maybe?* She unlatched the deadbolt and swung the door open, then looked down her wide front porch.

Jackson Stern sat slumped, his head propped in his hands, dozing on her porch swing.

"Dr. Morgan?" A little boy about six stood at the foot of her steps, wearing jeans, a striped shirt, and his baseball cap tugged down over his ears, shading his eyes. "It's me, Justin."

"Hi, Justin." She swept her tussled hair back from her face. "Did you ring my doorbell?"

"Uh huh." He nodded hard enough to crack his neck. "There's a man sleeping on your porch." His words whistled through a gap where his front teeth should have been. "My mom says strangers could be crazy or vinaigrette, and I got worried. So I wanted you to know he was there."

Vinaigrette? She thought, translated. "A *vagrant?*" His mother would have heart failure if she knew he'd come over with a strange man on the porch. Too many perverts on the loose.

"Uh huh." He scratched his neck. "I think so. It started with that sound anyway." He sighed his frustration. "I forgot."

"It's okay, Justin." She tried not to smile. "I know what you mean. Thanks for watching out for me, but I want you to be safe. Next time you see a stranger here, tell your mom and have her call me instead of coming over yourself, okay?"

"Okay, Dr. Morgan." Justin took off running back across the street to his home.

Jackson sat up. "I've been called a lot of things, but salad dressing is new to me."

Watching Justin go inside, Morgan grinned. "There's consolation. You could also be crazy."

"I'm not crazy," Jackson said, "but another night like last night, and I think I'd probably welcome the reprieve."

"I'm pretty sure you're safe from that." Unless God was napping, she'd pretty much bet on it. She walked down to his end of the porch. The shaded slats were cool under her feet. "Good morning again, Jackson."

"I'm sorry to bother you," he said, then hauled himself to his feet. "I, um, didn't know where else to go. Can't go to the boat, to Bruce's, and—"

"It's no bother," she lied. Odds of her getting back to sleep were nil, but he looked so lost. "I'm glad you're here," she said and meant it. "Come on in, and I'll make us some coffee. Do you drink coffee?"

He nodded. "Thanks." He walked over and passed her to enter the house.

Morgan wondered what had happened but sensed nothing. He was focused on her home. She looked at it through his eyes. Cluttered but clean, with a menagerie of cushy and comfortable furnishings that weren't at all pretentious. She sensed the word *welcoming* come to his mind.

Pleased by that, she lifted a hand. "Kitchen is this way," she said, and then led him through the entry and living room, across an open-columned hallway—dining room to the left, study to the right—and to the sunny yellow kitchen that overlooked the bay. Beyond the wide windows and the lawn, the water glistened, sun-spangled and inviting. "Have a seat. Your choice." She motioned to the bar and to the oak table and chairs beyond it.

He chose the bar and sat on a stool with a little grunt.

"Sorry to wake you." He rubbed at the back of his neck. "I didn't expect your little guardian to come over and ring the bell."

"Chivalry is alive and well, at least in pints." She smiled. "I'm surprised you aren't asleep." She paused and leaned against the counter. With Laura and Bruce, how could he sleep? "Mind won't shut down?" she asked, opening the door in case he needed to talk.

"That, too, but honestly I haven't had the chance to test it. The VOQ was booked."

That she hadn't expected. "I don't understand. Taylor Lee reserved and confirmed your room before you went over."

"She did," he said, letting her off the hook. "It was a clerical error on their end. No room at the inn, or at any other inn anywhere around. The desk clerk looked for an hour. All the way up to the Alabama state line. But even the fleabags were booked solid."

"Ouch." Morgan winced. "Holiday weekends can be that way." Considering his circumstances, this really sucked. In the last twenty-four hours, he hadn't been able to catch a break with a net and both hands. "I'm so sorry, Jackson."

"Me, too," Jackson responded earnestly.

Morgan filled the coffeepot with water, put in a filter, and added gourmet Columbian grounds. She loved good coffee.

Jackson continued, "But at least someone left a bag for me at the desk."

Alarm slammed through her. "A bag?"

"It's okay. It's just clothes and personal items," he swiftly assured her. "It's my black duffle off the *Sunrise*. I left it out on the porch by the swing."

Her mind relieved, she turned back to his motel dilemma. "You should have come over right away."

"I did." He shrugged. "But you weren't home yet, and I didn't hear you come in."

A little embarrassed, he leaned an arm on the bar. "Guess I dozed off pretty quick. It's a comfortable swing."

That would embarrass an operative. They, like other Special Forces folks, were trained to perform and be ready for anything at all times. *Interesting.* "A local woodcarver made the swing. He custom designs them." When she'd driven up, she hadn't seen Jackson on her porch, but she hadn't left the light on, either. And he had been on her mind, so even if she'd intuited him, she would have automatically attributed it to him being in her thoughts and dismissed it. She flipped the switch to turn on the coffeemaker. "Are you hungry?"

"No, but if I could take a shower, I'd appreciate it. Salt water makes my skin itch."

"Sure." She started to direct him to the bathroom, but wanted to address something else first. "Jackson, I'm sorry I had to shoot you."

"I know, Morgan." Betrayal still stung, but it wasn't directed at her. It was directed at the system. "In your shoes, I would have executed the order, too."

Their eyes met and held. Her pulse quickened. "Thank you." He hadn't had to be gracious. And he wasn't being kind because she was investigating Bruce and Laura's cases. He genuinely understood. "Are you always so gracious?"

"Honestly, no, I'm not." He paused to glance out on the water, gather himself. "But you're not the enemy in all this. I know that. You're just doing your job."

"It's a little more than that for me, Jackson," she confessed, having no idea why. "Laura came to me for help. I need to know if I missed something that caused her death."

"Don't borrow guilt," he advised her. His tone said he'd been there, done that, and it hadn't been a pleasant experience. "Enough finds us on its own."

"I need to know the truth."

"Yes." He understood completely. "So do I." He didn't blink or look away. "If we're going to sort through this and stop whatever Kunz plans, we need each other, Morgan."

Knowing he was right, she nodded. "The shower is down that hallway," she said. "First door on the right."

"Thanks." He left the kitchen, retrieved his duffle from the front porch, and then headed into her guest suite.

Minutes later, she heard the water running. Pouring herself a cup of coffee, she sat down at the bar and resigned herself to the fact that more sleep was not in her immediate future. Oddly, with Jackson there, she didn't feel groggy, or weary, or tired. She felt aware. Aware and alert and alive.

Oh, that's a wickedly bad sign, woman. You're going way

over the line. So far over it, you can't even see it anymore. He could be working with Kunz.

That's ridiculous. Joan had debriefed him. If he had been a Kunz operative, it would have come out then. It hadn't. She had nothing to fear from him.

Except maybe your heart. And making a damn fool of yourself.

Shut up.

The phone rang. Morgan slid off the stool and answered it on its second ring.

"Hey," Taylor Lee said. "Sorry if I woke you—"

"I wasn't asleep."

"Oh, well, okay. Anyway, I've been thinking."

"About what?"

She hesitated, then asked, "Are you on a secure line?"

All three of the phone lines into Morgan's house, including her fax line, were secure lines. "Yes." She moved back to the stool. Her stomach growled. When had she last eaten?

"You need to order a DNA sample on Bruce, the one in the brig."

"Hasn't one been ordered already?" Morgan sipped from her cup and resisted the urge to hold it against her forehead to see if the heat would help dissipate a dull ache that fear and doubt about Jackson had put there. "Surely Darcy did that."

"No, she didn't," Taylor Lee said, clearly surprised. "I

just checked."

"Odd." With Darcy's total recall, she usually didn't miss a thing. So why hadn't she run a DNA on Bruce? "Why do you want it run?" Morgan asked Taylor Lee. Had she drawn the same conclusion?

"To positively ID him, the guy in the brig. So we know if he's Bruce or a double."

Obviously she'd gotten her two hours and was already back at it. Morgan relayed orders. "Have Dr. Vargus go to the correctional facility and pull the blood himself. Warn him to not relinquish possession of it to anyone, or to let the sample out of his sight even for a second. He'll have to do it all, including run the test at the lab himself."

"Got it."

Now came the disappointing part. "You do understand that this alone won't give us a positive ID on the man incarcerated, right?" Morgan warned.

"Why the hell not?" Taylor Lee asked, blustering. "Kunz can't change a man's DNA. He can do plastic surgery and behavioral modifications, but no one can do that."

"True, but Kunz has successfully substituted false and alternate DNA test results in our computer systems before," she said. "I mentioned it during the conference, but there was a lot going on."

Taylor Lee's reaction took a substantial time coming. Clearly, she realized the magnanimity of Morgan's disclosure, and it worried her as much as it should. "How do we ever prove . . . Morgan, can we ever know for a fact who we're dealing with in any of these cases with Kunz?"

"We get creative." It wouldn't be easy to determine whether they had Bruce Stern or his double in this case—or any person or a double in any other case. But it could be done. Necessity had demanded they find ways, and they had. Morgan refilled her coffee cup, then returned to the bar and slid onto her padded stool. "We've had this problem before," she said. "We have methods."

"What? If DNA won't do it, what does?"

"Joan Foster, doing just what she did for us last night."

"Oh, hell, Morgan. We can't let Joan put this incarcerated guy through the paces." Taylor heaved a sigh. "If we bring her to the brig and she does her thing, word will be all over kingdom come in an hour. And we'd set off so many alarms, they'd still be blaring a month from now." Taylor Lee huffed, shooting static through the phone. "You know as well as I do that jerk of a commander running Providence isn't going to lift a finger to help us. There's no way he'd release the suspect into our custody to bring him to her at the hospital. He wants us to fail."

He did. Well, he wanted Sally Drake to fail. *Pissing contests are so stupid*, Morgan thought.

Taylor Lee grunted. "We're screwed."

She was right, at least insofar as she went. "True on all

fronts," Morgan said. "But—"

Jackson walked out of the guest bedroom and into the kitchen, wearing a pair of khaki slacks and a soft blue golf shirt. Freshly shaven, smelling of soap, he reached up to adjust his collar.

"Don't worry. Seriously," she said into the phone, knowing a way around this. "We have a secret weapon." She smiled at Jackson. "I'll handle it."

"Handle what? What can we do?"

"It's all relative," she said, not wanting to be overtly blunt until she'd gained Jackson's agreement. "I'll let you know as soon as I've worked out the details."

"Whatever you say," Taylor told her, then shared an update on other pertinent information.

"Thanks," Morgan said, mentally noting all she'd been told. She hung up the phone, poured Jackson a cup of coffee, and then warmed up her own. "I need something from you, Jackson." She passed him the cup.

"Sure." He sat down and accepted it. "What?"

Morgan looked him right in the eye. "Your blood."

His hand stilled, and the cup stopped halfway to his mouth. "Do I get to know why?"

Her face went hot. "Can we leave it with, 'because I asked'?" She could tell him anything, but she needed to know where things stood between them now, not later when she might be relying on him to cover her back.

He stared at her a long moment. "You're asking me

for a lot."

"I am."

"To trust a woman who shot me twice, drugged me, and then abducted me—"

"I remember."

"Without any explanation whatsoever . . ."

"Not really." She gave him a little shrug. "I'm guilty on all counts of everything you said. There's no dispute." Her honestly shone in her eyes. "But I'm also the woman trying to save your brother's life and to find your sister-in-law's murderer."

Slowly, Jackson set down his cup, looked at it a long second, and then stuck out his arm, his palm up and the vein at his inner elbow exposed. "Take all you need."

Trust. Morgan's chest swelled. It wasn't uncommon for her patients to come to trust her, but Jackson wasn't her patient, and he didn't have the benefit of first getting to know her well. Their first interactions had been adversarial and fierce, then intense and emotionally hyper-charged. They had crosscut a lot of the usual bonding that formed in relationships, zipping past the normal introductory phase and rocketing along at warp speed.

Touched, Morgan had to work to keep her voice level. "Thank you, Jackson," she said and genuinely meant it. Trust couldn't come easily to him after a lifetime that included no support. Why Bruce hadn't been there for Jackson confounded her, because he certainly had been for his brother. In time, she needed to be able to answer that question. But for now, it was more than enough that Jackson had somehow reached beyond all those issues and the baggage he carried because of them. Somehow, he had justified giving his trust to her. Knowing what that had to have cost him, how could she not react to it? Not be touched? Moved? Honored and humbled? And really, really surprised?

She touched his arm, gently pressed down, lowering it to the bar and resting her fingertips against his skin. "We'll drop by the hospital on the way to see Bruce after we eat something."

"All right." He looked at her fingertips on his arm, and an odd expression crossed his face. He blinked, buried it, but didn't move.

He liked her touching him. A thrill skimmed through her. She lifted her fingers, and he pulled his arm back, dropped it close to his body.

"I know you said you weren't hungry, but I need fuel." She walked to the fridge, cracked open the door. "It's a decent meal now, or I'll be looking for doughnuts or anything sweet and shoving them down my throat all day."

"I hate it when I do that," he confessed.

"Me, too," she said. "I hit the treadmill for an extra mile, which is hardly enough."

He tilted his head. "You're working me, Morgan Cabot, so I eat."

"Yeah, I guess I am. But every word was true." She pulled fresh onions and tomatoes out of the fridge, eggs and mushrooms and cheese—all the things needed for her favorite omelets.

"At least you're honest about it," he said more to himself than to her, then drank half a cup of coffee in silence, watching her work at the stove. "Ah."

"Ah?" she asked, setting a plate before him filled with a fluffy omelet and two slices of whole wheat toast.

"You know for a fact I'm Jackson Stern. Now you're going to compare my blood with Bruce's to make sure that he's my blood brother . . . in case he isn't."

Morgan looked away. The man was too sharp for his own good. She added her eggs to the pan and heard the little sizzle.

"There wasn't a question in that remark, Morgan. You can relax," he said.

"Good." She folded the omelet, feeling a slight tremor in her hand and hoping he didn't notice it.

"But I do have another comment . . ."

Smelling the green peppers, she flipped the omelet from the pan to her plate. "What's that?"

Jackson waited until she looked at him to ask. "You're clearly afraid Bruce—the guy in the brig—isn't my brother," Jackson said, his gaze boring, his expression far more sober than curious.

She blinked, and then blinked again. "That was also a

remark, not a question," she said.

"Yes, but there is a question, Morgan," Jackson warned her, "and I do want it answered."

She set her plate down and leaned against the bar for support. He seemed emotionally stable enough to handle whatever came up, and she had the authorization for full disclosure, but was he ready? Really? He had been through an enormous amount of devastation in the past twenty-four hours. "All right. I'll do my best."

He rimmed his cup with his thumb. "If the man arrested isn't Bruce, then who is he? And where is my brother?"

That she could answer honestly. Jackson wouldn't like what she would say, but it would be the truth. "I don't know whether or not he's Bruce," she confessed. "That's why I need your blood—to compare it to the detainee's to make that determination. And if he isn't Bruce, then I don't know who he is, or where your brother is located."

Jackson obviously hadn't expected an answer that frank. His jaw dropped open, and he just stared at her. It took a moment for him to recover, and when he did, he tossed down the gauntlet of challenge. "*Yet*. You don't know *yet*, right?"

"Yes, that is correct." She stiffened and accepted it. "I don't know *yet*."

CHAPTER 5

The brig was actually a minimum-security prison located less than a mile from the hospital on Providence Air Force Base.

The facility itself was a muddy-colored, multistory square brick building like most of those on the base, but unlike the others, it was surrounded by an eight-foot fence topped with razor wire. One gate led into it and its associated cluster of buildings, and long before reaching any of them, an entrant was detained at a manned gate until given authorization to continue on inside.

Morgan braked to a stop outside the brick and dark-glass guard shack positioned in the middle of the road, and rolled down her window, ID badge in hand. Jackson rolled a hip to remove his wallet from his slacks' pocket.

A young airman walked outside to her car door. He was armed with a gun and a scanner. First, he examined her ID; then he examined her. "Would you please remove your sunglasses, Dr. Cabot?"

She did and then held still. Through the open window, he flashed a scanner over her left iris and then her right. When she cleared the security check, he walked around the front of the car to the passenger's side, checked Jackson's ID card, scanned him, then returned to Morgan's side of the vehicle.

"I thought this was a minimum security facility," Jackson said softly so only she could hear. The air conditioner blew bits of his hair over his forehead.

"It is, but it's a minimum security federal prison at Providence." Catching Jackson's blank look, she added, "It's under Colonel Gray's command, and he's . . ."

"Anal?"

"And then some," she confessed, hoping it didn't come back to haunt her.

The airman continued watching his screen, pretending to be stone deaf. No doubt he also had stories to tell on Gray, but he kept them to himself. Probably wise, considering the man had the power to make his life a living hell. Finally, he said, "Okay, you're clear." He looked at Morgan. "Drive straight ahead and park in row C, Dr. Cabot. If you park anywhere else, your car will be impounded and you'll have to get clearance from the base commander to get it back." His tone promised it wouldn't be a pleasant experience.

"Row C. Got it. Thanks." She rolled up her window, pulled out, and glanced over at Jackson. "In case you had any doubts that I was unfairly biased against Colonel Gray, that policy should prove I wasn't. He's . . . slightly rigid."

"Slightly?" Jackson asked, cutting loose his sarcasm.

"I was being gracious."

"Don't waste your energy," he said. "It's obvious he's still at war with Commander Drake and flexing his muscles wherever he can just to needle her."

"You know about that?"

"Doesn't everyone?"

"Uh, no. Most people have no idea Commander Drake is even here."

"Not so," Jackson countered. "Everyone knows where she is and that Gray's shorts are in a wad because she beat him out of a plum Special Forces command. Though very few know that the plum command entails the S.A.S.S. units."

How Jackson had access to this highly classified information was anyone's guess. But it was right on target, which meant he'd been briefed from above and not learned it through the underground grapevine below. "That pretty well covers it."

"She's the better commander, and he should grow up."

"He should, but considering he's about to retire, I don't

hold out much hope for the growing-up part."

"Ah, the voice of personal experience from dealing with the man."

Crossing the D row, Morgan glanced at Jackson.

"Gray hates Commander Drake because he lost out to her," Jackson explained. "He coveted that job, and there's only one reason he hasn't already retired. He was supposed to go last year but pulled his papers."

"I didn't know that." Being a civilian consultant, Morgan didn't hear all the gossip, though she picked up on a lot during her counseling sessions. "So what's the one reason?"

"The Providence command," Jackson said. "These days, his purpose in life is to make everyone under Drake's command miserable, which naturally includes you." Jackson's disgust was evident. "Damn shame. At one time, Gray was a decent officer."

So Jackson knew about that, too. Her curiosity about how he'd come to know so much grew in leaps. "Have you ever worked under him?"

"No." He let out a humorless laugh. "Not bloody likely."

That was pretty adamant talk for a career military officer. They were routinely handed assignments they didn't want and were given no choice but to take them and give 100 percent on the job. She let out a noncommittal murmur and then decided to just straight out ask what she most wanted to know. "What exactly do you do these days?"

"Officially, I fly into hurricanes. Weather recon." His eyes smiled, but his lips remained flat. "Unofficially, I dabble."

"Dabble?" She waited, and he nodded; then she pushed further. "Which means you're involved in whatever, wherever, whenever," she surmised, figuring he was assigned directly to the Secretary of Defense or else to General Shaw, and his Hurricane Hunter job was a cover. He was probably assigned to the secretary; he had been the one who first authorized Colonel Drake to grant Jackson full disclosure. General Shaw had only later confirmed it.

Jackson didn't respond.

She didn't really expect that he would, but she couldn't stop herself from nudging him a little more. "You do know that you're at liberty to talk to me about anything, right? It's all authorized and totally confidential."

"I'm aware of that, yes."

So since their last meeting, he'd been briefed on her, too. She turned the radio down a notch. "That's what I do," she said, "listen to people talk about things they need to talk about but can't discuss with anyone else."

Morgan pulled into her assigned space in Row C and slid the gearshift into *park.* She left the engine running to keep the air conditioner going. It was melt-you-in-five-seconds hot outside and muggy as hell.

Jackson, ignoring Morgan's last comment, turned to another subject. "I think Laura knew something was seriously wrong with Bruce, Morgan. I can't prove it, but it's the only way most of what's happened makes any sense."

"Why do you think so?"

Jackson turned the radio off and unsnapped his safety belt. It clicked loudly in the silence. "Because she came to you," he said, twisting in his seat to face her. "And because coming to you would be a career-killer for Bruce, and she knew it."

It wasn't really, unless the stress of the job was deemed too much a burden for the individual carrying it. That could compromise the military member and national security. "Not necessarily, Jackson. In three years, I've had to recommend fewer than five transfers to less demanding positions." *Ones where high-level security clearances weren't required and their absence didn't create command issues.*

"Trust me on this," he countered. "In Bruce's job, talking to anyone is a career-killer, and Laura knew it. That's why her coming to you, especially in an official capacity, has bugged the hell out of me since I first heard it. She wouldn't do it. She would never do something she knew would kill his career. It meant everything to him, and he meant everything to her."

Jackson believed what he was saying, and as connected as he was, if he believed it, she'd be a fool not to believe it, too. "But she did come to me." Surprise trickled up Morgan's back, and two questions burned in her mind. She doubted Jackson would answer either of them, but she had to ask. "What is Bruce's job?"

Jackson nodded *no*.

Disappointment shot through her, and she backed off then tried a different approach. "Do you think Laura wanted Bruce reassigned to a less demanding job? One where maybe he would be less exposed and at home more?"

Fear flittered through Jackson's eyes, and he nodded. "That's possible."

A strong intuitive flash zapped Morgan, cramped her muscles, and she recalled Taylor Lee's impression of Bruce and Laura arguing and him grabbing her upper arms. He'd squeezed them so tightly they'd bruised.

It took Morgan a moment to recover and speak. "Her interfering with his career, maybe to the point that as a result he'd be removed from his job—you think that could be sufficient motive for Bruce to kill her."

Jackson's eyes shone overly bright, and he cleared his throat. "Bruce lived and breathed his job. He'd be lost without Laura, but without his work . . ." Jackson looked out through the windshield. "Bruce would rather be . . . dead."

Morgan's heart beat hard and fast. "So you think he killed her for talking to me?"

No answer. He dropped his gaze to the floorboard.

Morgan reached over, covered his hand with hers. "Jackson?" She waited until he looked up at her. The pain radiating from him staggered her. "Do you think Bruce killed Laura?"

Regret, remorse, and guilt—so much guilt—pounded

off him in deep, rolling waves. "I don't know what he's done," he said, "but to save his job . . ." Jackson dipped his chin to his chest and cupped his head in his hands. "God, forgive me."

Morgan stroked his shoulder. "Don't do this, Jackson," she whispered. "There's a lot at stake. You have to consider all possibilities."

"But he's my brother, Morgan," he said, his voice trembling with anguish. "My brother."

"And he will remain so, guilty or innocent," she reminded him.

"I owe him my loyalty. I owe him my faith in his innocence."

"You're wrong about that. The only thing you owe him *and* Laura is the truth," she said. "Seeking the truth when you don't know the outcome isn't being disloyal. It's the ultimate expression of faith. It says you don't fear your findings enough to avoid them."

"But I do fear them." He finally looked at her. "I fear them more than I've feared anything in my life."

"Because he might be guilty."

"Because Laura turned to me for help, and I didn't drop everything and come to her," Jackson said. "If Bruce is guilty, then Laura's death is my fault. If I'd been here, I could have stopped . . ."

"You don't know that," Morgan said, absently rubbing his forearm. "I can tell you from experience that if someone is of a mind to commit murder, they'll find a way to do it, Jackson. Nothing you could have done would have stopped it." She drew in a steadying breath. "But listen. Right now, we don't know if Bruce is guilty or innocent, and speculating isn't constructive to anyone, including him. So let's resolve to just not do it."

"How?" He looked at her as if he wanted to do what she suggested but had no idea how to make it happen.

"Let's keep an open mind and wait and see what the evidence tells us. Until then, we really don't know what to think or feel about any of this, other than sorrow that Laura is dead."

"And Bruce is in jail accused of killing her."

"We can feel sorrow about that, too. Either way," Morgan said. "We'll deal with everything beyond this when we know for a fact what happened."

Jackson nodded.

Morgan turned off the engine, and they got out of her Jeep and then walked across the parking lot to enter the facility. After the intense heat and humidity outside, the blast of cold air inside the door felt refreshing.

They cut across the open, expansive lobby with its gleaming floors and stopped at the front desk. A man about forty, armed to the teeth and wearing a sergeant's rank, looked up at them. "May I help you?"

"Good afternoon, Sergeant Dayton," Morgan said, reading his name tag, and offered him a smile. "Dr. Cabot and Captain Stern to see inmate Captain Bruce Stern."

He ran their names through his computer and passed over a clipboard. "You're both on the authorized visitor's list. You just need to sign in."

While they signed, the sergeant phoned to have Bruce brought to the interview room. When he got off the phone, he motioned to a young airman. "Parson, please escort Dr. Cabot and Captain Stern to Interview Room D."

Parson looked about twelve, tall and thin, with a nose that splattered halfway across his face. Definitely had been broken, likely more than once. "This way, please."

They followed him through a maze of bland corridors to a small room that was even more bland: unadorned white walls, floor, and ceiling, and a rickety table and four wooden chairs that sat dead center in the room. Sterile, and void of anything else. Not even a clock.

Bruce was escorted in shortly, wearing jeans, a blue denim work shirt, and white sneakers with no shoestrings. Commander Drake must have him on suicide watch. In person, his resemblance to Jackson was even more striking. He was obviously a few years younger, but from a distance, she doubted she could tell them apart.

He was curious about Morgan, but his eyes lit up when he spotted his brother. "Jackson."

They greeted each other awkwardly, both flushed and uncertain what to say. Finally, Jackson introduced Morgan.

"Bruce, this is Dr. Morgan Cabot."

He nodded, unsure if she was an ally or an enemy, but motioned for them to sit.

Morgan took a seat; then Bruce sat down across the scuffed table from her. His eyes clouded, and he focused on his brother. "I hoped they would call you," he said, his eyes welling up. "Laura is dead, Jax."

"I know." Jackson dropped into the chair beside Morgan and folded his hands atop the table. "I'm sorry, Bruce." A knot in his throat had him swallowing hard. "It doesn't seem like enough to say, but you know . . ."

"Yeah." Bruce blinked hard and fast. "I know."

Morgan watched the men, fascinated by the relationship dynamic between them. Interesting, to say the least. More like parent and child than brothers. Captivated by that oddity, Morgan kept quiet and just let them talk. Often she learned far more by listening than by interrogating, and she hoped that would be the case now.

"I have to ask, bro." Jackson locked gazes with Bruce. "Did you kill her?"

"No." Bruce's voice was strong, emphatic, and resentful enough to be sincere, but he didn't hold Jackson's gaze, which honestly could have shattered stone. "I did not."

Jackson pursed his lips and nodded. "So who did?"

Bruce looked him in the eye. "I don't know."

"Why not?" Jackson asked. "Where were you when she died?"

Bruce's jaw trembled, and hurt flashed in his eyes. "I

can't believe I have to put up with this from you, too. I thought you, of all people, would know better."

"Sorry. You're my brother and I love you, but there are no free rides on this one. I loved her, too." Jackson sat back, watched Bruce for a long second, and then added, "I want answers. No half-truths, no professional diversionary tactics, no posturing, and no damn games. I expect the truth, and if you loved Laura, you'll want me to have it and you'll give it to me."

"I loved her," Bruce insisted, trembling all over. He'd been mentally counting on Jackson's unqualified support. His disappointment at not getting it was palpable. "You know I loved her."

"I know she loved you as much as you love yourself," Jackson countered. "If you loved her, then answer my damn questions and tell me the truth. Where were you when Laura was murdered?"

Bruce's temper flared. He stared at the ceiling for a long moment, reining the anger in, then rolled his neck and glared daggers into an eye-level spot on the wall, avoiding looking at Jackson. "I was at a bar on Highway 98."

"Alone?"

"Yes, alone," Bruce snapped and stiffened. "What the hell kind of question is that?"

"A fair one." Jackson didn't ease up a bit. "You're a married man. What are you doing in a bar alone when your wife's waiting at home? Were you meeting some of the guys, or what?"

"No, I wasn't meeting anyone." He licked his lips. "I needed some time to myself."

"Why?" Jackson didn't break his gaze.

Unrelenting. The force of it had Morgan squirming, and it wasn't even directed at her.

It knocked the defiance right out of Bruce. He slumped in his chair, and his jaw quivered. "Laura and I had an argument, a bad one."

"About the job?" Jackson asked. He had more insight than one would expect from a brother not directly involved in their daily lives.

"Yeah." Bruce nodded. "I got pissed and left."

"You got pissed, grabbed her by the upper arms, and then left," Jackson corrected him.

Regret too deep to be anything but sincere shadowed Bruce's eyes. "Yes. One of my many regrets."

"Grabbing her, or leaving her at home alone?"

"Both," he said simply, his voice cracking. "I wish I hadn't done either, but I did, and now it's too late. Can't take it back." He cleared his throat, forced himself to meet that unrelenting gaze. "Can't change anything . . ."

"Did you hit her?"

Morgan curled her fingers into fists in her lap. No one could miss the tightly leashed restraint in Jackson, and if Bruce had hit Laura, Morgan doubted anything but a bullet between the eyes would keep Jackson from killing his brother with his bare hands.

"No way." Bruce hotly defended himself on that one.

It was a steadfast rule. Men didn't hit women under any circumstances. Morgan picked that up from both of them and wondered what had instilled it. Abuse? A strong mother who had instructed them? Could be either, or something else entirely.

Jackson went on. "When did you come home?"

Bruce glared at his brother. "I've had about enough of your questions."

"Sorry to hear that, because I've got a lot more of them." He tapped his laced hands on the scuffed table. "You can either answer them for me, so maybe I can help you avoid the needle, or you can answer them for someone who doesn't give a damn if you live or die." Jackson shrugged. "Up to you."

The heat leaked out of Bruce. His shoulders slumped. "I came home after the bar closed, at about four."

"You stayed in the bar, alone, until four in the morning?" Jackson had asked the question in a civil manner, but the skepticism in his voice proved he didn't believe what he'd been told.

And clearly Bruce knew it. "No, I didn't, and I didn't say that I did."

Jackson's jaw clamped tight. "I told you not to play around with me, Bruce. This is your last warning. Jack me around again, and you're on your own."

That stunned Bruce; Morgan felt the shock ripple through him.

He lowered his gaze to the table, dragged his thumb across its edge. "I left the bar about midnight."

Good thing Jackson was explicit. If he hadn't been, Bruce wouldn't have volunteered that information. After being warned against diversions, why had he tried to pull that nonsense with Jackson? Especially knowing he was trying to help him. Morgan thought about it from different angles, but it just didn't make sense.

Jackson's next question claimed her attention. "After you left the bar, where did you go?"

"I drove around a little, then stopped down on the beach by the harbor." Remembering that night had him regretting what he'd done and hadn't done. The tension in him strengthened, and he squeezed his eyes shut.

"You sat in the car?"

"No," he looked at Jackson. "I walked down the pier and just hung out." He hiked a shoulder. "It was quiet. The water lapping at the pilings . . . it calmed me down."

"You hung out alone?"

Bruce's jaw tightened, but he nodded. "Until about four." Sweeping a hand over his forehead, he blinked hard. "The bar was too noisy. I didn't want company, Jax. I wanted someplace quiet to think. Normally, I'd have gone to the *Sunrise*, but you had it, so I walked down to the sand, sat down, and, well, thought."

"About what?"

Morgan watched the brothers. She sensed that Jackson believed Bruce, and his body language confirmed it. The dynamic between them surpassed interesting. It was fascinating. Bruce had a wicked temper he had to work at to control. He deeply resented Jackson's questions, but the very moment Jackson had revealed that he would be trying to save Bruce's ass, he acquiesced and the dynamic shifted from rivaling brothers jockeying for the upper hand back to a parent and child relationship. Morgan saw this type of thing often in single-parent families but seldom found it in ones where both parents had been present, and both had been present in the Stern household.

"I asked what you were thinking about, Bruce," Jackson said.

"I know."

"Then answer me, damn it."

"It's not that easy. You won't understand."

"So tell me anyway."

Bruce hesitated a long time. He feared the truth would upset Jackson and leave him in a bad light.

"Laura is dead, and I'm not playing games, Bruce," Jackson said. "Don't make me ask you again."

His eyes flashed anger, and he shot Jackson a withering look. "I was trying to figure out how to force Laura to divorce me."

"What?"

"You heard me," Bruce said. "I'd already tried everything I knew to try, but nothing worked. She refused to leave me."

"Everything?" Jackson asked. "Does that include knocking her around? Choking her? Squeezing her damn arms so tight you left bruises?"

"Hell, no. Have you gone crazy?" Bruce paled. "I'd never hit Laura. I never choked her, either."

"But you grabbed her by her upper arms and bruised her."

No answer.

"Don't lie to me, or I swear to God I'll walk out of here and never look back."

Morgan held her breath. Jackson wasn't bluffing. Did Bruce realize that? If he did cross the line, how could she intervene and soothe the rift enough to make Jackson stay? She'd have to, because she was learning far more from Jackson questioning his brother than she'd ever learn on her own—at least, this quickly. *Come on, Bruce. Talk straight. Please, talk straight.*

Bruce blinked hard and fast. "I . . . I grabbed her, trying to shake some sense into her." He licked his lips, and remorse set in. "But when I looked into her eyes and saw she was afraid of me. I . . . I couldn't stand it, Jax." A tear coursed down Bruce's cheek. He pretended not to notice it had fallen, and went on. "I told her she had no choice. I would have a divorce, and I wanted her out of the house and out of Magnolia Beach right away." The words burned his throat. "Then I left the house."

That surprised Jackson. "*You* wanted a divorce?"

Bruce chewed at his inner lip, but wouldn't meet Jackson's eyes. "It was . . . for the best."

"For whom?"

That question earned Jackson another glare. "Honestly?"

"Nothing less will do," Jackson said, not fazed in the least.

Bruce frowned. "For both of us."

Definitely a motivated response and a motivated action. But what—or whom—could motivate Bruce into believing that divorce was the best option?

Jackson recognized the underpinnings in Bruce's response, too, and he pushed for more of an answer. "Because . . ."

His expression turned wooden, and Bruce refused to answer.

Undeterred, Jackson backed off then regrouped and headed back in, trying a different approach. "You two loved each other," he said. "Given that, and that your marriage has been a solid one for nearly a decade, I have to ask. Were the reasons you considered a divorce personal or professional?"

Again Bruce refused to answer.

Sensing that it was time, and that she'd made an

assumption she now needed to verify, Morgan interceded. "Bruce, you are aware of the fact that Laura was my patient, correct?"

"Your patient?" He blinked. "No, I didn't know she'd been to a doctor. Was she ill?"

Jackson grunted. "You're her husband, damn it. If she was sick, wouldn't you know it?"

Bruce didn't look away from Morgan. "Not necessarily," he said, then asked Morgan. "Why was she seeing you? What kind of doctor are you?"

"I'm a psychologist, Bruce."

He sucked in a sharp breath. "Oh, no. Then she told you . . ."

So much for Jackson's theory that Bruce had killed her to save his job. Bruce's reaction was too blunt and genuine to not be honest, and it tossed the theory right out the window. "Told me what?"

He didn't answer.

"She didn't fear you," Morgan said. "But she did fear what was happening to you and to your marriage."

Remorse flooded his eyes, put lines of strain on his face alongside his mouth. "You have no idea how much I regret that."

Jackson muttered his thoughts. "What did you do to her? What did you break and expect her to fix?"

Anger flashed in Bruce's eyes and flushed his skin. "It wasn't my fault, Jackson."

Jackson had wanted to test Bruce's reaction and, while he had responded in a way Morgan expected Jackson would approve, he clearly didn't.

"It never is, bro." Jackson stood up, shoved his chair under the table. "That's the problem. You do what you want, everyone around you pays the price and limps on, and you walk out shining like a diamond—except for this time. This time, Laura paid with her life." Jackson turned for the door.

"It's wasn't like that," Bruce called after him. "Listen to me. Jax, wait. It wasn't like that!"

But Jackson didn't listen. He kept walking, left the room, and shut the door behind him.

Morgan felt the disappointment in Bruce. It was as strong as, if not stronger than, Jackson's disappointment in his brother.

Bruce turned to her. "It's not like that," he said. "I swear it."

"What is it like?" Morgan asked, deliberately keeping her tone level and her voice soft and nonthreatening.

"What's the difference? He won't listen."

"Maybe your freedom is the difference," she said. "Bruce, your brother is as torn about this as you would be if your positions were reversed. You can't expect him to blow off answers to questions, no matter how hard they are for either of you."

"I don't." He started to say something, changed his

mind, and fell silent.

"What do you have to say that you want me to hear?"

Her insight into him surprised him, and it showed. He debated and elected not to share it. But it didn't matter. "Let me tell you," she offered. "You want me to know that you loved your wife and that you're innocent."

He ran his tongue up against the roof of his mouth and nodded.

"I hear you." Morgan sat back and rubbed a clammy hand over her thigh. "I'm going to need a blood sample from you. My associate, Dr. Vargus, will be here in about forty minutes to take it. Do you have any objections?"

"No." Bruce kept watching the door, as if he expected Jackson to come back through it.

Morgan could have spared him the hope. Jackson was maxed out and knew it. He wouldn't return until he had sorted through things on his own, and he had a lot to sort through. "Exactly when did you come back from Iraq?"

Bruce looked over at her. "I'm not at liberty to say."

"You do have the right to speak to me about anything, Captain," she said, then cited her position and clearances. Technically, he did, but she couldn't forget what Jackson had said about the reality of doing so and that it would cost Bruce his job. Now that Laura was gone, his work really was all he had left.

He didn't utter a word.

Morgan shifted subjects, as Jackson had, and took a

different approach. She and Bruce talked for a few minutes more, and then Morgan said, "I understand that you're facing special challenges, Captain. But if you want me to help save your ass, then I'm going to need a little help from you."

"Right. Sure thing." He gave her a sidelong look. "Everyone, including my own brother, is convinced I killed my wife. Why should I believe you're any different?"

"In all fairness, I'm not sure Jackson has made a decision yet on what he believes," Morgan said. "I, on the other hand, have decided." She paused, waited until he finally looked at her. "I don't believe you killed Laura."

Bruce swallowed hard. His Adam's apple bobbed in his throat. "You believe I'm innocent?"

His surprise was so sudden, so unexpected, it startled her. Jackson's walking out on Bruce had rattled him and exposed his soft underbelly in ways little else could. He felt vulnerable and lost, afraid to hope.

"I do believe you're innocent of murdering Laura." Morgan had chosen her words carefully to exclude his involvement in motivation. "In fact, Captain Stern, I *know* you didn't murder her."

"How do you know?" he asked. "Why do you believe me?"

She studied him a long moment. "Because I can."

Before he could respond with another question, she gathered her handbag from near her feet and then stood up. "The challenge is not in what I know but in proving that what I know is fact. The blood work will help with that." She moved across the tile floor, heading toward the door. Her heels clicked in the silence.

"Dr. Cabot?" He waited for her to stop and look back at him. "You were right."

"About what?"

"I wanted you to know that I loved my wife."

He did. It radiated from him, as did his grief. "I know you did, Bruce."

"And I didn't kill her."

"I know that, too." Morgan nodded, feeling the weight of his burden about his wife's death. His guilt, and something else. Something . . . odd.

Bruce Stern felt no fear.

Morgan walked out and thoughtfully closed the door. Detachment often accompanied grief. The worst that could happen already had, so what else possibly existed to fear? Yet she had never run across grief-related detachment in a situation where the person doing the grieving was accused of murdering the beloved departed. She would have expected to intuit fear from him.

Yet, Bruce's didn't feel like grief-related detachment. It felt different. Exactly how it was different, Morgan couldn't explain. She was as much at a loss to define it as Taylor Lee had been to define how she knew Bruce hadn't been at home when Laura was attacked and murdered—if in fact the evidence proved he hadn't been there. Taylor

Lee *saw* images and events. She might have seen that Bruce wasn't in an image, but that didn't explain how she knew he wasn't in the house. Still, she insisted he wasn't. Had he been? Not been?

Either way, Morgan left the interview room with what she needed to know intuitively. The man inside was Bruce Stern, and he had not killed his wife.

Though he hadn't voiced strong suspicions, he had plenty of them about who had killed Laura and why, and about that, he felt guilty. Unfortunately, that guilt raised an alarm Morgan couldn't ignore. The S.A.T.'s worst fears about this case weren't just fears or concerns; they were active in this case.

G.R.I.D.

Just down the hallway, Jackson waited for Morgan, standing with feet spread, shoulders rounded, tense and wary and angry as hell. *Round two . . .*

She shored up her patience and then walked to him. "You okay?"

He cast her a level look.

"Sorry." She apologized and then admitted, "Stupid question."

"I'm not sure what to do," Jackson confessed, falling into step beside her. "And I hate it."

They walked down the corridor toward the entrance, their escort following closely behind them. "You think Bruce is guilty," Morgan said, nodding to two armed guards they passed in the hallway.

They signed out at the front desk, then moved through security. After clearing the biometric scans and metal detectors, they nodded their thanks to their escort and then left the building.

"I know he's guilty," Jackson said, voice shaking. "I've seen it too many times."

Morgan wasn't tracking his meaning. "You've seen what too many times?"

"Bruce's victim look." Jackson shoved a hand into his pocket and moved into the parking lot. "He's done that since he was a kid."

The heat pounded off the concrete, the glare blinding. Morgan waited until they were seated in the Jeep to say anything more. Heat radiated off the dash, and the steering wheel was hot enough to raise blisters. She cranked the engine and turned the air conditioner on, kicking the fan up full blast. "Jackson, in these situations, it's not uncommon at all for the surviving spouse to feel guilty. Bruce is probably beating himself up because they argued and he left. Because he went to the bar. Because he stayed gone so long." She stowed her handbag behind the passenger's front seat. "Most of all, he's kicking himself because he wasn't there to protect Laura."

The heat had Morgan breaking into a sweat. She brushed at her damp forehead, tasted the salt on her lips. "He feels guilty, but that doesn't mean he murdered her."

"We'll see." Jackson buckled his seat belt and looked out the side window, face turned away from her. "I hope you're right, Morgan. I really do, but—"

"You have doubts." She clasped Jackson's hand. "I understand."

He squeezed her fingers tightly. "Do you?" He gave his head a little shake. "I doubt you can," he said. "Hell, I lived with it my whole life and I don't understand it."

"He's your brother, and you love him," she said. "You're afraid to hope that he's innocent and risk being proven wrong later on," she whispered. "It's a long way to fall."

"A very long way to fall." He clasped her hand in both of his. "Too far. I . . . I just can't do it."

Her cell phone rang.

She pulled back her hand, grabbed her purse, and then rifled through it for her cell. Snagging it, she flipped her phone open and then answered. "Dr. Cabot."

"Morgan, it's me, Jaz."

Morgan intuited Jazie's urgency, excitement. "What is it?"

Mindful of the non-secure communications, Jazie elected to be cryptic. "Our adversary."

G.R.I.D. Morgan's stomach clutched, and she gripped the steering wheel hard. "You're positive?"

"They're here, Morgan," Jazie said. "Three of them."

Morgan's heart thumped hard, banging against her ribs. "Do you have art?"

"Faxing it to your home now."

"We're on our way."

"The commander called to see if you got anything from the prisoner."

"Nothing that will stand up in a court of law."

"I'll pass the word," Jazie said, and then briefed Morgan on things she could pass along without benefit of a secure line.

"Thanks, Jazie." Morgan hung up, tossed her phone into her purse, and stuffed it back behind the seat. With a grunt, she straightened her back and then steered the car out of the parking lot and down the street leading to the guard shack.

A green Volvo was stopped, the driver talking to the guard. She braked until it pulled out, then moved up and notified the same guard who'd let them enter that she and Captain Stern were leaving the facility.

"Have a good day, Dr. Cabot." He saluted Jackson. "Captain, permission to exit granted."

Morgan hit the gas and drove down the road to the stop sign.

"Well?" Jackson had been patient, but now his curiosity had won. "What's going on?"

"The assassins we expected to greet you on arrival are definitely here."

"I figured." He mulled that over, and then asked, "Has the *Sunrise* been cut loose?"

"Forensics took it to the harbor marina about an hour ago."

"Good. If it wouldn't be too much trouble, I'd like to do a walk-through on Bruce and Laura's house. Before I go to the boat, I also want to see where her body was found," he said with apology in his tone. "I know you haven't gotten any sleep—"

"Don't worry about that," she said. "I'm fine. We need to do as much as we can as quickly as we can."

"In case the locals take possession of the body."

She nodded.

"After we check out those things, I'd appreciate a lift to the marina. No rentals available right now. I'll stay on the *Sunrise* and—"

"Staying on the *Sunrise* is definitely not a good idea, Jackson. Not with three G.R.I.D. assassins after your head."

"It's a very good idea, if they're after me and not mistaking me for Bruce," Jackson countered. "Geez, watch that idiot driving the blue truck." He pointed to the right, two cars up. "He's tailgating and talking on the phone. Bad combination."

"Thanks," she said, watching the truck come too close to smacking into the back end of the SUV in front of it. "How can you being on the boat be a good idea?" She braked for a red light. The SUV was now beside them with its radio blaring hard rock. The two teens inside were arguing over something, though the loud music prevented her from hearing about what. Morgan wondered how they could hear each other. Just the reverberation had her teeth chattering. "I can't see it, Jackson."

"That's where they intended to take me out initially." He gave her a deadpan look. "I'll be in their kill zone."

Morgan's heart fluttered, and her mouth went dry. "The object is to stay out of kill zones, not to plant yourself in them," she reminded him. "So you, you know, keep breathing."

"The object is to survive," he corrected her. "The odds are better for it if you confront an enemy when you know they're coming." He glanced out his side window. "Trust me. I've been in this position before."

He had. Her senses screamed he'd been in this position many, many times. Why she found that comforting when it should scare her to death, she had no idea, and she was just coward enough at the moment to not explore it. It was those damn tingles again.

Irritated with herself, she flicked at the signal light with her pinky then turned right at the corner.

"Where are we going?" Jackson asked, watching her follow the sign to enter Providence Air Force Base. "The base gate is straight ahead. Take a wrong turn?"

"No, I didn't. Laura's body was found on base," Morgan reminded him. Across from the gas station, she made a left then pulled to a stop near a building being constructed.

Yellow crime-scene tape stretched out twenty yards in a loose circle around a dumpster half full of construction debris. Morgan stopped and cut the engine, wishing she could have avoided bringing him here.

He took in his surroundings. The hill of dirt, the stacks of brick and pipe, the dumpster . . . His eyes stretched wide, flooded with horror. "Oh, no." Jackson darted his gaze to her. "Tell me Laura wasn't found in a filthy dumpster. Morgan, please tell me she wasn't . . ."

Morgan's chest went tight. "I'm so sorry, Jackson."

"Oh, God." A wild fury rose in him. He jerked the Jeep's door open and rolled out, his steps hard and heavy, angry. *Outraged.* "In a dumpster. On the frigging base." He stopped and glared back at Morgan. "Some bastard drops her body in a dumpster on the base, and no one *noticed*?"

Morgan had been just as surprised, and Commander Drake had been just as outraged. "We're still canvassing," Morgan said, deliberately softening her voice, "but so far we haven't located any witnesses."

He dragged a frustrated hand through his hair, visually examined the ground inside the yellow-tape circle. "Tell me forensics picked up DNA, shoeprints, tire tracks . . . *something.*"

"I wish I could." He had no idea how much she wished it. It was appalling to have to stand here and admit that they had nothing. Appalling. Humiliating. Frustrating to see someone in such pain, suffering, and to have nothing to offer. No comfort, nothing. "We're waiting for the official reports, but the preliminaries didn't reveal anything significant."

Jackson paced along the running tape, tension radiating from him hotter than a noonday sun. He shot Morgan a look so hard and unrelenting she nearly staggered. "Was Laura dead when the murderers brought her here?"

"The ME says she was."

"Thank God." He went quiet for a long minute. His expression tamed and tension leashed, he looked from the ground back to Morgan, sparing her the brunt of his upset. "Laura was . . ." He stopped, swallowed hard, and then went on. "She didn't like being messy. Even if she wasn't going anywhere, she was careful with her appearance."

"Because what she did, or didn't do, reflected on Bruce?" Morgan asked.

"Yes." Jackson nodded, his eyes bright. "From day one, Laura moved heaven and earth to be an asset to him."

"She loved him." Morgan squeezed her car keys in her palm, welcoming the feeling of the metal points digging into her flesh. The pressure deflected some of Jackson's pain assaulting her heart.

"Yes, she loved him." Jackson bit his lip, turned, and then walked back to the Jeep.

Morgan followed him, curious, thoughtful, and reflective. Her family had never been close; she was an oddball, and they just didn't know what to do with her, so they ignored her. But Jackson's family had been very close, and he clearly had taken his sister-in-law into his heart. Was their whole family there for each other through thick and thin, or was he an oddball, too?

Recalling the parent-child dynamic between Jackson and Bruce, Morgan wondered. As selfish and crazy as it was, considering the brothers' current turmoil and grief, Morgan suffered flashes of envy. She and her two sisters had nothing in common and by mutual, unspoken agreement stayed out of each other's way. Even now, they saw each other only at extended family members' funerals and every third year on Christmas. Their holidays together were nothing Norman Rockwell would have painted. For three days they resided in the same house, but they remained solidly in their own different worlds.

In all honesty, they were like polite strangers. Acquainted with the necessary essentials in the way of information about one another, but for all intents and purposes, they were totally disconnected. It wasn't that there'd been some major disagreement. There hadn't. They simply didn't like each other as people. So they went through the motions at command performances and avoided interaction otherwise. *Can't choose your relatives. You're stuck with the ones you get.*

Yet their non-relationship relationships had always worked for them. That didn't mean, however, when Morgan observed closeness in other families, bonds between siblings that only they fully understood, she didn't long for it or wish that closeness had been a part of her life. She'd tried several times to get to know her sisters, to integrate them into her inner world, but they were content with things as they were and didn't want anything more. She'd been ignored, rebuffed, and finally admonished for making the effort. That's when she'd said to hell with it, built her own life with people who wanted to be a part of it, and accepted that her sisters were merely women with whom she'd shared parents and happened to grow up in the same house. To them, she was weird because of her sensory gift, and she expected she would be until the day she died.

Sad about that, Morgan cursed herself as a fool for giving a damn and drove south toward Magnolia Beach. She had to get her mind off her family situation. Nothing would change, and that made it an energy drain.

Plug it. Think of Jackson.

Yes, she thought. *Jackson.* He needed her attention and focus right now. He and Laura and poor Bruce, who loved Laura and was accused of the most god-awful violation of love possible. And it was gnawing at the marrow of Jackson's bones. He hadn't said a word since leaving the dumpster.

Morgan looked over at him. "You hungry?"

He indicated that he wasn't.

Morgan left him to his thoughts. He was hurting, so much so she wondered how he stayed upright. So many emotional shifts and hard knocks in such a short period of time. He was strong. And she hoped he proved to be even stronger because, God love him, he needed to be. He probably thought the shocks were over on each pivotal point since she'd shot him. But as soon as he absorbed one, there came another, chasing its heels. Laura's death had nearly put him on his knees. Bruce's arrest hadn't. But her body being discarded like trash in a dumpster. That lack of respect toward her offended him in ways Morgan couldn't even put into words. But, oh, could she feel them. Crippled, but he was holding himself together, dealing with the shocks and not trying to repress them, which was good. But he was human, and he did need a little breathing room to reassess, regroup, and recover his balance. The grief and upset and pain would be with him for a long time to come—maybe forever—but he could find a new sense of balance where he carried all that without it breaking him.

"I've got to pick up a fax from Jazie." Morgan pulled into her driveway and left the car out of the garage a short distance from the front porch. "Do you want to come in for something to drink or anything?"

He didn't answer. But he did get out of the Jeep.

Morgan unlocked the front door and coded the alarm, disarming it. "Help yourself, Jackson. I'm just going to grab that fax from my office, and then I'll be right in."

He walked through to the kitchen and, before she got to her home office, she heard ice clinking into glasses.

The fax was there, in the machine. Three pages with a note from Darcy encrypted in a simple three, two, one code that read: Merk, Stick, and Payton, respectively. All suspected G.R.I.D. operatives. Intel specialty identified: Assassins. *Extreme caution.*

A shockwave rippled through Morgan's body from head to toe. Knowing this and seeing it confirmed created two entirely different reactions in her. Knowing set her teeth on edge, made her wary and cautious. Seeing it confirmed did all that . . . and also curdled her blood.

"G.R.I.D. trained. Specializing in assassinations. And Jackson wants to deliberately plant himself in the kill zone . . ."

How are you going to stop him?

She shook from head to toe, having no idea.

CHAPTER 6

Jackson stood at Morgan's kitchen sink, downing a glass of ice water.

"There are sodas in the fridge," she told him, brushing at the sleeve of her soft pink top. "Iced tea and juice, too."

"I need the water," he said. "High humidity and this heat . . . You need it, too." He passed her a chilled glass with a lavender orchid etched into its side.

"Thank you." She took a drink and then laid out the photos on the gray granite bar.

Jackson leaned over to take a look. "These our G.R.I.D. assassins?"

"Yes, they are." The first man was thin, had a nerdish quality to him, and a totally forgettable face—unless you knew he was out to kill you. "Merk," she said, pointing to his photo with her fingertip.

"No last names?"

"No, not on any of them." While Merk looked like he could be the typical man next door, "Stick" looked like the neighborhood thug everyone wanted to avoid. He had nothing in common with a stick, either. How had he gotten that name? He was big, brawny; his sunglasses hid his eyes and magnified his cocky attitude. *Obnoxious.* It came to Morgan's mind and stayed.

"Bad to the bone, that one," Jackson said.

"Mmm, definitely." She nodded her agreement, moving on to the final third. "Payton." He was anything but nondescript. His head was shaved; his suit, classic Saville Row. In a crowd, he'd be seen as a CEO, a powerful executive, or a sports team owner. He probably could have been any of those things or one of a thousand others, but an assassin? Nothing about him fit anyone's stereotypical description. That was unnerving.

"Nice dresser," Jackson said about Payton. "Good for about four grand a pop."

"Or more," Morgan agreed. She took in specific details from each photo and committed them to memory. "But a pig in silk is still a pig." She turned toward Jackson.

He stood closer than she expected; she smelled his skin, the trace of aftershave clinging to him. A little flutter in her stomach warmed and she lifted her gaze, looked up at him, into his eyes, and her determination to save him from himself doubled. "These men mean to kill you, Jackson. Whether because you're you or because they think you're Bruce, we don't yet know. But either way, they want you dead."

"Yes." He looked down at her upturned face and searched her eyes. "They want me dead."

Close. So close. Too close. Her breath caught and a warning sounded in her head, urging her to back away. But too tempted to kiss him, she stood fast and swallowed hard. "Jackson?"

"Mmmm?" His flattened lips softened, slightly parted.

"Don't let them, okay?"

The distance in his eyes faded, welcoming her. "Worried about having more work to do?"

She started to say yes, but that wasn't the reason, and they both knew it. "That, too."

"Why else?" He let out a little grunt. The skin wrinkled between his eyebrows above his nose. He waited, but she didn't answer, so he prodded her, "Because . . ."

"Because I need to know you," she finally admitted.

"Need to?" He didn't flinch. "Or want to?"

"Both," she confessed, afraid to move, afraid to breathe for fear it would break this intimacy and the moment would be gone, lost forever.

"You know I'm attracted to you." He lifted a fingertip to her face; let it skim along her jaw, down to her chin.

She should deny it. What if this more-than-attraction

feeling in her was all one-sided? What if she'd misread him, and he wasn't interested in her beyond attraction and what she could do to help him and his brother? She turned her face into his hand. "Yes, I know."

"And you know that in our present circumstances, getting involved with each other is nothing short of insanity."

His hand was warm on her face. Caressing her. "I know that, too, Jackson."

"So." He cupped her face in his hands and looked into her eyes. "Are we intentionally going to be insane?"

"Definitely." She didn't hesitate, leaned into him, pressing her hand to his chest and lifting her mouth to his.

He met her halfway. Their kiss was tentative, trembly and tender, warm and wistful. She curled her arms around his neck, let her fingertips splay on his broad shoulders, and sank into it.

He groaned against her mouth, parted his lips, and his heated breath fanned over her face. "You're beautiful, Morgan," he whispered, his throat thick, his voice husky.

All too soon, he loosened his hold on her and moved to pull away. Her emotions churning in full riot, she refused to let him go, tugged him closer, and took their kiss deeper instead, exploring, opening herself completely to all of his anger and worry and outrage and grief . . . so much grief . . . so many regrets . . . and so much fear. She stroked his nape, his chin, his chest with lingering fingertips, wanting to comfort and soothe, to quench the fire burning low in her stomach, and embraced his passion. Emotionally staggering, she let out a sound she didn't recognize as her own, and he sighed softly against her lips, pleasantly content. He rubbed his nose against hers and then pulled back to look at her.

Reeling, she let him, held his gaze . . . and smiled.

He smiled back, pulled her tighter into the circle of his arms, and gently squeezed her. "If anyone had told me twenty-four hours ago I'd be kissing a gorgeous woman who'd shot me twice and then abducted me, I'd have sworn that they'd lost their mind."

She nipped at her lower lip. "If anyone had told me twenty-four hours ago that I'd be kissing a man I'd shot twice and abducted who takes my breath away with a mere glance, I'd have thought that they'd lost their mind."

"Anyone else, maybe." His eyes sparkled. "But you knew, Morgan."

She tensed, not wanting to ruin this—whatever it was—between them before it started. "What did I know?"

"That it would be good." He swept a lock of her hair back from her face and tucked it behind her ear. "We would be good. Special."

"I did?" How could he know that? He couldn't know that. She had known it from the first sign of attraction on the *Sunrise*. From that first erotic tingle. Those rare glimpses just didn't happen in her everyday life.

He nodded. "You're very intuitive. Of course, you knew."

Shock rippled through her. Had he already been told about her special ability skills, or was he talking about the average, typical level of women's intuition? She waited for a hint.

He didn't give her one.

Regardless, she could admit that she had known they'd be magical together, and not lie. "I suspected we would be . . . compatible."

He let out a laugh. "More like combustible."

She smiled again. "That, too."

Looking into her eyes, his gaze softened and he leaned forward and pressed a chaste kiss to her cheek. "Thank you."

She scrunched her brows in an unasked question.

"For giving me something good to hold on to during all this."

She couldn't let him think this was manufactured for convenience. "Oh, Jackson, wait." She grabbed a breath, made sure she had his full attention, then went on. "This with us isn't situational. I mean, the situation didn't induce it. It's—"

"Shh, I know that. Give me a little credit, Morgan."

"I didn't mean to insult you. It's just that you can't think . . ."

"I can think. That's what I'm trying to tell you." He waited for her to look up into his eyes. "It wouldn't matter what we were involved in."

He did get it. He understood. And he was okay with it. "No, it wouldn't matter." She stroked his face. "But we do need to stay focused to keep you alive." She let him see her resolve. "We will find the answers you need. I promise you that."

Grief settled again in his eyes. "Laura would have liked you very much."

She had liked Laura, too. In another time, they could have been friends. "You were very close to her . . ."

"I admired and respected her," Jackson said easily. "She was loving and kind and gentle and as hard as nails when she needed to be, which was way too often, being married to my brother."

"I saw all those things in her in our session." Morgan said. She had—and a lot more.

He blinked. "I have a hard time believing a woman that sharp wouldn't know she was living with a double. Laura was no lightweight on any front, and that's a fact. She'd have known it, especially with her being as attuned to Bruce as she was. She had to have known it."

"Maybe you're right," Morgan said, considering it. "Maybe that's why she came to see me. Because she did know, or she suspected he wasn't Bruce, and she wanted him checked out without asking for it to be done." Reluctant though Morgan was to leave Jackson's arms, she moved away and then grabbed two juices out of the fridge. She passed one to him. "If Laura knew the man with her wasn't

Bruce—let's face it, if no other time, during sex she would definitely have known—she would want to know where the real Bruce was, and she wouldn't want him mucking up Bruce's job. It's the most important thing in the world to him." Realizing what she'd said, Morgan blushed. "Laura aside, of course," she added, feeling obligated.

"Don't start lying to me," Jackson said. "With Bruce, Laura came after his job. She knew it, and she was all right with it. Why? I don't know and won't speculate. But she did know, and it was okay with her."

"Amazing woman," Morgan said.

"Yes."

His simple agreement without adornment spoke volumes about him and about Laura.

"That would explain her coming to you," Jackson said. "Nothing else does. She wouldn't jeopardize his job under any circumstances. But if she knew the man wasn't Bruce, then I could see her coming to you. She wouldn't have a clue how to locate Bruce. She wouldn't have an explanation for how a double could have been substituted for him either. But she would believe you would figure it out and find the real Bruce," Jackson said. "I am certain of one thing."

Morgan unscrewed the top off the juice bottle. It popped. "What's that?"

"If she did know or suspect the man in her house was a body double, then there's no way in hell she'd ever leave him without knowing where to find Bruce. He was her only link, and she'd die before breaking it."

Morgan stilled. *Help Bruce.*

"What is it?" Jackson asked. "Morgan? What's wrong?"

"Nothing." She took a drink from the bottle. The cranberry flavor washed down her throat. "I'm, um, fine."

"You're not fine," he argued. "You look as if you've seen a ghost."

Maybe she had. "It's really nothing," she insisted, giving him a little smile. "But if we want daylight when we check out Laura and Bruce's home, then we'd better get going."

"Let me grab my duffle." He headed for the guest room. "Save us a trip back here before dropping me off at the boat."

The kill zone. When he returned, Morgan again addressed that topic. "I wish you'd reconsider staying on the *Sunrise.* You know as well as I do that G.R.I.D. assassins are experts. Facing them one at a time would give you reasonable odds of success, but three on one? Those are not good odds, Jackson. I don't give a damn how good you are."

"I need to be in the kill zone," he insisted, walking to the front door. "But try not to worry."

"I know." She sighed, locked the door, set the alarm, and closed up. "You've faced worse odds before."

He nodded. "You're very intuitive. I like that in a woman." He shot her a smile, walked out, and then got into the Jeep.

Yeah. Intuitive, but crazy as hell for not falling for a guy with a quiet little life and a safe nine-to-five job who didn't put his neck on the line intentionally with a damn track record of bad odds.

Unfortunately, the heart and not the head made the who-to-fall-for call, and apparently hers had decided on him. How strange. Until now, only two men in her entire life had kissed her breath away. She had buried one and had watched the second marry another woman, certain she would never experience that sensation again. And then along comes Jackson Stern. And she experiences the sensation again—stronger and more intense than ever before. And she'd known him less than twenty-four hours.

Unbelievable.

Definitely the heart making the call.

Was it too much to hope that her heart was both intuitive and not crazy?

On the way to Bruce and Linda's home, Morgan checked in with Home Base on her cell phone.

Darcy was manning the operations desk, and she verified that Dr. Vargus had taken the blood sample from the incarcerated Bruce Stern and that the ME had run a DNA on the scrapings found under Laura's cracked nails. The results wouldn't be in until sometime tomorrow.

"Okay, thanks, Darcy," Morgan said. "Jackson and I are on our way to the Sterns' home. We want to look around."

"I'll note it in the record," she said. "The guard is gone from there. Forensics finished up earlier this afternoon and released the house."

Morgan braked to a stop at a four-way. "Did they find anything of note?"

"Afraid not," Darcy said, clearly disappointed. "Did you get the fax?"

The photos of Merk, Stick, and Payton. "Yes, I did." Morgan hung a left onto Highway 98 and then turned north on Main. Tropical Storm Lil had changed paths, cutting a sharp turn to the west. Mississippi and Louisiana were taking the brunt of it, and Mobile was getting a little rain. Florida had been spared, and while Morgan wouldn't wish a storm on anyone, she was grateful they didn't have to deal with that now, too. "Has Lil been downgraded yet?"

"Next advisory, it will be," Darcy said. "Those poor people in Pass Christian are still in FEMA trailers from Hurricane Katrina and now they're having to deal with Lil. It's just not fair."

"No, it isn't." Bruce and Laura's home was located in Seascape Estates, just a few blocks off the beach. Morgan tapped her signal and turned right at the corner, then drove through the bricked entrance to the subdivision. "Does anyone have any idea where these men are now?" She avoided using keywords that would be picked up by Intel. Darcy would know Morgan was talking about the assassins.

"None." Darcy sighed her frustration over that one. "But we have verified that they didn't fly out of Magnolia Beach, Destin, Fort Walton, Pensacola, or Mobile. If they've gone anywhere, it's been by car or boat."

Morgan would feel a lot better, especially considering Jackson's insistence about staying aboard the *Sunrise*, if the S.A.S.S. knew where the assassins were currently located. "Do we have anyone posted at the harbor?"

"Not authorized," Darcy said. "Until we can prove a direct connection with hard evidence, we can't assign assets there."

That connection would be between G.R.I.D. and the Sterns. Frustration swam through Morgan. She, Jazie, and Taylor Lee knew the connection was there, but they couldn't prove it with physical evidence—only with their special abilities. "I see." She did. Jackson had been removed from the equation before the assassins could make the attempt to kill him, so there was no hard evidence that he was a target. Therefore, the *Sunrise* wasn't officially in jeopardy and neither was Jackson. "Let me guess. Colonel Gray's orders."

"Got it in one." Darcy confirmed that the Providence base commander, who had authority over the personnel necessary for the assignment, was sticking it to Commander

Drake. *Again.* "Is the guy in jail *our* guy or *theirs*?"

"I don't know yet, but I think he's ours," Morgan said, slowing down for two little girls riding their bikes on the edge of the street.

Darcy would translate that response to mean that Morgan believed the man in custody was the real Bruce, though she couldn't yet prove it. "Did he kill her?"

"No. My findings agree with Taylor Lee's on that. All the way." Morgan hoped for Bruce's sake and Jackson's that she was right about that. "I'll update you after visiting the house."

"Proof will come in good time," Darcy said.

Provided G.R.I.D. didn't kill Jackson, or Morgan, or both of them *before* she could find that proof. "Call me on the cell with any updates."

"Will do."

Morgan closed her phone, dropped it into her purse, and then paused at the foot of the Sterns' driveway. Some instinct warned her not to pull in. Having learned long ago to respect those quiet nudges, she drove down the street a couple houses and then parked at the curb.

Jackson cast her a puzzled look. "Why didn't you use the driveway?"

"I don't know," she admitted, risking probably more than she should. "I started to, but had a funny feeling."

"Invasive?" he guessed.

Close enough. She nodded.

"Sometimes you have to invade to resolve, Morgan.

But you already know that." He grabbed the handle and tugged, opening the door.

"Jackson." She stopped his exit from the car with a hand on his forearm. "You're right, I do know it. And I know that sometimes, no matter how strong and determined we are, we have to back off a bit and regroup before we can go on." Man, she hoped he took this in the spirit intended, but some men really objected to being reminded that they were mere mortals. "Are you sure you're ready for this? There's no shame in saying it's too much to deal with right now."

"Hell, Morgan," he answered bluntly. "I haven't been ready for anything that's happened since you shot me on the *Sunrise*. Who could be?"

Valid point. "Of course." He was proud but real, too, and his mental health was her domain by honcho decree. She had to do her best and give him an out. "You can do this later, you know."

"No, I can't. Time is against us already. We don't need degraded evidence, and you know as well as I do that the longer we wait, the more it will degrade."

Morgan had the distinct feeling that what there had been in the way of evidence, the G.R.I.D. assassins had destroyed. Thomas Kunz hired only the best, and the best didn't screw up often or leave calling cards. They operated in stealth-mode and rarely made mistakes. That, and each assassin's or operative's knowledge and access being limited to a specific segment of the operation—only Kunz knew the entire operation and his overall plan—made his employees extremely elusive.

"I know," she finally said. "I'm just concerned that you're overloaded."

Her concern surprised and touched him; she saw it in his face and felt it in her heart.

"Don't worry." He stroked her face with a gentle hand. "I am overloaded, but I'm dealing with it and I won't endanger you anymore than you are already."

"I wasn't concerned about that," she said. "I was concerned about you."

"Oh." That really did surprise him. "I'm, um, all right."

Endearing, that. "If you weren't, would you tell me?" she asked.

He almost smiled. "You know, I think I would."

Jackson Stern didn't confide in many people, and the fact that he trusted her was special.

"Okay," she said. Feeling better, she opened the Jeep's door and slid out. The air was hot, heavy with a balmy breeze blowing inland over the few blocks from the coast.

"You look exhausted." Jackson walked with her toward the front entry. "I should be asking if *you're* okay."

"I've had a full couple of days," she said, opening her senses and looking at the welcoming brick, ranch-style home. Large baskets of lush ferns hung from studs flanking the front door. Farther down the tiled porch was a little wrought-iron chair and matching table. Just off its edge, nestled among thick green bushes, a stacked-stone fountain bubbled. Its sounds were soothing, so at odds with the violence Laura Stern's body proved she'd been through. It was easy to imagine her sitting at the table, sipping sweet tea and reading a book, or just being still and peaceful, watching her neighbors weed their flower beds and the kids ride their bikes and play ball on their front lawns. She knew her neighbors, kept an eye out for them, and prided herself on always having extra sugar, eggs, and ketchup on hand to lend, sparing others last-minute runs to the grocery store. And she made it her business to be first in line to drop by and welcome a newcomer to the neighborhood.

A special woman. Thoughtful, considerate, compassionate . . .

Determined to prove her worth.

"Morgan?" Standing beside her, Jackson touched her arm. "Where are you?"

Startled, she jerked. "I'm sorry. I got lost in thought." Her face warmed. "It's very peaceful here."

"Laura," he said, pulling a key ring from his pocket. "She had a thing about serenity and comfort." Picking a key, he inserted it into the door. "It's as important as air."

"Ah. Wise woman."

"In many ways she was, but I think her history had a lot to do with it. She had a hellish home life growing up."

Morgan nodded. "So she made sure her home was a sanctuary."

"Right." He turned the key. The lock snapped, and he opened the door.

"Good thing you had a key," Morgan said. "I totally forgot to drive out to headquarters and pick one up." Ordinarily she'd berate herself for that, but it was after 6:00 P.M. and she was running on sheer will and adrenaline. Her energy low-level light had been flashing nonstop for a couple of hours.

"Disturb as little as possible." Jackson opened the door and walked into the entryway. "I'm sure forensics has been over every inch of space, but—"

"I'm familiar, and forensics released the house a few hours ago. They're done here."

In the entryway, Morgan looked at the family portraits hanging on the wall. Bruce. Jackson. A woman who resembled them too strongly to be anyone but their mother. Morgan moved on, deeper into the house. Bruce and Laura's wedding photo. Wearing a red sweater, a floppy-eared puppy that hadn't yet grown into his feet. A diamond-shaped cluster of group photos of the four of them: Jackson, their mom, Bruce, and Laura. *God, they looked so happy . . . What was that?*

Two frames from the end in the second row hung a photo of Jackson. He had his arm wrapped around the waist of a woman who wasn't his mother or Laura. He had never been married, so Morgan hadn't expected to see a "couple" photo of him on the wall, but there one was. The woman was gorgeous, too.

Naturally. A pang of envy stabbed Morgan. She chided herself for being ridiculous. It didn't help. The woman had long, thick, red hair, flashing green eyes, and a wicked smile that must have enchanted Jackson.

"Aren't you going to ask?" he said from just behind Morgan's shoulder.

For a long second, she debated. She could pretend not to understand what he meant, but that would be insulting to them both, so instead she lifted a fingertip and motioned. "Your mother, Laura and Bruce, of course, you, the family pet—"

"Moxy," Jackson supplied the pup's name. "Laura loved that dog."

"Did she pass away?"

"No." He stood for a moment, a bittersweet smile touching his lips. "Laura gave her to a neighbor at their last base." He looked from the photo to Laura. "Fred was a widower. He, Laura, and Bruce were close. It was a surrogate family situation; he had no family of his own."

Sanctuary. Laura.

"When he found out they'd gotten orders to move here, Fred was pretty torn up."

"So Laura left Moxy with him."

Jackson's mouth curved into a soft, sad smile. "She

called him every Saturday to check on her."

Morgan smiled, liking Laura more all the time. "But she was really checking on him."

"Actually, she was checking on both of them. Fred and Moxy." Jackson sniffed. "Laura was like that."

He *was* going to make Morgan ask about the woman in the picture. Curiosity had gotten the best of her, so she gave into it. "And the redhead?"

"She's a friend of Laura's," he said, clearly enjoying Morgan's asking far too much. "Judy something. I don't remember. I only met her that once."

A totally illogical bubble of happiness burst in Morgan. The woman—Judy whatever—hadn't been important to him. "So she's not one of your lost loves?"

"No." He let out a little grunt. "I have no lost loves, Morgan."

She looked back at him over her shoulder. "Why not?"

"Excuse me?"

"Don't, okay? You know your assets. I'm just a little surprised there hasn't been a love or two you've left behind."

His mouth flattened, and he sobered. "Think for a second. Love and my line of work aren't exactly compatible."

"Ah." She'd run into this far too often with her patients. "You have to keep too many secrets."

"Among other things."

She cast him a look from under her lashes. "Tell me you're not a commitment-phobe."

"Not at all." He puffed up, genuinely offended. "I'm very committed."

"To your work."

"And to my family." He scanned the photos on the wall. "Especially to my family."

"But you have had relationships." Morgan couldn't imagine a man his age with his looks and personality not having several of them.

"Sure I have." He paused and then shrugged. "Just none that endured long enough to make it onto the wall."

In their line of work, there was a lot to be endured. Secrets, danger, unexplained absences, long-term separations, and much more. His situation was, unfortunately, all too common.

They moved on into the kitchen. Magnets on the fridge. Fresh fruit in a bowl on the counter. Car keys on a hook embedded in a note board next to the phone. Its pen was still in place. A card from Laura's dentist—she had an appointment next Thursday at two o'clock—thumb-tacked to it. "Fred's birthday" circled in red on the calendar. Normal . . . Normal . . . Normal . . .

Intuitive insights thus far were limited to low-level arguing. Mundane discussion. Not so much as a niggle of anything violent. Not between Laura and Bruce, or between Laura and anyone else.

Disappointing but not surprising, considering how

many people had been through here since the murder.

"I'm surprised Laura didn't have a houseful of kids."

"One of those things," Jackson said, answering without revealing or violating Laura and Bruce's privacy. If there was a reason, Jackson either didn't know it or refuted it. Either way, even his thoughts were leashed and schooled on that subject.

There it was again. That level of loyalty she had begun to believe had become extinct.

Glad it still existed in at least one man, Morgan walked through the dining room, admired the antique claw-footed table and high-back chairs, the hutch displaying cups and saucers and intricate miniature crystal figurines. Laura had dozens of them—boats, dragons, a treasure chest, animals, and an anchor—quite a collection.

An ordinary life.

An extraordinary woman, living an ordinary life.

Moving on, Morgan walked down the hallway and flipped the switch to turn on the overhead light in Laura's bedroom.

Something crashed. *Inside the house. In the living room.*

"Jack—?" A hand slapped over her mouth.

Her heart slammed against her breastbone. She automatically positioned to jerk away, but a whisper near her ear stopped her cold.

"Shh . . ." He moved around so she could see his face.

Jackson. Relief weakened her knees. Then it hit her: he

hadn't created the crash she'd heard in the living room.

He lifted a pointed fingertip, pressed it to his lips, and then motioned for her to get into the closet. Leaning in close, he whispered in her ear, "Intruder. Get in, and don't come out until I come to get you."

Morgan didn't argue, just ignored his instructions. Instead, she reached into her purse and pulled out her .38.

CHAPTER 7

"Sorry," Jackson whispered, clicking the light off. "Forgot who you were for a second."

Footfalls moved through the house. Morgan took up a position to the right of the door and prepared to fire.

Jackson moved over to the unmade bed, eased a hand under the edge of the mattress. Judging by the items on the nightstand, it was Bruce's side. He pulled out a .45, shoved it into the back of his slacks at the waist, crawled over to the other side, and pulled out a .38. *Laura's.* Then he motioned to Morgan to get behind the bed and use it as a shield.

"It's empty." A man's voice carried down the hallway and into the room. "Find the damn thing, and let's get out of here."

A second man responded. "If it ever was here, the cops

got it. This is a waste of time."

"Shut up and look," the first man said, voice booming, echoing off the walls. "He wants it, okay? You wanna be the one to tell him you don't have it?"

Two of them, shuffling through the house, opening and closing doors, drawers, and cabinets. It was only a matter of time before they reached the bedroom, though they seemed to be focusing intently on Laura's little office. Morgan would lay odds the booming voice belonged to Payton, and the second man was either Merk or Stick. Which one, she didn't have a clue. They were both fixated on finding . . . something.

"Nothing. It's not here," Merk or Stick said. "Let's go."

Silence.

A shot blasted, barely missing Jackson's head. The bullet hit the sheetrock in the wall behind him. Dust flew.

Morgan dropped behind the bed for cover, watched the door. A man's silhouette filled the doorway. *Bad angle.* She fired three times in rapid succession.

"I'm hit. I'm hit." Merk or Stick grabbed his shoulder, rolled back, then ran down the hall.

Jackson lifted two fingers, motioning for her to stay put.

He was worried about the other man. He hadn't needed to tell her; she wasn't moving. She'd yet to hear the second set of footfalls, signaling retreat. One of the bastards was still in the house.

Jackson shoved back the drapes, revealing a French

door. He opened it, scanned the yard, and then motioned with his gun barrel for Morgan to go outside.

She slipped out the door, looked both ways, but saw nothing that didn't belong: trees, bushes, a kid's swing set next door. Gardening supplies and a grill on the patio . . .

Jackson joined her in the backyard and then pulled the French doors closed behind him. "Go left," he told her, and then moved right.

Dusk clung to everything, distorting, creating shadows. Morgan left her senses wide open, scanned constantly in all directions, and made her way to the corner of the house, then paused and grabbed a quick look down the driveway. No car parked there or on the street, and no one in sight. No sounds or smells that struck her as strange or out of place. Her heart thudded hard against her ribs. She made the corner and swept as far as she could see in steeped twilight.

A street lamp at the end of the driveway spilled amber-tinted light on the pavement. Morgan listened, but heard only frogs croaking and the buzz of mosquitoes.

In a cold sweat, she blew out a silent breath and then crossed to a row of bushes on the far side of the driveway. Shoving through them, she hunched down and followed the shrubs down toward the street.

A black sedan was parked at the curb halfway down the block. Its engine was running, its lights off. *The third man? G.R.I.D.*

The back door of the sedan opened, a man rolled into

the car, and the driver hit the gas hard. Tires squealed, churned smoke, and the car sped past Morgan, careening down the street and taking a hard left at the corner onto a cross street; then it disappeared from sight.

Without a confirmed visual on the target, she couldn't do a thing but watch them go.

Jackson came running around the far corner of the house and called out to her. "Morgan?" Fear riddled his voice. "Morgan?"

"I'm here." She stepped into the light.

He sprinted over to her, shoved his gun into the waist of his slacks above the zipper. "Did you get a look at them?"

"Too dark," she said, her brow damp with sweat. "I couldn't even see how many of them there were for a fact."

"Three." Jackson swiped at a bug on his cheek. "One stayed in the car. Two searched the house."

Blood drops stained the driveway. "I winged one of them," she said. "Left shoulder." She'd also blown two holes in Bruce Stern's hallway wall.

"Better report it." He looked back to the house. "If he shows up at the hospital, we'll be notified."

He wouldn't show up in the hospital. The other two would kill him first and dump his body. But she went back to the Jeep anyway, retrieved her cell phone, and then phoned Darcy, not sure how the commander would want to handle this. She might or might not prefer to involve the locals in the home invasion.

Morgan was still shaking when she got off the phone with Darcy. "She's going to call back with instructions."

Jackson looked relaxed, leaning against the Jeep's front fender. "Do you know what they were after?"

Clearly, he had a history of being shot at that far exceeded Morgan's. "No idea. But it's odd as hell that they bypassed Bruce's home office and ripped up Laura's."

"That struck me as strange, too." Jackson rubbed at his neck, a habit of his, she'd noticed, when he was troubled or puzzled. "It doesn't make a lot of sense. What could she have had that they want?"

Morgan wondered that and more. "You know, we've been looking at G.R.I.D. and Thomas Kunz's involvement in this from a single perspective. We logically assumed Kunz's attack was sparked by Bruce's job. But what if it wasn't?"

"G.R.I.D. brokers intelligence," Jackson reminded her. "Bruce has access to very high levels of technology and assets that Thomas Kunz would love to get his hands on and sell on the black market." Jackson lifted both hands. "Laura is a homemaker and wife. What could she have had that Kunz wants?"

"I don't know. But I'm thinking maybe we'd better start looking at this from that perspective, too."

"Bruce is the logical choice."

"He is," Morgan agreed. "But since when has Kunz limited himself to the logical?"

"Good point." Jackson gazed off, thinking. "So what could Kunz want?"

Morgan lifted her brows. "Laura."

Jackson frowned, totally baffled. "She loved gardening and cooking and sewing and calligraphy. What in that would interest Thomas Kunz?"

"I don't know," Morgan admitted. "Maybe nothing. Or maybe something significant enough for him to kill her."

Jackson plucked a brown leaf off a dense green bush, crushed it between his forefinger and thumb. "I understand why you're shifting your thinking in this direction, but I honestly can't see Kunz targeting Laura. It just doesn't make sense."

"But they searched *her* hobby room, or office, or whatever she called it. It was *her* space they swarmed, not Bruce's," Morgan said, insistent that the G.R.I.D. operatives' actions had to be significant.

Jackson thought about it a long minute. "They had probably already searched Bruce's space, Morgan. And they probably figured, since they didn't find whatever it is they're after, that Bruce stashed it somewhere else. Like in Laura's office. That's the only way any of this makes sense. Laura was amazing, but Kunz is into money and damaging the U.S. Laura's sphere of influence wouldn't empower him to do that in ways many others' would. I can't see it. Sorry."

"Our answer probably lies in that room, or they

wouldn't have come back and ripped into it," Morgan insisted. "Let's go back inside and see if maybe we can find what they couldn't."

"All right." Jackson made no secret of his doubt that they'd find anything of value to them, but he led the way anyway.

They walked back in through the front entryway, down the hallway, passing the two bullet holes Morgan had put in the wall. "Bruce is going to be pissed about that," Jackson predicted.

"I doubt he'll give it much thought, considering everything else on his mind." Morgan headed straight into Laura's little room. "I'll take the desk," Morgan said, motioning with a raised hand. "You take the closet."

Morgan methodically searched the desk drawers running down the left to the floor—nothing odd or of interest—then the one that ran the width across the center just under the desktop. Pencils, pens, extra nibs for her calligraphy, scissors—all the usual items you'd expect to see, but nothing that didn't fit in.

Jackson cursed, and Morgan twisted on the chair to look back over her shoulder at him. "What's wrong?"

"There's film in this camera." He lifted a Canon toward Morgan. "Forensics didn't pull the film."

They'd had no reason to suspect anything recorded on it had a connection to the murder. Still, they should have pulled it. "Is it a digital or film?"

"Film. Laura refused to enter the digital age."

Morgan stood up. "Let's go get it developed and see what's there."

He nodded, looked down at the floor at something shiny, then bent to pick it up. "What is that?" Morgan asked.

"A coin," he said. "A gold coin from Cook Island." Jackson grunted, rubbed at his neck. "Now where the hell did that come from?"

"Vacation memorabilia?" Morgan suggested. "Or maybe a collection. A lot of people collect coins."

"Not Laura. She and Bruce would have talked about any trip. She'd have sent me her itinerary, travel log, photographs—the whole nine yards."

She would have. Morgan frowned, searched her memory, and came up dry. "Where is Cook Island?"

"I don't know." He looked up from the coin to Morgan. "Never heard of it."

Morgan's interest was piqued. "Did you and Laura talk while Bruce was in Iraq?"

"Of course," Jackson said. "We checked in with each other at least once a week."

Morgan walked over to the closet, straightened a nest of books and a photo album sitting on a tabletop next to a padded rocking chair along the way. "Did you call her, or did she call you?"

Jackson got a strange look on his face. "She called me.

They had a free long-distance plan."

Morgan flipped open the photo album, saw a picture of Laura and the redhead in the entryway photo with Jackson, the woman she'd thought he'd been interested in. Judy somebody. They stood arms linked, laughing, at a location that looked like a tropical resort. Hawaii, maybe? Somewhere with that Pacific Island flavor, gauging by the sand and surf and their beach attire. It was a recent photo, too. Laura looked the same as she had in Morgan's office, and her hair was styled the same way and the same length. She'd been on a trip somewhere. Maybe to this Cook Island . . .

Closing the book, Morgan thought for a second. "So you don't know for a fact that Laura was here when she called you. She really could have been anywhere."

"I suppose. I can't say I paid any attention at all to caller ID. Had no reason to, you know?" He shrugged, as if the thought that she hadn't been at home had never occurred to him.

But why should it? Bruce was on temporary duty in Iraq. Wives waited, kept the home fires burning, especially wives dedicated to their husbands, like Laura.

Morgan pulled out her cell and dialed Darcy at Home Base. When she answered, Morgan asked, "Darcy, have you pulled the phone records on the Stern residence?"

"You bet. I scanned the house and both cell phones for foreign calls, considering . . ."

"Did you find any?"

"No, not even one." Darcy made a noise from her throat and then added, "Why are you asking?"

"Just a hunch," Morgan said, downplaying her zinging intuition on this. "Can you run a check to see how many times Laura phoned Jackson while Bruce was in Iraq?" She covered the mouthpiece and told Jackson, "I need your number."

He relayed his home, office, and cell numbers. "She usually called me at home."

Within seconds, Darcy relayed her findings. "During that time, there were no calls from the Stern residence or from either cell phone to any of those numbers."

Not good. Not good. Jackson was clearly waiting to hear Darcy's findings. Morgan nodded, sharing the news that there had been no calls recorded.

Jackson frowned. "She couldn't have checked that fast. Tell her to slow down and look again." He tapped his palm with his index finger. "Laura phoned me every single Saturday, Morgan. Every single Saturday."

Morgan nodded, acknowledging that she'd heard him. He looked ready to go off like a rocket, so she paused to explain. "Hang on a second, Darcy."

"Sure thing."

Morgan covered the mic in the phone with her hand so her words wouldn't carry through to Home Base. "Jackson, you don't understand. Darcy doesn't need to double-check."

"Apparently, she does. She's dead-damn wrong."

"No, she isn't," Morgan insisted. "Darcy has total recall. She reviews something once, and it's in her head verbatim for life. Laura made no calls from this house or either of their cell phones. That's a Darcy-verified fact I'd bet my life on."

"I see."

She thought maybe he did.

He bit his inner lip. "So where the hell was she? Where did she call from and why didn't she tell me she wasn't at home?"

"I don't know, but we'd better find out." Morgan put the phone back to her ear. "Thanks for waiting, Darcy."

"No problem."

"Can you run a reverse check on Jackson's home phone?"

"Do we have his permission?"

A courtesy. In a murder investigation, they could get the necessary authorizations and had most of them already. Still, Morgan looked at him. "Jackson, do I have your permission?"

"Yes, you do," he said loudly enough for Darcy to hear. "Whatever of mine you want to examine, pull it."

"Trusting guy," Darcy said.

"Not really."

"Ah, you're special."

Morgan murmured. "One can but hope."

"Jazie said he was special and you had the hots for him."

She could deny it, but why bother? Facts were facts. No sense shooting her credibility for nothing; they knew the truth. "Yes."

"Ouch, he's right there, right?"

"Yes."

She laughed. "Okay, then. "What exactly do you need?"

Relaxing now that the topic had shifted off her personal life and back to business, Morgan said, "I want a complete listing of all incoming calls for every Saturday during Bruce's absence . . . no. No, wait." She paused and rethought the request, then amended it. "I want a complete listing of all incoming calls for every Saturday from the time Bruce left for Iraq until three weeks ago."

"I'm on it."

"Thanks, Darcy." Morgan hung up.

Jackson leaned against the doorframe. "This situation is turning into a pretzel."

"It started out like a pretzel. Now it's becoming a whole bag of them." Morgan motioned to Laura's camera. "Let's get that film processed and see what's on it."

Jackson removed it from the camera and tossed it to Morgan. "Catch."

She did and then dropped it into an evidence bag inside her purse.

"We're not going to find anyplace to process the film tonight," he said, glancing at his watch. "Why don't you drop me off at the *Sunrise* and we'll resume in the morning?"

He was right about the film. It was just after 10:00 P.M. Short of driving up to Home Base at Regret, which was forty miles from Magnolia Beach, there wasn't a place open to process it. "Works for me."

They locked up the house, walked to the car, and then Morgan drove to the harbor. Parking was atrocious; the clubs were packed, and the marina was as jammed as Grand Central. Morgan looped the parking lot three times without seeing a single parking space.

Finally, on round four, Jackson spotted a car backing out. "There." He pointed.

Morgan zipped into the vacated space and then pushed the gearshift into *park*. "I still wish you'd change your mind about being out here." Her instincts screamed it was a bad idea. Should she stay and watch his back?

"I'll be fine, and no hanging around to cover my sixes. I'd be in more trouble trying to protect myself and you."

God, was she that transparent? "Okay, but I don't like this."

"Noted."

And it didn't make a damn bit of difference except to feed his ego. That would irk her, but honestly she sensed he needed it. He needed a little TLC and nurturing. "Shall I pick you up?"

He slid her a killer smile. "Anytime you like, Morgan."

She laughed. It felt foreign and good, and clearly it

did to him, too. "I'll hold that thought," she promised, and then sobered, remembering where they were and who else might be here with them. "You should reconsider and stay in my guest room." He'd tagged the *Sunrise* the G.R.I.D. kill zone, and Morgan totally agreed with him on that. Of everywhere in the world, right now, this was the most dangerous place for him to be, and leaving him there set her raw nerves on edge.

"Tempting offer, but no thanks." He lifted a hand and stroked her cheek.

"You're hell-bent on keeping your friends close and your enemies closer?" Morgan said, recalling the old cliché.

"Something like that." He glanced out the window. "Actually, I was thinking of checking out a couple of the bars."

Surprise flitted through her. "Trolling for women?"

His eyes glinted steel. "Trolling for G.R.I.D. operatives."

She moved to turn off the ignition. "I'll come with you." He should have backup, in case he did run into them.

"Morgan, no." He stayed her hand on the ignition, kept her from turning off the engine. The green lights on the dashboard reflected on his face. "I wasn't kidding. This is the G.R.I.D. kill zone, and they are after me. I'd prefer you not be here at all, much less be here with me."

"It doesn't matter where I am," she said in a voice she forced level. "I'm in the kill zone, too, Jackson." She paused and let that seep into his mind, giving him time to see the truth in it. "We can't prove it, but we know those were G.R.I.D. assassins at Bruce and Laura's tonight. I put a bullet in one of their shoulders. I'm as much a target as you are."

"Not necessarily," he countered. "They're professionals. Kunz's professionals. They're not going to let personal vendettas interfere with their work for him. He wouldn't tolerate it, and they know it."

"I'm a professional, too," she said softly. "Do you think he doesn't know about me? Come on, Jackson. He knows who we are, all of us. He's infiltrated our systems. We know that for a fact."

"But that doesn't mean *they* know. He holds everything he possibly can tight to his chest. It's how he survives. And the room was dark. His goons might not have seen your face. You didn't see theirs."

"True, but they did see my Jeep parked in the street. Once they discovered people inside the house, how long do you think it took them to run the plates on all the cars around there? The third guy in the car surely pulled the plate numbers on all the vehicles in the vicinity." If he hadn't, he'd been a damn fool. "No, they've identified me already. I know it, and I'd be derelict in my job not to admit it."

He didn't like it and searched his mind for an objection that would stand up against her logic, but failed to find one. "Okay, then." He let out a resigned sigh. "At least if you're with me, I can watch your back."

"My thoughts exactly." *Only reversed. I can watch yours.*

He opened the door. "Let's go."

They hit two clubs on the pier, ordered drinks they didn't touch, scanned the places, saw no one of interest, and then left to scout out a third.

Papa Bear's. Inside, they walked over crushed peanut shells on the wooden floor—totally impractical for a beachside club with all the sand. They skirted the perimeter, which gave them a clear view of everyone present, and didn't see any of the three assassins.

Morgan nodded toward the door, Jackson acknowledged, and they went outside. "Let's call it a night," Morgan suggested. "If they don't want to be seen down here, they won't be. It's easy to get lost in this sea of people." The dockside was packed.

"All right. I'll walk you back to the Jeep." Jackson fell into step beside her, shouldered a path between people until it thinned out, and they got to the parking lot. "Will seven o'clock in the morning work for you?"

She hit the button on her key chain to unlock the door. "Sure." Sliding into her seat, she clicked her seat belt into place, then keyed the ignition. Her gaze lowered, down his chest. He'd untucked his shirt to hide the imprints of the guns he'd confiscated from Laura's. "Do you have your cell phone?"

He reached to his hip, felt it there, and nodded.

"Put me on speed dial, and call if you need me."

He smiled, hesitated a second, then leaned in and pecked a gentle kiss on her lips. "You, too."

"Jackson?" It was a question she had to ask. She was too tired to intuit it on her own with any certainty of accuracy, and if she didn't ask, she could kiss off sleeping a wink. Too weary to bother with subtleties, she got direct. "Do you still believe Bruce killed Laura?"

"I honestly don't know," he admitted, though having to voice doubt cost him. "I do think the assassins were checking out Laura's space at the house, but I still think all of this somehow relates to Bruce's job. I wish I could say he didn't do it, but I don't know it, and I can't prove it."

"I might agree with you," Morgan said with a trace of bitterness, "if I knew what Bruce's job was, at least when he was in Iraq. Not knowing, I'm floundering at making those connections."

Forearms propped at her window, Jackson looked down at the ground. "I can't disclose what I know about that," Jackson said, the wheels of his mind turning in his eyes. "Let me say this. Thomas Kunz has built a multinational empire selling intelligence on U.S. personnel and weaponry systems and other assets. Bruce is an internationally known authority on biowarfare. That's about all I can say."

So Bruce had been checking out something that Intel had determined Kunz was interested in acquiring or exploiting. "Okay," she said.

"It appears as if G.R.I.D. killed Laura," Jackson continued. "But all things considered, odds rank off the charts that they killed her to manipulate Bruce."

That, Morgan didn't accept. "Kunz doesn't go around when he can go direct," she said. "I've been involved in one way or another on five G.R.I.D. related missions, and in every one of them, he's gone for the jugular, straight for whatever he wanted."

Jackson nodded. "That's consistent with my experience," he said, revealing that he'd had previous experience with G.R.I.D. and Kunz, too. "But when you consider that Bruce refused to answer our questions and give us what we need to work this, you have to also consider that Kunz or one of his bastard henchmen tried to go direct. My guess is they tried Bruce first and failed, and then—"

"Killed Laura to coerce Bruce into doing whatever it is Kunz wants done?"

Jackson nodded.

Revulsion slithered through Morgan. Kunz had done that before. Dr. Joan Foster had refused to work for him, so he'd killed her parents and grandparents to coerce her, and then he'd threatened to kill her husband and son. She was an expert on psychological warfare, memory manipulation, programming and deprogramming, which meant she had all the tools available to anyone to fight Kunz, and yet she'd folded.

Laura was dead. Assassins had been after Jackson.

Bruce had been framed—and likely could be cleared if he agreed to cooperate with Kunz and tell him what he wanted to know. The coercion theory would fit if . . .

"Jackson, do you and Bruce have any other living relatives?"

"No, we don't. Our mother passed away two years ago. We're all that's left."

Morgan's heart beat hard and fast. Then coercion did fit. Everything that had happened fit within known Kunz and G.R.I.D. tactics.

"Let's pick this up in the morning, okay? We're both wiped out," he said, stepping back from the Jeep. "Night."

"Night." Morgan closed her window, reversed out of the parking space, and then drove away, glancing back in her rearview at Jackson watching her go. He was an amazingly strong man and very perceptive. Damn gorgeous, too. She smiled to herself and turned onto Highway 98. *God, please. When tomorrow comes, let him still be alive . . .*

Halfway home, she decided that though Jackson's line of logic on coercion tactics fit, that didn't mean it was accurate. It'd be clean and efficient if it was, but Morgan's intuition said to keep digging.

Dig deep.

Morgan blew out a weary breath. One thing came through loud and clear.

The truth had not yet been revealed . . .

CHAPTER 8

Morgan punched in the alarm code, entered her house, and then reset the alarm. Her skin crawled; she was on edge and uneasy, and she wasn't used to feeling edgy and uneasy in her own home.

She blew out a resentful breath, set down her handbag, and carried her car keys with her. If push came to shove, she could sound the car alarm. That surely would get at least Justin's mom's attention. *There was an upside to having a nosy neighbor.*

The answering machine's blinking red light snagged her attention. Morgan slid off her shoes and tapped the button to listen to her messages.

A hang-up call at 10:25 P.M.—*after* Morgan had left the Stern residence. By then, the G.R.I.D. assassins would have had more than ample time to run the plates on her car and find out who she was and where she lived.

An uneasy shiver crept up her back.

She tapped *forward* and then listened to the next call.

"Morgan, it's Taylor Lee. I'm coming up dry on every front, and I don't mind telling you it's pissing me off." Her sigh crackled static through the phone. "Something's not right on this whole Bruce thing. I don't know what it is, but as deep as we're digging, *something* should be floating to the surface, you know? But it's not. It's almost like someone's making sure it can't. Even Snow White wasn't this damn clean." Another pause, then, "You know what? I've had it for the night. I'm going to grab Rick and go dancing, burn off some stress. Oh, don't worry. I remember whom we're up against. No drinking. That's a promise, so don't worry."

Click. Taylor Lee had hung up.

Taylor Lee often drank to wash away the images she saw. It had to be hell to see the horrors inside someone's mind. Shopping malls brought on three-margarita binges. Sometimes one binge would dull the images enough that she could bear them; sometimes a double binge was required. Morgan and Jazie understood and did what they could to protect Taylor Lee when she needed binge relief. So far, that had worked out fine. Taylor Lee was acidic and blunt and sometimes a royal pain in the ass, but she kept her promises. Confident she would this time, Morgan went on to the next call.

"Hey, Morgan. It's me, Jazie, checking in. I've been thinking about that "help Bruce" message. I took it that Laura wanted us to help him but, you know, I'm wondering now if maybe she wasn't telling us that he had recruited her to help him with something." Jazie paused to think on that supposition a second and then added, "Otherwise, what's going on here . . . well, the puzzle pieces just don't fit." She mumbled something she obviously didn't mean to convey to Morgan, and then continued. "The silence is deafening on this entire case. I don't have to tell you how weird that is, Morgan. There's got to be a reason we haven't thought of yet, and whatever it is, I think it might be key to figuring it all out." Jazie let out a sigh that was half yawn. "Anyway, I've got to crash now, or I'm going to burn. Think about what I said, okay? We'll talk it over in the morning."

Morgan unbuttoned her blouse. Jazie had a point Morgan hadn't considered. What if Bruce had recruited Laura to help him?

Would he do that?

It wouldn't be an extraordinary action between a man and his wife. *He has a problem. They discuss it and then work through it together as a team. Teamwork is what marriage is all about.*

Whoa, wait a minute, Morgan. Think classified information. G.R.I.D. Thomas Kunz, master torturer and mass murderer. Would Bruce really bring Laura in on that? Willingly?

Ordinarily, she'd bet against it. He was into his job,

and he loved her. But as a last resort . . . *He might, if she was unwittingly dragged into it and he couldn't prevent it.*

Morgan wondered, and again Joan Foster and her situation came to Morgan's mind. She glanced at the clock. After eleven. She hated to call so late, especially with Joan being pregnant and up all night last night, but she likely had slept today and odds were decent that she was still awake. Morgan squelched her reluctance and dialed the phone.

Joan answered, sounding groggy. "Foster."

Morgan winced. "Did I wake you?"

"I was getting up anyway," she said. "Time for my every-half-hour trip to the bathroom."

"The joys of pregnancy, huh?"

"This child is constantly bouncing on my bladder. I swear it."

Morgan chuckled. "I'm sorry to bother you, but I wanted to ask a question only you can answer."

"Okay. But you have to either wait a minute or go with me to the bathroom."

"I'll wait." Morgan laughed again and walked into her bedroom, stripping off her slacks and top. She snagged her robe from its hook and slid into it.

"Ah, much better," Joan said, returning to the phone. "Sorry about that, but now I can actually think."

Morgan tied the sash at her waist and returned to the office, then sat down in her chair and swiveled back and forth. "When Kunz was trying to push you into working for him, did you consider telling Simon about what was happening?" Simon was Joan's husband, a truly good man in Morgan's book.

"Not at first," Joan said. "I was too afraid. But after my grandparents were killed, well, I figured the odds were high that we were all going to die and Simon at least deserved to know why."

Morgan tapped the floor with her bare toe, stopping the chair. "So you did talk to him about it."

"I said I considered talking to him. I didn't say I'd done it," she corrected Morgan. "Because if I said I had done it, then I'd be admitting that I violated my security clearance." She paused long enough to let Morgan digest that comment. "We both know how strongly the powers that be frown on that."

She had talked to Simon. Definitely. But both she and Morgan had to be careful here. "Can we discuss a hypothetical situation, then? You're the closest I've got to the real thing."

"Sure."

Okay, the ground rules had been laid and acknowledged. Now they were free to talk turkey. "Hypothetically, if when you were in this situation you had talked to Simon," Morgan said, protecting Joan's security clearance, "when do you think you would have done so?"

Joan didn't pause to think; just responded. "Probably after my parents were killed."

"Why then?"

"Kunz had come to me through an emissary, and of course that didn't work. So he killed my grandparents to force the issue. When that didn't work either, he murdered my parents. I thought they were safe. I stashed them, Morgan. No one could connect either of them or me to the place they were hiding. But he found them—I still have no idea how—and he killed them." Bitterness stole into her voice. "I nearly lost my mind then."

"Feeling responsible for the death of someone you love is hell."

"Multiply that times four." She grunted to cover a crack in her voice. "Being responsible is worse than hell. You think getting really good at what you do is an asset until something like this happens. Then you wish you were cleaning toilets for a living. No one kills anyone to find out how to clean toilets."

She had a point. "So, hypothetically, you would have considered talking with Simon then?"

"Hypothetically, yes, I would have."

"If you had disclosed the situation to him then—or at any other time—would it have been to seek his help in resolving it?"

Joan let out a little laugh devoid of humor. "No, Morgan. My Simon is a brilliant man, and God knows how dear he is to me, but the simple fact is that no man resolves any situation with Thomas Kunz. If you kill him, you win. If you don't, you lose. If you're lucky, he kills you. If not, well, you hope to hell you're strong enough to suffer torture well and you live with the guilt of causing loved ones to die."

Regret. Remorse. Self-hatred. Morgan sensed it all, and it was so unfair and so strong it nearly bent her double. "You survived, Joan."

"Yes, I did. But what it cost my family . . ." She sucked in a sharp breath and dropped her voice. "Speaking honestly? There isn't a moment in a single day of my life, asleep or awake, that I'm not afraid."

"Of what?"

"Kunz coming back for me. Of him hurting my family." Joan's voice trembled. "He could at any time. And let's face it—there's nothing I can do to stop him."

Feeling Joan's fear, dread, and mental anguish aroused compassion in Morgan. Her throat tightened, and her voice turned dusty and thick. "How do you stand it?"

"A minute at a time," she said, repeating the words she'd said to Morgan at the hospital.

Morgan's eyes burned. The back of her nose tingled, and her vision blurred. "Hypothetically, if you had talked to Simon, would he still be afraid, too?"

"Absolutely," she said with complete candor. "No parent or spouse could avoid it, and Simon is both."

In light of all this, there was something Morgan just didn't understand. "But you're comfortable enough in your life to have a new baby."

"I wish that were true, but it's not. Oh, the baby coming is real enough, but I'm never comfortable, Morgan. Kunz chills my blood. More than most others, I saw firsthand what he's capable of doing and the extraordinary measures he'll take to reach his objective. I might not be in his custody anymore, but I'm still his prisoner. I will be until one of us is dead."

"But the baby?"

Joan paused, then confessed, "Some things aren't planned."

Morgan grabbed a glass from the kitchen cabinet and filled it with water. "I appreciate your being so frank with me . . . about your considerations and helping me with this hypothetical situation."

"I'm assuming that the reason you asked wasn't idle curiosity."

"No," Morgan admitted. "It's not idle curiosity. But I'm not sure enough of anything yet to get into what it is. I need more time."

"Well, you know where I am if you need me."

"Thanks, Joan."

"Do remember my every-half-hour pit stops. Allow me an extra ring or two."

Morgan smiled through a yawn. "You bet. Night."

"Night."

Morgan hung up, went to her bedroom's bath, brushed

her teeth, and then finger-smoothed her hair in the mirror. The humidity had made it wild.

Joan's disclosure and insights had her mind spinning. Bruce had relied on Laura; she was totally supportive of him, and of his career. Odds were high that if Kunz had approached him— putting it gently—Bruce would have busted security at some point and talked to Laura about it, and Kunz might have killed her because Bruce hadn't become a believer and wasn't cooperating.

So had Kunz sent the G.R.I.D. assassins to kill Jackson for the same reason—to coerce Bruce?

For one significant reason, that didn't fit. Kunz wouldn't go through all the trouble of framing Bruce for Laura's murder unless he'd played out his hand with Bruce and his double and he simply wanted Bruce taken out of the game. But from the Intel intercepts, they knew for a fact that Kunz had cut his killers loose on Jackson before he had murdered Laura and framed Bruce.

That made it far more likely that the assassins really had been after Bruce. The intercepts had been on Captain Stern, which didn't confirm or dismiss either of the brothers as the specific target.

Which likely had poor Jackson half out of his mind, worried that Laura had been killed because of him. And Bruce totally out of his mind, feeling regret, remorse, resentment, and guilt—all the feelings that Joan Foster lived with so intensely that she would not have deliberately conceived a baby to bring into this world.

It didn't feel quite right to Morgan, but she was getting closer to the truth. She sensed it in the very marrow of her bones. For Jackson's sake, she wished she had the evidence to back it up and prove Bruce innocent.

She clicked off the bathroom light and returned to the answering machine with one thing troubling her deeply. If Bruce had been framed, and he had been the target, and Laura had been murdered to let Bruce know that Kunz meant business, then Thomas Kunz had to know that Bruce was in the brig *before* the *Sunrise* was due at Magnolia Beach harbor, which meant . . .

Oh, God. Kunz *had* been targeting Jackson.

The question was, *why?*

Not knowing set Morgan's teeth on edge, but her intuition strummed strong. There were still facets of the situation that hadn't yet surfaced.

Knowing that as well as she knew her own name, she tapped the button to listen to the remaining messages. An unrelated patient with a routine question. A medical supplier wanting to know if she had reviewed the materials he'd left at the office with Jazie.

And another hang-up call.

The fine hair on Morgan's neck stood on end. She checked the time it had come in. Just minutes before she'd actually arrived home.

Intuitive warnings flashed danger signs, slammed

them one upon another through her mind. The men at the Sterns' house *had* been Kunz's men. The man she'd shot in the shoulder *had* been a G.R.I.D. assassin. They *had* picked up her license plate number and run it. They *did* know who she was and where she lived. And they *were* monitoring her.

Morgan shook and mentally debated on a course of action. She knew what she intuited would prove to be fact, but at the moment she couldn't prove it. And that left her with no course of action to take outside of alerting Home Base and being vigilant and aware.

She left a message for Darcy on their non-emergency line, then grabbed her car keys and cell phone. The urge to test her alarm system hit her hard. She resisted pressing the panic button, and forced herself to go on to bed. Before she got in, she lifted the edge of the mattress and pulled out the .38 she kept there for personal protection. As tired as she was— it'd been nearly forty-eight hours since she'd really slept—she couldn't be sure she would awaken easily. But when she did, if the need warranted, she would awaken loudly.

Gun in one hand, car keys in the other, and cell phone next to her hip, Morgan settled back against the pillows. The house alarm was her first line of defense. She glanced at the monitor on the wall near the light switch. Its red button glowed in the dark. It was armed.

And so was she.

The phone rang.

Reflex kicked in before she opened her eyes, and Morgan hit the panic button on her car alarm. Even being at the far end of the house, she could hear it—*too* clearly.

The sound was wrong. *Wrong, wrong, wrong.* Her car sounded as if it was outside. Not in the garage where she'd left it.

She snagged the phone, rolled to the floor and over to the edge of the room. Sliding up, she hugged the wall beside the window and peeked outside. Her Jeep was parked at the end of the driveway. Morning had come with a vengeance. Bright sunlight glinted off the vehicle's front bumper.

"What the hell?" She clicked the button to answer the persistently ringing phone. "Yes, what?"

"Morgan?" Jackson sounded worried. "What's wrong?"

"Someone's taken my Jeep out of the garage and parked it at the end of my driveway."

"You sure you garaged it?"

She frowned into the phone, slung on a pair of jeans, propping the phone between her shoulder and ear. "I'm sure. Totally sure," she said again, adding weight to her claim. "I was tired, Jackson, not drunk."

"Don't touch it," he said. "It's probably rigged with explosives."

She tucked her weapon into her waistband and looked outside again. *Nosey's* little boy was walking across the street toward her Jeep. "Call the bomb squad at Providence," she gushed. "I've got to go."

"What is it?"

"Justin—the kid across the street—he's by the damn Jeep." She tossed down the phone and took off running.

"Morgan, don't touch that car!"

Jackson's shout followed her to the front door. She jerked it open, setting off the house alarm, which turned out to be a good thing. It startled the boy into stopping a full five feet away from the Jeep.

"Justin!" she shouted, running outside, the car and house alarms wailing. "Don't touch that car!"

He cocked his head, looked at her oddly, and shouted over the sirens, "I wasn't gonna touch it, Dr. Morgan."

"Back up, honey." She reached him and grasped his shoulder. "Get back across the street. All the way, okay?"

"Why?" He dragged his feet, not wanting to go home. "I wasn't gonna hurt anything, I swear." He hollered to make sure she had heard him. "I just wanted to see your flat tires."

She guided him back to his own front yard and then glanced back at her vehicle. Indeed, all four tires were flat. "Stay here." She looked him right in the eyes. "Justin, stay here. Do you understand me? It's dangerous, and I don't want you to get hurt."

"From a flat tire?"

"Somebody messed with my car, honey. I don't know what else they did."

"All right." He stubbed his sneaker's toe on the concrete curb. "But it wasn't me," he said, clearly figuring he was in trouble. "I promise I didn't touch nothing."

Several of her neighbors spilled out onto the street to see what all the racket was about. Morgan sprinted back to her house and turned the house alarm off, then went back outside and apologized, eager to get the neighbors back inside their homes and out of harm's way as quickly as possible.

They listened to her request to retreat, but all the curtains up and down the block were spread open and people were peeking out to see what was happening.

Within minutes, a bomb squad arrived. Morgan met the team at the curb, and she briefly explained that she was a psychologist and one of her patients had apparently gone off the deep end. Satisfied, they began sweeping the Jeep.

Before they finished, a white-faced Jackson arrived in a beat-up blue truck. Who did it belong to?

"Morgan!" He leapt out at the curb and ran over to her. "Are you okay?"

She nodded, and he blew out a steadying breath, but his hands on her arms still shook. "What happened?"

"I don't know," she admitted. "You called. The phone ringing startled me awake, and I guess I hit the panic button on my key ring." How humiliating to have to admit she'd been sleeping with it in her hand! "The alarm was louder than it should have been with the Jeep in the garage, so I looked out the window and saw it'd been moved to the foot of the driveway. Justin was heading toward it, to look at the flat tires." She nodded at the boy sitting on his front porch watching intently.

The same boy who had told her Jackson was sleeping on her front porch.

Jackson's jaw went rigid. "Were they in the house?"

He didn't have to identify whom he meant. They both knew he was talking about the G.R.I.D. assassins.

"I don't know. I haven't checked yet." She blocked the glare of the baking sun with a cupped hand at her brow.

"What has the bomb squad found?" Jackson motioned to the team with a nod.

"So far, a device on the ignition, one that would activate on depressing the gas pedal, and another one set to explode when the driver's door opened," she said, swallowing convulsively. "But they're not done yet."

The color leaked out of Jackson's face again. "Three?"

She shivered and rubbed at her arms. "So far."

He wrapped an arm around her shoulder and led her into the house. "They'll take care of this. You go finish getting dressed."

She looked down, only then becoming aware that she had on jeans and her thin robe—which in the sunlight was transparent. "Oh, great." She'd been flashing the entire neighborhood, including the kid across the street.

"Terrific view, but some are a little young." Jackson smiled.

Morgan growled at him. "How can you smile about this?" Feeling unjustly betrayed, she glared at him and then at her Jeep. "They found three freaking bombs on my car."

"So far."

Next to the front door, she turned toward him and let her voice carry a warning that resonated down to her soul, "Jackson . . ."

"Three devices," he reiterated, stepping up onto the porch to stand beside her, "and four flat tires, which guaranteed that you wouldn't be driving the Jeep to detonate any of them."

That stopped her cold. "What's your point?"

He glanced at her. "They invaded your space to scare the hell out of you, Morgan. They didn't mean to kill you, at least not this time."

How reassuring. "Well, they succeeded. I am scared." Her jaw quivered. "What if that child had opened the car door? He could have been killed."

Jackson dropped his voice. "He wasn't."

"But he could have been," she insisted.

"But he wasn't, Morgan. And I'll bet the door was locked." Jackson led her inside and then walked her toward her bedroom. "You get dressed while I have a look around."

"Be careful, okay?" She paused. "If they were in the garage, then they could have been anywhere."

He paused to look back at her. "The garage is under the security system, too?"

"Yes. They had to disarm and then rearm the alarm after they got the Jeep out."

His eyes narrowed. "And you didn't hear anything?"

"Nothing," she confessed. "Which is pretty damn spooky." How could she sleep in peace ever again, knowing someone had beaten her alarm and gotten in, and she hadn't known a thing about it?

She changed into aqua slacks and a white top trimmed in the same shade, then slid into matching sandals. Pivoting her foot in the mirror, she considered how many times she and Jackson had had to run yesterday and the way today had started out with her running.

Screw style. You need mobility, woman.

She reluctantly gave up her sandals—they made the outfit—then bent down and pulled her white sneakers out of the closet. As far as sacrifices went, this one was pretty painless. She sat down on the edge of the bed and shoved her foot into the right shoe.

Something cold and hard snagged her toe.

God, had they been in here, too?

She jerked her foot out, dumped the shoe upside down, and tapped it against the floor.

A gold coin spilled out and rolled across the hardwood floor.

Morgan watched it, transfixed, until it hit the wall, fell over, and stopped. When she recaptured her senses, she called out. "Jackson!" Her voice sounded weak, shaky, and hollow. She regrouped and tried again. "Jackson!"

He ran around the corner and into her room, saw her sitting on the edge of the bed, and frowned. "You bellowed?"

"Look." She pointed at the coin, flat on the floor next to the wall.

He dropped his gaze. "Where did you get that?"

She looked up at him, trying not to let the fear jackhammering through her completely steal her control. "It was in my shoe."

Seeing how upset she was, he walked over to her. "You didn't put it in your shoe, did you?"

She shook her head. "Would I be upset if I'd put it in there?"

"Sorry. You've had a tense morning, you know? Just wanted to verify."

"Well, now you have, okay?"

"Sorry." He apologized again, then clasped her hand and pressed a chaste kiss to her temple. "You've never seen the coin before, either, I take it."

Again, she shook her head. Tears were welling, and she fought like hell to keep them from falling and making her seem like an unprofessional fool but, damn it, this was her home and she was so scared, and even more angry.

Jackson sucked in a breath so sharp it expanded his chest. "It's all right, Morgan."

"It's not all right." Her voice cracked. "They were in my house. The sons of bitches were in my bedroom, Jackson. Right next to me, and I didn't even know it."

He kept his voice low, level. "They're gone now."

"But they could have killed me." Didn't he get it? The level of outrage you felt at being invaded, your space violated. She was at home, her safe place and refuge from the world—her sanctuary—and in her own damn bed. A woman should be safe in her own damn bed.

"They didn't hurt you." He cupped her face in his hands, and she felt him trembling. "They didn't hurt you."

He wasn't unaffected; he was worried sick, and he'd been terrified for her. And that, on top of everything else he was going through, ignited an even deeper outrage in her. One so deep that a sudden burst of unbridled fury erupted, and she scrambled to her feet. "They've gone too far, Jackson. Way too far."

"Yes." The anger in his eyes burned as deep as hers. "And they'll pay for it." He let her see that truth, its promise in his eyes, before he stood up. Then he moved over to the coin, but he didn't touch it. "Where the hell is this thing minted?"

"I have no idea." She picked it up, careful to only touch its edges. "But I'm going to scan it into my computer and shoot it over to Darcy. If anyone knows where it's from, she will."

"And if she doesn't know?" he asked.

"She'll find out," Morgan said with total confidence, and then headed to the computer.

Minutes later, she tapped the *send* button. At the same time, her doorbell rang.

Jackson answered it, and the bomb squad specialist standing on the doorstep introduced himself as Frank Garvey. He and Jackson shook hands, and Jackson asked, "You finished up?"

"Yeah, finally," he said. "There were a total of seven devices on the vehicle. Damnedest amount of overkill I've ever seen, and I've been at this twenty-one years."

"You were informed that Dr. Cabot is a psychologist with Providence affiliations, right?"

"That's why we're here." He parked a hand on his hip. "If she's a head doctor, then we're probably looking at a patient, just like she suspected. No one sane would bother with that kind of redundancy."

It was definitely not the work of a patient, but letting Frank Garvey believe it had been was easier for Jackson or Morgan than coming up with a logical cover story.

Morgan sniffed. "Someone wanted to punctuate a point, I'm afraid," she said, pausing so that the idea could root in Garvey's mind. "People do strange things when they're stressed out."

He nodded, but doubt burned in his eyes.

"I appreciate your help."

"No problem, Doc. I'll turn the report in to Colonel Gray immediately," Garvey said. "The commander wants to be kept abreast of all events. He'll probably call you in a bit. Usually does anytime we respond to a call."

"Thank you."

Morgan's home phone rang. She left Jackson and Garvey talking at the door and went to answer it, hoping it wasn't another hang-up call. With everything that had happened, she was already about to jump out of her skin.

"I got your message and attachment," Darcy told Morgan. "The coin is actual currency used predominantly in a small group of islands in the South Pacific."

"You sure it's not some kind of doubloon, like for Mardi Gras?" Morgan had felt that festive sensation so strongly when touching the coin.

"No, it's cash. No doubt about it."

Interesting, and apparently one instance of Morgan's thirteen-percentage-point stats when her intuition was on hiatus.

"So why is it important?"

Morgan would answer Darcy's question and report this freaking home intrusion, but the stir it would cause was one she would definitely have preferred to live without.

When she'd finished the briefing, Darcy withheld comment, although on hearing Colonel Gray, the Providence base commander, would likely be calling Morgan, Darcy had groaned like someone dying. The pissing contest between Gray and Drake had her shielding her unit operatives and consultants as much as humanly possible.

"You'd better assemble your team," Darcy said. "The commander is going to want a group conference ASAP."

"At Providence?"

"Hang on." Darcy's line went silent, and a few moments later, she returned. "Hospital conference room at nine o'clock this morning. Drs. Foster and Vargus will be consulting."

Morgan interpreted. Blood work results on Bruce were back and the ME's report had been released to Joan. "Is Jackson supposed to be there, too?"

"He was at the residence when shots were fired, correct?"

Bruce and Laura's residence. "Yes."

"Absolutely, then."

"Okay," Morgan said. "Thanks."

Darcy hung up, and Morgan hit *flash* on her phone then placed a conference call with Jazie and Taylor Lee. Jazie was obviously up and about, well rested, and sunny. Taylor Lee sounded half dead and barely conscious. "Are you all right?" Morgan asked, afraid Taylor Lee had broken her promise after all.

"I'm fine," she said. "We were out late. Dancing, not drinking."

That, at least, was good news. But where she'd found the extra energy after their last two days, Morgan had no idea. "I'd like some of your stamina."

"None to spare at the moment, but I'll keep that in mind for future reference."

Morgan grunted. "Jazie, maybe you'd better reschedule our patients at the clinic today. Actually, go ahead and reschedule tomorrow's, too." The pretzel was spawning new twists by the second. "I think this situation might take a little time to clear up."

"Will do," Jazie said. "Who's covering?"

"Anyone you can find who's upright and semi-willing," Morgan said. "Be at the hospital at nine sharp."

"I'll be there," Jazie said.

"Damn." Taylor Lee grunted.

Morgan took that as the best confirmation she was going to get.

CHAPTER 9

Morgan spent the next hour phone shopping for a rental car. Finally, she located one, and she and Jackson had breakfast while waiting for it to be delivered. The rental service assured her she would have a car in her driveway no later than 8:00 A.M.

Greg LaGrange, the owner and chief mechanic from LaGrange's Automotive, picked up the Jeep at seven thirty, assuring her he'd have new tires on it—since all four had been slashed in several places—and check the Jeep out bumper-to-bumper himself before the end of Morgan's workday. He was a jewel.

She swallowed the last of the pancakes and sausage Jackson had prepared while she had been taking care of business, and then set down her fork. "Very good." She smiled. "Thanks."

"No problem." He drained his juice glass and then refilled it. "The side door to the garage was jimmied open, but there are no signs that anyone tampered with the locks or entered the house."

"Except for the coin in my shoe."

He grunted. "The alarm wasn't turned off and then reset. I checked with the monitoring service. There's no record of any interruptions before it went off, when you ran outside after the kid across the street."

"The coin was in my shoe. The shoe was in my closet, Jackson. Someone had to get into the house to put it there."

"I'm not disputing that the coin was there," he said, lifting her plate from the table and taking it to the sink. "I am disputing that G.R.I.D. or anyone else came into the house while you were asleep and dropped the coin in your shoe."

That was fair. "Okay." She cleared the rest of the table and then nudged at him with her hip at the sink to take over loading the dishes in the dishwasher.

He cleared the counter. "It's a foreign coin, not exactly popular in these parts. Yet Laura had one, too."

"Yes, she did." And that didn't strike Morgan odd so much as significant. "So did someone plant the coin in her office, too?" Morgan asked Jackson.

"It's possible." Jackson snagged the dishcloth and wiped down the counter.

It was possible, of course, but there was another possibility that also warranted consideration. "Would you say"—Morgan poured soap into the dishwasher, then closed the door and pushed the button to start the cycle—"that's more or less possible than Laura breaking into my house and planting the coin in my shoe?"

From the goofy look he slung her way, that idea struck him as silly. "Laura breaking into anything, anywhere, is beyond ridiculous."

Morgan rinsed her hands and wiped up the water she'd splashed on the sink's stainless rim. "Would it still be beyond ridiculous if she did it to help Bruce?"

Jackson didn't hesitate, just reacted. His expression sobered, and the light in his eyes darkened. "That could be different."

Morgan stilled, leaned back against the cabinet, and stared off at a point beyond the ceiling.

"What are you thinking?" he asked.

"I'm trying to remember exactly when I last wore those shoes." She searched her mind, thinking back day to day for the last clear memory. Since G.R.I.D. had reared its nasty head in those Intel intercepts, her running schedule had been decimated. *A week.* It'd been a week. The last time she'd had them with her had been the day . . . She gasped.

"You've pegged it." Jackson interrupted, clearly dreading what he was about to say. "When do you run?"

Oh, God. He was already heading in the same direction.

"After work. I run on the beach."

He leaned back against the bar, across from her. "When did you last run wearing those shoes?"

Definitely heading in the same direction. Morgan decided she might as well make it easier—and less time-consuming—for them both. "I intended to run the day Laura came to see me in the office, but I had an emergency come up and it preempted my plans."

He crossed his arms over his chest. "So your running shoes were in your office."

She nodded. Laura had been late, and Morgan had figured she'd cancelled. She had just taken out her bag with her running gear to change clothes when Laura had arrived. They'd talked thirty or forty-five minutes, and then Taylor Lee had interrupted their discussion with an emergency call.

Morgan had gone to the consult room to take it so she could enter her orders in the computer system in private. "I did leave the office while she was there," Morgan told Jackson. "Laura had access. She could have put the coin in my shoe then. I didn't run that day, so I wouldn't have noticed."

Jackson refilled his glass with water and took a long drink before responding. "Okay, let's suppose she did put the coin in your shoe then." He emptied his glass and set it in the sink. "Why did she do it? What is significant about those coins?"

Morgan had no idea. She snagged a paper towel, dampened it, and then dabbed at a dot of syrup on Jackson's shirtfront. "I have no idea," she admitted on a sigh, and tossed the paper towel into the trash.

Jackson caught her arm, the edge of his mouth lifting. "You're a nurturer."

How he felt about that wasn't clear. He looked a little amused, but his voice had a hard edge.

"I guess." She shrugged. "Selectively."

"I like it."

She stilled and glanced up into his eyes. "You don't look as if you like it. Actually, you look a little put out about it."

"I don't like liking it," he confessed.

"Why not?" She was baffled. "Tender touches . . ."

"Are too easy to get used to, and then if they depart the fix, a man's left missing them."

Depart the fix. Pilot lingo for leaving. So he flew, too. She wondered what type of aircraft. Helicopters? Planes? Both? "Jackson?" Morgan reacted on gut instinct. "You have abandonment issues, don't you?"

He pulled her to him, until he rested against the cabinet and she rested against him, then he met and held her gaze. "I never have," he admitted. "But I think I could be developing them."

Her heart skipped a full beat and then thudded. "So what do you need?" If he said for her to back off, she was going to be one very unhappy woman.

"I don't know." Blunt and honest, he looped his arms around her waist. "Maybe to know how you're feeling about what's happening between us. That could help resolve some things in my mind."

"I'm not sure, to tell you the truth." She fought to give her feelings voice. "I like you. I'm very attracted to you, and I feel connected to you. But we're in intense times, and that's not the best time to try to sort out these things."

How would he react to her special abilities? Would he back off? Run? Others had and, like him, they'd been strong men. Unlike them, he was not a man she ever wanted to lose. Sounded crazy considering the short time they'd known each other, but sometimes a woman recognized things at deeper levels than consciously or logically made sense, and this—whatever this was—with her and Jackson was deeper . . . and it was right.

"Life is intense, Morgan." He tucked her hair behind her ears. "There are no perfect conditions, especially not for people in our professions."

"That's true, but still . . ."

He dipped his chin. "Stop being logical and professional about this. It's personal, damned personal, and logic has nothing to do with the heart. In your profession, you surely know that."

"I do. And because it is personal, that's all the more reason to be careful." She rested her hands on his chest. "I don't want to hurt you, and I damn sure don't want to be hurt, Jackson."

"Who does?" he asked but didn't wait for an answer. "I know you're not a coward, honey, so why don't you just admit you're crazy about me? I'll admit I'm crazy about you, and we can be insane together and call it done."

She fingered the collar of his shirt. "I did admit I was in for the insanity," she reminded him. Was there a distinction between that and being crazy about him?

"You did." He gave her that. "Trouble is you really do consider what's happening between us insane." He sounded a little irked by that.

"And you consider it crazy," she countered. "Which is better or worse?"

He ignored her question and stared at her mouth. "I like you. A lot."

She smiled. "I like you a lot, too."

"That's better." He touched her chin with his fingertip and then kissed her breathless.

The saving grace was that he was left breathless, too. "Much better." He grinned. "Ready to dump logic and go for it?" The twinkle in his eye was as enticing as his kiss.

"Getting closer all the time."

"Now that's much better," he said, pulling her closer still, and then kissing her again.

The conference room was cold.

Morgan and Jackson walked in, acknowledged the others with nods, and took the two available seats beside each other, across from Taylor Lee and Jazie. The commander sat at the head of the table, Joan Foster at the foot, and Dr. Vargus on her left, across from an empty seat beside Jackson.

"Everyone knows everyone, so let's get started," Commander Drake said. "Dr. Vargus?"

"At Morgan's request, I took a blood sample from the incarcerated Captain Bruce Stern and ran various tests on it, including his DNA." The doctor plucked his thin black-frame glasses from his white jacket pocket and eased them onto his nose, then thumped the bridge to seat them into place. "The DNA of the man incarcerated matches the DNA we have on record for Bruce Stern."

That meant less than nothing since Thomas Kunz had successfully substituted medical records, DNA results, X-rays, and other lab studies into the government's system in the past. Morgan patiently waited for the test results that could tell them Bruce was actually Bruce: Jackson's DNA.

"I also ran similar studies on Captain Jackson Stern," Dr. Vargus said. "His DNA has distinct similarities to that of the incarcerated man, but they are not a perfect match." He avoided looking at Jackson. "As full blood brothers, they should be."

Everyone, including Morgan, let his or her gaze drift from the doctor to Jackson. Betrayed and deceived, she asked, "Jackson, what does this mean?"

His expression turned dark and guilt radiated from him, swamping Morgan. "It means what it means, Morgan," he said sharply, clearly embarrassed and resentful. "Bruce and I are not full brothers, and neither of us ever claimed anything to the contrary."

Morgan was content to wait and let him explain this in his own way.

The commander wasn't, and cut to the chase. "Dr. Vargus? What conclusions have you drawn?"

"The two men share a mother, Commander."

There was nothing about his parents divorcing in his file. In fact, they had remained married until his father's death, which meant . . . *Oh, hell.* His mother had had an affair.

Was that the source of Jackson's guilt? It couldn't be. He would have had no control over his mother's activities. Yet children commonly took on parents' responsibilities as their own.

Joan Foster cleared her throat. "So Bruce Stern is Bruce Stern."

"Oh, yes." Dr. Vargus nodded, giving them affirmation beyond just his words.

"That's settled then." Joan Foster stepped in, not looking Jackson's way, doing what she could to help the uncomfortable moment pass. "The ME hasn't officially released his report or authorized the release of Laura's body for burial, but unofficially, he's told me that she died from a stab wound to the heart."

"She was stabbed *and* strangled?" Jackson asked, shock in his voice.

"I'm so sorry, Jackson," Joan said. "I thought you'd viewed the body."

"I did," he said softly. "What was exposed anyway. She was my sister-in-law," he reminded Joan. "It didn't seem proper to move the sheet when it wasn't absolutely necessary."

"I totally agree," she said. "I wish I'd been more gentle. I didn't know . . ."

He slid her a flat look. "There is no gentle way to say she was stabbed and strangled, Joan, but I appreciate the thought."

She nodded and then looked down the table at the commander. "Perhaps it would be best to discuss the balance of the ME's findings privately?"

"No," Jackson said, then cleared his throat and looked at Commander Drake. "I didn't realize she'd been stabbed; that's all. Please, just go ahead."

The commander sent Joan a look Morgan had no trouble interpreting. *Omit the specifics.* Everyone except Jackson knew Laura had thirty-one stab wounds, and no good would come from revealing it to him right at the moment.

Joan continued. "There was sufficient skin and blood

under Laura's nails to run a DNA test."

Jackson stiffened beside her, and Morgan felt the tension coil tightly in him.

"It doesn't match Bruce's DNA," she added quickly, looking at Jackson. "Bruce didn't attack her."

Jackson's expression didn't change, but Morgan felt the tension drain out of his body and she was grateful for it. At least that was one worry off his mind.

Taylor Lee intervened. "Does anything rule out Bruce stabbing her?"

"No, I'm afraid not," Joan said. "Without the weapon, we can't be sure. But we are sure that Bruce is within the killer's height range—"

"Him and five million other men," Jazie said. "That doesn't prove anything."

"That's true; it doesn't." Joan nodded her agreement. "Both Bruce and the killer are right handed," she went on, and then hesitated, giving Morgan an apologetic look. "We do know that Bruce is responsible for the bruises on Laura's upper arms—"

"He's admitted grabbing her during an argument, Colonel," Taylor Lee said. "He never meant to leave bruises, of course. Things heated up, and they were both upset. He didn't realize he'd squeezed her that hard."

"Was he aware that he'd bruised her?" Drake asked.

"No, he wasn't," Jazie said, revealing that both she and Taylor Lee had spoken with Bruce. "Not until we told him."

Commander Drake twirled her pen between her fingertips. The pad in front of her was blank. "What was his reaction?"

"Remorseful," Jazie said.

"He was disgusted," Taylor Lee added. "Genuinely disgusted with himself."

Morgan was relieved to hear that, and so was Jackson. He rolled his shoulders and sat back in his seat. For the first time since they'd entered the room, he didn't look as if he wanted to throw up.

Tapping her pen against the paper, Commander Drake let her gaze wander between them. "Does anyone at this table think Bruce killed his wife?"

"I don't," Joan Foster said. "Nothing in the findings supports it, Commander."

Dr. Vargus lifted his hands. "No judgment, but as an observer, I'd have to say no. He's grieving, Sally. No one knows better than we do that you can't fake grief—not at that level."

Morgan agreed.

"In my opinion," Taylor Lee said, next in line going around the table. "He's not totally innocent. But he's not guilty either. It's tough to explain."

"Mmmm." Jazie let out a little moan. "He didn't do it, Commander," she said, voicing her opinion. "That much is abundantly clear from . . . er, the evidence. But I get where Taylor Lee is picking up that he's not totally innocent."

Jazie tilted her head. "He feels as if Laura's death is his fault, not because he was directly involved in her murder, I don't think. But maybe because he couldn't stop it from happening."

Jackson stared at Jazie in awe and surprise.

"Captain Stern?" The commander addressed Jackson, who was next in line. "Have you formed an opinion on this that you would feel comfortable sharing with us?"

The tension came back in him, and doubled. "Family loyalty would insist I swear he's innocent," Jackson said. "But if I said he was, that's what it would be—loyalty, not fact." Jackson hated saying the words. It vibrated through him to everyone at the table. "The truth is, I don't know if he killed her. He loved her. I'm certain of that. But Thomas Kunz and G.R.I.D. . . ." He went silent a second, then added, "Well, right now, Commander, too much remains unexplained. I can't have an opinion I have any faith in. Not yet." Jackson swallowed. "Believe me, I wish I could. I would love nothing more than to look you in the eye and tell you I know Bruce is innocent."

"But . . ." she prodded.

"But I can't. I don't know." His voice took on a sharp edge. "I don't believe we have all the questions yet, much less all the answers."

Morgan watched the commander closely and was taken aback because she wasn't surprised. Not at all. It was as if she'd expected Jackson to voice uncertainty . . . and maybe she had. And maybe Morgan should have expected it, too. Jackson loved them both—Bruce and Laura. He would be conflicted. And yet this uncertainty went deeper, into something beyond Morgan's scope of understanding. She felt it; she just couldn't identify or explain it because she lacked a frame of reference for it.

"I understand, Jackson," Commander Drake said. "I don't think there's anyone wearing a uniform who doesn't comprehend the conflict between love for family and dedication to duty. You don't want to poorly serve either."

"No, ma'am, I don't." He said in a flat tone.

Of course, Morgan thought, feeling easier now that she'd gotten a firm fix on it. *Of course.*

"Morgan?" Commander Drake dragged a hand through her short, spiky hair. "Your take?"

"He didn't kill her," she said simply. "But there is credible evidence that Bruce has a double and we're not sure which man was where when—though we are certain and now have confirmation that the real Bruce Stern is in the brig—or was when the blood was drawn."

"He's on full monitoring now, Morgan."

She nodded at Darcy. "Glad to hear it."

"Commander," Jackson said. "I can verify that Bruce didn't return home until three weeks ago. I know it for a fact because I met with him in Iraq."

She propped an elbow on her chair arm and dropped her chin into one palm. "Captain, we've just required DNA testing to prove he's your brother to know for a fact who we have in jail. Can you be absolutely certain it was Bruce and not one of Kunz's doubles you met with in Iraq?"

"Yes, ma'am, I can."

"How?"

"His soul's in his eyes, Commander," Jackson explained. "Kunz can use surgeons to change a man's appearance. He can use psychological warfare techniques to manipulate his mind, behavioral modifications to change his habits, and body language and coaching to change his manner of speaking and a thousand other things. But nothing Thomas Kunz or a hospital full of doctors can do can change what's in a man's soul. It hasn't been mapped by mortals. And Bruce wears his soul in his eyes. He has his whole life."

Jazie was impressed by that insight. Taylor Lee was skeptical of it. Morgan was enthralled by it and fascinated by the man who thought in those terms, and she was more certain than ever that Jackson possessed elevated attunement and intuitive skills, though he'd likely call them well-honed gut instincts.

"Well, it happens that you're right, Captain," Commander Drake said. "I've gone up the chain of command with our dilemma on this and, while the powers that be resolutely refuse to disclose specifics, they have verified that Bruce returned from Iraq three weeks ago."

"Now this is bizarre," Joan Foster said, eyes flashing

with questions. "Kunz had Bruce's double here with Laura instead of in the field gathering intelligence?" She sat back and rested her hands on her distended stomach. "How very, very bizarre."

Colonel Drake frowned. "So far as we know, it's another first. Any insight you can share, Joan . . ."

"A double inserted with a spouse is totally outside anything I've seen," she said. "There can be only one reason, Commander. Bruce wasn't Kunz's target."

Shock rippled around the table. "Are you saying Kunz was after Laura?"

"Yeah, I am." Joan nodded to punctuate her claim. "The double was after intelligence, but not from Bruce. From Laura."

"Be patient with me," the commander said. "I'm trying to wrap my mind around this." She lifted a finger. "Kunz wanted intelligence information Bruce had shared with Laura? Is that what you're saying?"

"I won't go that far speculating," Joan said. "I will say I think Kunz wanted something from Laura. Whether it was intelligence from Bruce or something separate from him, I have no way of knowing. But I do know Thomas Kunz, and, traditionally, he tortures or kills family members to force information from the source. He targets the source, not secondary people. I've never known him to accept intelligence from anyone other than a direct source. Unless something significant has changed, he put the double with

Laura because he wanted something from her."

Jackson looked at Morgan, his puzzlement expanding, filling the distance between them. "What could Laura possibly know that Kunz would consider *that* important?"

"Let's speculate after we've heard all the facts," the commander said. "What else do we know, Morgan?"

She related events from the Stern residence, the fact that the Jeep had been removed from her garage and rigged with seven explosive devices, and then the issue of the coins. However, she didn't mention Laura's having the opportunity to plant the one found in her shoe. If Jazie or Taylor Lee picked up on anything about that, it would be more valuable to the S.A.T. team if it came unsolicited. It was also an opportunity to test their skills, which they were encouraged to do whenever possible.

Morgan put the two evidence bags on the table. "One was found at the Stern residence. The other in mine."

Jazie reached for the bag on the left.

Taylor picked up the one on the right.

Morgan waited a long tense moment and then added, "Darcy identified them as actual currency predominately used in an island chain in the South Pacific."

"Laura," Jazie said.

Taylor Lee nodded her agreement. "There's no evidence G.R.I.D. was inside your house?"

"No, there isn't." Morgan's nerves jangled. Jackson didn't know about the team's special abilities and she would prefer he not learn about them here. Discovering Laura had been stabbed and strangled, he'd already suffered enough shocks in this meeting. "Just in the garage," she said.

"Laura wanted you to find this," Jazie said.

"We've surmised that," Morgan said. "But we're not sure why, though we found some film in her camera—the coin found at her home was positioned on top of the camera, right, Jackson?"

He nodded. "When I picked the camera up from the closet shelf, the coin fell off it and onto the floor."

"We're hoping," Morgan continued, "that whatever is on the film will offer some answers as to why the coins are significant."

"Where's the film?" the commander asked.

"At the base lab being processed," Morgan said, adjusting her cuff. "They'll have prints ready in about thirty minutes. Darcy will get secure digitals within the hour."

"All right." Commander Drake set her pen down, then braced her hands on the tabletop. "Anything else?"

Jazie addressed the group. "Darcy and I have been coordinating on the G.R.I.D. assassins. We had a possible sighting on Stick—"

"The one with the shaved head?" Dr. Vargus asked and then motioned to his jacket front. "Expensive dresser?"

"Stick's the big, bald bruiser, Merk's the nerd, and Payton is the business exec," Jazie said, giving the doc a quick recap. "A car rental agency said a man offered to pay her triple the standard rates for a car. She thinks it was Stick, but couldn't be positive."

"There are no rentals available anywhere in the three surrounding counties," Jackson said.

"True, Commander," Morgan said. "My mechanic had to get me one from his private stock." She turned to Jackson. "Who owns the blue truck you've been driving?"

"I borrowed it from a guy at the marina," Jackson said. "We were eating breakfast together when I called you this morning. He picked up on the emergency, and we traded. He's holding the keys to the *Sunrise* and hoping, I'm sure, I never return."

"I checked out two dozen clubs last night," Taylor Lee said. "No sign of the G.R.I.D. men in any of them."

So much for Taylor Lee's dancing for the sake of dancing. Morgan should have known. Taylor Lee loved to party, but loved her work even more.

"Okay, then. Thanks, everybody. Keep at it on all fronts, and report details as you get them." Sally Drake stood up and then left the table.

Morgan issued her team a few secondary orders. "Jazie, you keep working the local aspect. Hotels, restaurants . . . Even G.R.I.D. assassins have to sleep and eat."

"You got it."

"Taylor Lee, dig into Bruce and Laura's finances. See if her spending was in line with their assets. And if she did any traveling while Bruce was in Iraq, I want to know it."

Those phone calls to Jackson every Saturday from somewhere other than Laura's own phones gnawed at Morgan and had to be explained.

"If we can do anything here, just say the word," Joan told Morgan.

"Absolutely," Dr. Vargus added, then looked at Jackson. "I realize you have a lot going on right now, but I think Bruce would really appreciate a few minutes of your time."

Jackson nodded. "He'll appreciate us proving his innocence more, but I'll make an effort, Doctor. Thanks for your concern."

"Of course." Dr. Vargus left the table and then the room.

Morgan checked her watch, which showed 9:45. "Phone conference at four." She grabbed her handbag. "Jackson, let's go get those photos."

Out in the hall, Commander Drake intercepted Morgan. "A moment, please."

Morgan told Jackson, "I'll be right back," then joined the commander, and they walked a few paces down the hall.

"I'm having Darcy check deeper into these coins," Sally Drake said, eyes shining. "I'd like to put Amanda on it, but she's tied up with her wedding and she's pretty stressed out about that . . ."

"Understandable considering the abuse in her history, Commander," Morgan whispered.

"Totally," she agreed and blew out a sigh. "Tell your

team to expect an invitation to her bridal shower, and warn them that Kate's giving it."

Surprise shuddered through Morgan. "Kate?" She was the last person Morgan expected would throw a bridal shower. She'd consider them ridiculous frou-frou fluff.

Judging by Commander Drake's expression, she apparently agreed Kate doing it was beyond odd. "Expect Blue Bell Double Chocolate Fudge Brownie ice cream, a cake shaped like some weapon, and drinks with umbrellas in them."

"That's quite a mix." Morgan chuckled. "Umbrellas?"

"She's been on a tropical kick since she and Nathan have been rendezvousing on some island somewhere close to wherever they are every four weeks." Commander Drake sighed again. Deeper. "I'm doing my damnedest to get General Shaw to assign him to Providence."

"What would Nathan do at Providence?" Morgan asked.

A twinkle lit in Sally Drake's eyes. "Command the base."

"What about Colonel Gray?" Morgan hated to mention the name of the commander's nemesis, but it couldn't be avoided.

"He'll be retiring in less than a year." Glee flitted across her face. "We're marking off the days on the Home Base calendar out at Regret," she added. "When that jerk retires is when I'll throw a party."

He was an ass; Morgan had to agree, and she didn't cross paths with him nearly so often as Commander Drake did. "I hope you're successful," she said. "And Amanda's shower should be an experience."

"With Kate at the helm, you can bet on it." Sally Drake smiled. "Morgan, she had Darcy pull research to see what to do at a bridal shower, and after she read the notes, she had fifteen pages of questions. Darcy was ready to commit murder."

Morgan laughed. "I'll bet she was, but you've got to give it to Kate. She's trying to do things right for Amanda and Mark."

"Yeah, but she is so out of her depth. The woman can take apart a bomb or build anything that explodes, but she can't order a cake without a congressional act. It's a riot."

It was. "I'll warn the others to expect anything."

"Especially Taylor Lee. Jazie is more diplomatic—"

"Taylor Lee is diplomatic, too."

Commander Drake slid Morgan a deadpan look. "The woman has the tact of a Mack truck."

Morgan couldn't deny it, so she said nothing.

"If Taylor Lee should happen to say the wrong thing, with Kate's, er, let's say, short fuse, there could be bad trouble, and with Amanda being skittish about all this wedding and marriage business, anyway . . ."

"It wouldn't be good," Morgan filled in the blank.

"Not good at all." Commander Drake grunted. "If there's bloodletting at her bridal shower, Amanda's bound to take it as a bad sign and . . ."

"Mark will wear out a dozen pairs of running shoes trying to catch her."

"Exactly." Sally Drake reached into her purse, pulled out an apple, and took a little bite. "That would cause an unwelcome distraction in my command."

And that meant there'd be hell to pay. Sally Drake was a good woman and a strong commander, but mess with her command, and she was hell on wheels. "I'll talk to Taylor Lee. An ounce of prevention is worth a pound of cure." It was. Especially when the cure could be painful for many.

"Good." Commander Drake took another bite of apple and then swallowed before going on. "I wasn't sure where you'd placed Jackson on your need-to-know list."

"Front and center," Morgan said. "He's too perceptive to be anywhere else."

She nodded, worrying her lower lip. "Any conflicts?"

"None." Morgan didn't hesitate. "If anything, he's more skeptical about Bruce than the rest of us."

"Picked up on that." She twirled the apple in her hand, thinking. "You bend over backward to be objective and end up being unfair to those who mean most to you."

Morgan nodded. "It's a rough position to be in."

"It's hell." Sally ran her tongue over her teeth, making sure no apple bits were clinging to them.

Morgan hiked her handbag's strap on her shoulder. "So what's Darcy doing on the coins?"

If the commander was surprised that Morgan had intuited there was more, she didn't show it. "It's valid currency, but a commemorative coin. Not circulated. They minted it for a festival and distributed it largely to collectors throughout the region."

Morgan knew a festival had been involved. Reassured about her sensory perception on that, she prodded. "So it won't pinpoint a single island for us?"

"No, but that was too much to expect anyway. There are over nine hundred islands in that area, and just under four hundred of them are inhabited."

Morgan digested that and then stilled. Uninhabited islands. G.R.I.D. compounds. Kunz had used remote places before—Kate had clashed with him in a compound built in an underwater cave. "Are you thinking what I'm thinking?"

"Probably. Laura is pointing us to the festival, not to the island." Sally Drake worried her lip with her teeth. "From what Joan said, Kunz hit his primary target every time. What I need to know is why Laura Stern, a wife and homemaker who was not a government employee, was on the radar of the world's largest black market intelligence broker."

"I'll do what I can, Commander. If Laura were alive, we'd be able to pick up on a lot more than we can with her dead. That's especially true, across the board, when a victim dies violently. At the moment of death, their entire focus—all their energy—is pinpointed on their survival. So not much else is there to be intuited or seen or heard. Know what I mean?"

"Yes, I do. When Kenneth died, I was intensely focused, too."

Morgan nodded. "Laura wanted us to see that film. She went to a lot of trouble seeing to it that we did."

"I can't prove it, Morgan, but I think she thought it was important enough to die for, which makes it pretty frigging important to me, and I expect it'll be even more important to Bruce." Sally Drake slicked back her spiky hair. "I'm going to keep Bruce incarcerated, by the way. We could release him based on the DNA evidence not matching up, but with those G.R.I.D. goons around looking for a fight, I think the man's safer in jail than out of it."

"I agree. It's bad enough to have to worry about Jackson, Commander. He continually insists on putting himself in the kill zone."

"Where he can see them coming," she surmised. "There's solid strategic logic in that line of thinking."

"Yes, there is, but it still scares the hell out of me, and I would rather not be sidetracked by them both being on the loose and in the kill zone." There wasn't a doubt in Morgan's mind that if Bruce was set free, he'd be right there with Jackson.

A speculative gleam shone in the commander's eyes. "Is there anything going on between you and Jackson that I need to worry about?"

"Worry about? No, not at all." Morgan started to shun further disclosure, but reconsidered. The commander had picked up on their attraction and she would be fine with it, provided it didn't come with lies. In her command, omission definitely rated as a lie, and lies were always unwise. "I like him, Sally." Morgan deliberately used the commander's first name, making the matter personal rather than keeping it on a professional footing. That was something she rarely did.

"You like him?"

Morgan nodded. "A lot. He's a good man."

"Okay, then." She gave Morgan a steely look. "I'm glad you two like each other. A lot. But don't go stupid on me. Your heart and hormones can flutter all they want—later. Right now, you're dealing with G.R.I.D. Thomas Kunz is a master at emotional manipulation, and to protect his interests, he'll kill you, Morgan. Don't let Cupid make it easy for him."

The same lecture Morgan had been giving herself all along. "I won't." She nodded to Jackson, who waited just down the hall, indicating she'd be just a minute more. "I'm not even sure it isn't the intensity of the case at this point."

"Good." Sally Drake shrugged. "It should be considered. It changes the complexion of things."

It did. And honestly Morgan couldn't decide at present if the thing with Jackson was right or good. But she did want to explore and find out.

"Keep me posted."

"I will." Morgan walked away, back down the hallway to Jackson. "Ready?"

"Yeah." He fell into step beside her. "Everything okay?"

"Perfect," she said. "Just a little operational housekeeping."

"And a warning not to get so close to me that you don't see the forest for the trees."

There it was again. That sharp, uncanny perceptiveness of his. "That, too," she admitted.

"You don't have to worry, Morgan. I'm safe."

Safe? The man could break her heart in ways no man ever had. But she trusted him, and she smiled her appreciation for his reassurance, brushing a hand over his forearm. "But Thomas Kunz and his G.R.I.D. assassins are not. That's who the commander is worried about."

He waited for a woman carrying a lab box to walk past them in the hall. When she had, he said, "We're paying attention."

"We'd better."

He stepped outside and held the door. "By the time we get to the lab, the photos should be ready."

Morgan walked out into the heat. The glare was blinding. She grabbed her sunglasses from her purse and put them on. "I hope to hell they tell us something."

"They will," he said, and then leveled her with an unwavering look that sent a little chill down her back. "I don't pretend to understand this, but Laura's actions have been very deliberate. That changes the question. It isn't *if* the photos will tell us anything, but if we'll be sharp enough to decipher what the photos tell us."

Morgan slid in behind the wheel of the rental Camry, certain Jackson was exactly right. She cranked the engine and turned up the air conditioner full blast. It was already pushing ninety degrees outside, and the full heat of the day was still hours away.

"I need to make a quick call," she said, then pulled out her cell and dialed.

"Jazie Craig."

"It's Morgan." The parking lot was emptier than usual for this time of morning. The hospital must be working a field disaster exercise or something. "Are you researching from the office or from home right now?"

"The office. Secure tracking seemed prudent."

"Excellent," Morgan said. "Check to see when there was a festival of the arts in the coin's immediate area of distribution."

"Travel there would be pretty much airlines or boat," Jackson said. "For what it's worth."

Which was a great deal, considering the line of thought

it spurred. "When you narrow the time, check travel from here to that general area—air and boat in particular—and let's see who turns up."

"That's going to take awhile," Jazie said. "Pretty big area—several island chains."

"But hopefully not so many festivals that warrant a coin being minted to commemorate them."

"That should help substantially," she said. "I'll get back to you."

Morgan dropped her phone back into her handbag, then reached for the gearshift and looked over at Jackson. "Now, let's see about those photos."

CHAPTER 10

The photo lab was located in the central area of the base, which should have been crowded on a weekday morning. Morgan checked her watch—11:10.

"Something's wrong." Jackson placed a hand on her thigh. "Stay away from the building."

She had the same instinctive feeling. Was it from him, or—?

The building exploded.

The impact knocked the Camry thirty degrees right. Morgan fought for control and stomped the gas. "Get my cell. Speed dial one."

Jackson scrambled for the phone, hit the button, and then passed over the phone.

"Morgan?" Sally Drake said in a rush. "What the hell

is going on? It sounds like you're in a war zone."

"We are, Commander." She hit the brakes and came to a hard stop at the foot of the parking lot.

"Where are you?" She shouted, "Darcy, activate Big Brother on Cabot—now!"

Big Brother was a satellite locator system enabled by a chip embedded in Morgan—and every other S.A.S.S. operative's neck—and activating it made the chip susceptible to interception. "No, Commander. I'm at Providence, on base outside what used to be the photo lab."

"Darcy, cancel that Big Brother order," she said, and then spoke to Morgan, "Used to be?"

Sirens sounded in the distance.

"Base emergency personnel are responding," Jackson said. "Clear out of here."

"The lab's gone. Blown up. Kate needs to be here, to run fingerprints and see who created the device." They were very specific, and even in rubble a lot could be learned about who had made the bomb. Morgan's money was on G.R.I.D.

"The film?" the commander asked.

"Gone." Disappointment hit Morgan hard, and she squeezed her eyes shut. Laura might have died to get that information to them. It was so unfair. So damned unfair for it to be lost forever.

Jackson touched her arm.

She looked over and saw he was holding something in

his upturned palm. Stunned, she stared at it, at him. "Hold on a minute," she told Commander Drake. "Is that—?"

"The film," he said. "I'm sorry, Morgan. I had a bad feeling. G.R.I.D. hasn't been diligent in pursuing us, and that's atypical for them. Normally we'd be under constant attack until they killed us or stopped us or did whatever their mission is to do. So I switched the film. I was going to tell you, but we didn't get any private time so I could—"

"I heard that," the commander said. "Morgan, chew his ass out for deceiving you later. Right now get that damn film to the processing plant on 98 by the marina. I'll call ahead. Stand there with it and wait for those damn photos. Eyes on all the way."

"Yes, ma'am."

"And get the hell away from the lab before Gray gets me on the phone wanting to question you to see if you blew it up."

"They're getting close, Morgan," Jackson added. "Go, go, go—now!"

Morgan hit the gas and cleared the parking lot, then turned on a side street. "We're out, Commander." They were four blocks down the street before the first fire truck passed them.

"Uh, you didn't do it, right?" Commander Drake asked.

"No, ma'am, I didn't."

"And you vouch for Jackson?"

Morgan tilted the phone. "Did you put explosives in the film canister or plant any other device to cause the lab explosion?"

"No." He smiled. "I didn't."

She smiled back at him. "No, ma'am. Neither of us blew up the lab."

"Darcy, where's Kate?" The line went dead.

The commander was done. "Don't take offense to that question, Jackson."

"I didn't," he said. "She asked you, too. But I'm taking serious offense to your driving. Would you please slow down?"

Morgan backed off the gas. "Seventy?"

"Yeah." He was gripping the dash. "In a thirty zone."

"Sorry." She drove out of the base gate moments before the gate guards scrambled out of the guard shack and closed it.

Colonel Gray had Providence Air Force Base on lockdown.

Jackson looked back in the passenger side mirror. "Too late," he predicted. "They're long gone."

"G.R.I.D.?"

"Who else?" He tumbled the film canister in his hand. "What the hell could be on this film that has Kunz so afraid?"

"We'll soon find out." Morgan drove down to the main drag in Magnolia Beach, then turned left on Highway 98 and headed for the marina.

When they came up on the photo lab's processing plant, Jackson said, "Circle the block."

Morgan kept going. "Jackson, if G.R.I.D. is responsible for the lab explosion, they think they got the film. They aren't going to be looking for us to show up at a photo lab, especially one open to the public. They haven't had time to figure out that you switched the film."

"You willing to bet your life on it?" He looked out the window, left then right, scanning cars and those occupying them. "How freaking assassins got base access is what I want to know."

The gate guards at Providence pulled a 100 percent ID check as a matter of routine and had since 9/11. That was one of Gray's policies Morgan appreciated. "There are doubles we know about but haven't yet accounted for or located," she said. "Last count, forty-three of them."

"I know that," he admitted. "What I mean is how did they get on *this* base *this* morning?"

"I don't understand." Doubles were in jobs where they would have access. Braked at a stop sign, Morgan looked over at him.

His hand fisted around the film canister, and his knuckles went white. "Where's Bruce's double now?" he asked. "He was here while Bruce was in Iraq. He was gone when Bruce returned home three weeks ago, and Laura and Bruce no doubt talked about that. So when Bruce's double disappeared on Bruce's return, where did he go?"

"I expect somewhere out of the country," Morgan said, following a green SUV down the street. "That's been the pattern."

"I wouldn't bet on it," Jackson said. "My guess is Kunz broke the pattern. I expect Bruce ran into him, and if he did—"

"What the hell are you saying, Jackson?"

"I'm saying that if Laura and Bruce spoke ten words to each other, he knew she thought he'd been home for three months as well as he knew he hadn't been. So bear with me on this."

"Okay, go ahead."

"If we were married, and you came home and I talked about things that had gone on during the past few months, what would be the first thing you'd do?"

Morgan pulled off the road and stopped, bubbles rippling in her stomach. "Report the security breach."

"But Bruce didn't report it, did he?"

"No, he didn't."

"There. It's what you would have done, what I would have done, what any officer would have done. But Bruce didn't. Why not?" Jackson asked with a lift of his eyebrows.

"I don't know," Morgan said, watching him closely. "But I think you might."

"Bruce wasn't here, Morgan. That's the only way this makes sense. Bruce wasn't here until right before Laura's murder."

She propped an arm on the steering wheel and swept her hair back from her face. "So Bruce left Iraq three weeks ago, but he didn't get home three weeks ago?" she asked, having a hard time getting a grip on it. "After being away from his home and his wife for months, he's cut loose to come home and he takes a side trip first?"

"I'd bet the bank on it." Jackson frowned and looked around to make sure they weren't being followed or watched. "I didn't say he took the scenic route willingly, but I do think he took it."

Realizing they were sitting ducks, Morgan pulled out into traffic, drove down to a Winn-Dixie parking lot, pulled in, stopped, and then gave Jackson her rapt attention. "You think Kunz snatched him?"

Jackson nodded. "If I'm right, then that would explain the guilt."

"How could Bruce do that?"

"You don't understand him, Morgan, or why he's like he is." Jackson obviously would rather not talk about it, but it was important to Morgan's understanding. "My father knew that Bruce wasn't his son, and he never let him forget it. He hated Bruce."

"Hated him? But he was an innocent child."

"He hated him," Jackson repeated. "Every time he looked at Bruce, it was like acid in his face. He never forgot that my mother wasn't faithful to him, and he never let her or Bruce forget she'd been unfaithful." Jackson's neck turned red. "I ran interference. It was my job to keep Bruce out of Dad's path. He drank, Morgan, and when he did, he was a mean son of a bitch. I protected Bruce, and he let me. His whole life. He never took responsibility for anything he did. Ever. I don't blame him—hell, I trained him to hide behind me, and so did our mother. But Bruce never stopped hiding behind me." Jackson lifted a hand. "He grew up, left home, and he never stopped hiding behind me."

Morgan felt the pain of the boy who had tried to protect this brother, who had always taken the hits for his mistakes and misdeeds, and she understood what Jackson was telling her. "If Bruce reported any of this, he'd lose his clearance. He'd be out of a job."

"Yes."

And he loved his job. "So, instead, he'd hide. He'd hide and leave the U.S. and Laura exposed."

Jackson's eyes filled. "Because it's what he knows to do. I believe he would."

Morgan took this through to the next step. "And he would know that you knew he had."

"Which is why, I think, he was swimming in guilt when we saw him." Jackson looked away. "He was okay with not speaking up until he looked me in the face. Then he couldn't tell himself he wasn't hiding, and that's when he started feeling guilty as hell because his wife was dead and he did nothing to protect her. Nothing but to protect his own ass."

Bruce had been overwhelmed with guilt. About that, Morgan had no doubt. "If this is all true, then it still brings us right back to the original question." A woman rolled a shopping cart full of grocery bags across the lot. Its wheels crackled on the uneven pavement. She emptied her groceries into her car, slammed the trunk, then got in and pulled away. "Where was Bruce during that time, and where is his double now?"

"Have Darcy check the base gate's security tapes. Either one of the three G.R.I.D. assassins we know are here—Merk, Stick, and Payton—or Bruce's double likely planted the photo lab bomb."

Morgan made the call, and Darcy promised to check the tapes right away. "Awesome, Darcy, I appreciate it."

"Sure. Oh, and while I have you, the paperwork has come through on the Stern phone records. They're pulling them now."

"Thanks." Morgan hung up and then told Jackson, "We're about to get the phone records on Laura's calls to you."

Morgan realized what she had said. "Damn it."

"What?" Jackson asked.

Driving down the street, she glanced over. "What if Laura made that side trip *with* Bruce?"

"I hadn't thought of that," Jackson said. "You'd think they'd mention going on a trip—unless they were doing something wrong."

"Or something dangerous." It was possible. "They might have known you'd come running to save Bruce, and he might not have wanted to put you in danger, too."

"Possible," he said, more than a little skeptical. "It's not probable, but it is possible." Jackson sighed. "Either way, we'll soon find out."

"Will we?" she asked. "You know, Jackson, I'm having a hell of a time deciding if Bruce and Laura are our allies or our enemies. Half the time, I think they're really good and the other half, I'm convinced they're bad to the bone." She settled into pure frustration. "Are they friends or foes? Not being sure is making me crazy."

"I know what you mean." He rubbed at his thigh. "I'm in the same boat."

And his emotional investment was far, far greater. She clasped his hand and gave it a gentle squeeze. "I'm sorry, honey."

"Me, too." He laced their fingers and held on tight.

At the photo processing plant, she circled the block. "Anything?"

"No, we're okay." Jackson lifted his nose to the left. "Open parking spot over there."

Morgan parked, and then they went inside the little wooden building that probably had once been someone's fishing camp.

A kid who looked twelve addressed them from behind

the counter. "Help you?"

"I believe Commander Drake called and said we'd be coming."

"Yes, ma'am." He pointed to the edge of the counter. "She said you had to watch. Come on back."

Morgan walked over to the end of the counter, looped around it, and noticed Jackson wasn't following her.

"You go ahead, he said." "I'll wait here."

And keep watch. She heard the words that hadn't been spoken, and offered up a little prayer that nothing happened. They needed these photos. Desperately. Morgan was more and more convinced that Laura had died to get them to her.

The boy, Craig, ran the film through the machine and within thirty minutes, Morgan and Jackson had the pictures spread across the counter.

"They're definitely somewhere tropical," Morgan said. *Palm trees, sun, and beach.* "It looks as if it could be in the South Pacific." *Consistent with the coin.* "Darcy will know for sure." Morgan looked over at the boy seated at his computer. "Craig, I need a digital copy of these."

"A second one?" he asked, hitting the return key. "The commander told me to send one to an address she gave me."

Morgan walked over. "What's the address?"

He showed her. It was Darcy. "Can you forward a copy to me?" she asked, then gave him an email account she'd set up a year ago but had never used.

He hit the keys, then grinned up at her. "Done."

"Awesome." Morgan reached into her purse. "I'll need a bill."

Jackson gathered up the photos.

"Oh, no, ma'am. Commander Drake's taken care of it."

"How?" Morgan hadn't meant to ask, but it'd just slipped out.

"I do yard work for her," he said. "She lets me drive her Harley sometimes. I get paid cash *and* a full hour on the Harley for this."

Morgan grinned. "Wear a helmet."

"They changed that law."

"I'm a doctor, Craig. You know what we call motor-cycles whose riders ride without helmets?"

He hiked a shoulder, asking.

"Brain scramblers."

Craig pulled a sour face. "I'll wear a helmet."

"Good call." She walked over to the door where Jackson stood waiting, eager to review and discuss the photos privately with him.

Maybe they'd have better luck mulling over them together. In a quick glance, neither of them had picked up on anything significant, except that Bruce wasn't in them.

But the redhead photographed with Laura in the album Morgan had seen in Laura's office—the same redhead whose photo was on her entryway wall—was in most of the photographs—with Laura.

Jackson drove over to Morgan's, and they went inside; then she spread the photos out on the kitchen bar.

He helped himself to a glass of water and brought one to Morgan. "You don't drink enough."

"Thanks." She took the glass, pleased that he cared enough to look out for her and a little amused. His nurturing instincts were as strong as hers, but he obviously didn't see it.

"It's that Judy woman," he said. "Laura went on a vacation with her?"

"Apparently, she did. They are at some kind of festival on a tropical island. That's apparent." And a relief. Morgan's intuition had been right about that.

"Look at this one." He pointed to the third from the end in a row. "What's in Laura's hand?"

Morgan couldn't see it clearly. She grabbed a magnifying glass from her office and checked it again. "The coin." Her heart beat hard. "It's the coin."

"Morgan?" Jackson stilled, and his voice went deadly quiet.

So quiet she got chills and looked up from the photo.

"Who's taking the pictures?"

She moved down the long line of photos and found a clue. A man's left two fingers had crossed the lens. And on his second finger was a ring, turned to face the lens.

A ring bearing the commemorative coin.

"Does Bruce have a ring like that?" she asked.

"If he does, I've never seen it."

She pulled a plastic container of strawberries from the fridge, rinsed them, and dumped them into a bowl, then munched down on one. "Well, it's definitely a man's hand." She plucked another berry from the bowl. They were sweet and firm, awesome. "Is Judy *whatever* married?"

"She wasn't when I met her. But who knows?" Jackson ate a berry whole. "Maybe Laura went to this island for her wedding." He rubbed at his neck, puzzled. "She would have mentioned it. Until now, I thought she'd mention any trip. This is just weird."

A girlfriends' fling just didn't feel right. It wasn't Laura. So what was this, and why had she kept going secretly? "Mmmm." The phone rang.

Morgan answered it. "Cabot."

"Morgan." The commander's voice was two octaves higher than normal. "Have you seen the freaking photos?"

"We're looking at them now, Commander."

"The redhead—ask Jackson who she is."

"Already did," Morgan said. "Her photo is on the Stern's entryway hall and in a photo album in Laura's office."

"Ask him again."

Oddly, the commander sounded really rattled. Sally Drake could stare down the devil and didn't get rattled. Morgan turned. "Jackson, who is the redhead?"

"Judy," he said. "A friend of Laura's from college—I think it was college."

"Wrong," the commander said. "Well, right, but that's not all she is."

Morgan stiffened. "Who is she?"

"She used to be a security officer at Santa Bella Shopping Mall."

Kunz had attempted to release a deadly virus there as a capabilities demonstration, and if not for Maggie Holt, another S.A.S.S. agent assigned to one of Commander Drake's units, and Dr. Justin Crowe, who had developed an antidote to the lethal virus, Kunz would have succeeded. He had come damned close. "Well, what the hell is she doing with Laura? Were they really friends from school, or did they just meet at the mall?"

"Darcy's verified it. High school," the commander said. "But more important is what she became after leaving there."

Morgan felt ice cold inside. The commander had that "on a scale of one to ten, this is a twenty" tone. "What did she become?"

"Thomas Kunz's significant other," she said. "Judy Meyer is Thomas Kunz's significant other."

"Oh, my God." Morgan couldn't restrain herself. "So the guy wearing the ring in the photo isn't Bruce. He's Thomas Kunz!"

CHAPTER 11

Tropical Storm Lil had crawled ashore in Mississippi and Louisiana and then made a one-eighty and turned back to the gulf. Now it sat stalled out about forty miles offshore and, thanks to the warm water feeding it, it was gaining strength.

On hearing the five o'clock advisory, Morgan sensed it wouldn't be stalled out very long. It was about to shift directions, double back, and blast the Florida coast.

The 7:00 P.M. advisory confirmed it, and Lil had been upgraded to a category one hurricane.

"We're right in the middle of the projected path," Jackson said.

They were, and it was going to hit Magnolia Beach.

"I'd better get to the *Sunrise* and make preparations,

maybe move her inland to the bay."

Morgan nodded. "By dawn, the marina will be about empty." But tonight it would be slammed. Fishermen and pleasure boaters would be waiting in line to get out of the harbor, moving their boats to inland waterways for safety.

Jackson rubbed her upper arms. "I don't want to leave you alone here. G.R.I.D. has to know by now that we have the film. Kunz will want to stop us from taking it up to Regret."

"He'll know we sent Home Base digitals," Morgan predicted.

"Not from a nonsecure location," Jackson countered. "He'd never expect Sally Drake to authorize that."

Jackson was probably right about that. "Part of what makes her a strong S.A.S.S. commander is her willingness to take risks."

"It's also what makes us extra vulnerable right now," Jackson said. "Kunz will believe that if he stops us, he stops the photos from getting out."

"I just don't get this, Jackson. The S.A.S.S. knows what Kunz looks like now—Amanda discovered and revealed that—so what is it he's so hell-bent on hiding?"

"A G.R.I.D. compound?" he suggested.

Morgan shook her head, disagreeing. "There's nothing in the photos to pinpoint the location. The amount of topography and vegetation revealed is too narrow for us to get a fix."

"What if what he wants to hide isn't related to G.R.I.D.?" Jackson said. "What if it's more personal?"

Morgan's eyes glittered. "His home base. His retreat," she said, her heart thudding a drumming beat. Kunz was ruthless already. But how much further would he go to protect his sanctuary from the S.A.S.S.?

Jackson's hand moved in small, smooth circles against her arm. "He's going to come after us, Morgan."

"He already has." She shuddered. "But he'll attack with renewed vigor now."

"I'm not leaving you alone. Let's get the *Sunrise* storm-ready, and then we'll come back here and ride out the hurricane."

Relieved that she wouldn't have to face the worst of Kunz and a hurricane alone, she agreed. "Let me grab some different shoes. The deck will be slick," she said, already halfway down the hall. If it wasn't raining already—honestly, she'd been too focused on the photos to notice—it would be shortly. The weather would disintegrate quickly, and get a lot worse before it got better.

Running water sounded from the kitchen sink. Jackson getting a drink of water.

She didn't drink enough; he drank enough to float. Together, they were pretty well balanced.

Glass shattered.

Morgan flattened her back against the hall wall outside her bedroom.

"Morgan!" Jackson came barreling around the corner.

The smell of kerosene burned her nose. She was closer

to the door. Jackson pressed his weapon into her hands: an operative's ultimate expression of trust.

She took it and darted a fast look into her bedroom. Flames rose up from her bed a solid four feet, scorching the ceiling. "Fire. Call 911, Jackson." Obviously they'd taken out the smoke detector, or the alarm company would already have phoned.

He backtracked to the office, to the nearest phone, and dialed. "Fire," he said, then gave the address, dropped the phone, and returned to her, carrying her handbag.

She took it and retrieved her own gun, then returned his to him. "On three," she silently mouthed, then began the countdown.

"Three."

They burst into the room together, back to back, scanning and sweeping the walls, ready to fire. But the room was empty.

And the window was open.

"Hose." Morgan ran outside and around the side of the house, opened the water spigot, and then shoved the end of the garden hose through her bedroom window.

Jackson pulled it hard, and sprayed the bed.

Soon the fire was out.

The charred room stank of burn and smoke and the ceiling was cracked, its texture peeling from the heat. He wet it down to cool it. "Come in and call 911 back. We've got it under control, but they'll need to file a report."

Morgan stared at her bed, at the mess made of her room. And saw red streaks on the far wall. Streaks that spelled out a message.

You're next.

And the brazen bastard had signed it.

T.K.

The fire marshal insisted on checking out the attic to be sure there weren't any embers that would later ignite. Then he examined the ceiling, the walls, and helped remove the bed from her home to the curb, where it could be hauled away by the trash collector.

When he'd gotten all he needed for his report and had left her home, Morgan hugged Jackson. On seeing Kunz's message, her insides had gone liquid. "They opened that window while we were in the house. The alarm was on before then, so they had to do this while we were in the kitchen."

"Oh, no." Fear stretched Jackson's eyes wide. "The photos!"

They rushed into the kitchen and looked at the bar. Its granite top stretched the length of the room, slick and shiny and sheening the light reflected from the overhead.

No pictures.

While they'd dealt with the fire, one of the goons had stolen the photos.

Morgan reported the incident to Commander Drake, who was uncharacteristically shaken by the bold invasion it had required. "I want you out of that house now, Morgan. And don't go back until we resolve this. I mean it."

"But all the hotels are full, Commander."

"You can stay with me."

Jackson shook his head. "Her husband . . ."

Morgan knew what Jackson meant. Kenneth Drake had been killed in their home. He'd been in the wrong place at the wrong time. It'd been a G.R.I.D. hit, and Sally Drake, not Kenneth, had been the target. Kunz wasn't going to get Sally while targeting Morgan, or Morgan while targeting Sally. "No. We're not going to make a two-for-one easy for the bastard. I'll be with Jackson," Morgan said. "We're going to move the *Sunrise* into the bay before the storm comes; then . . ." She started to say they'd be on the boat, but thought better of it. The lines were supposed to be secure, but then so was her house. "I don't know where we'll be. I'll phone in, and you can reach me on—"

"I know," Sally said, obviously not wanting to disclose how they'd be communicating either.

Morgan would stop at a store, buy a couple disposable cells, and use them to communicate. She'd use her personal cell to transmit unrelated information to others and take the batteries out when it wasn't in use. It wasn't a perfect method to avoid being tracked, but it was the best available. She thought about the hurricane. *Lil,* she thought, *don't you dare knock out those towers.*

"Okay," Sally said. "But stay away from your house."

"I will." Her sanctuary was gone. Violated and gone.

Sally's blown breath relayed crackling static through the phone. "Morgan, I swear there's a special place in hell for that bastard."

"I vote we send him there just as soon as possible, Commander."

"I'll second that," she said with heart. "Keep me posted."

Morgan hung up and started gathering a few things. "Why did he burn my bed?"

"It's flammable and away from the kitchen. It was a diversion, honey. That's all."

Hatred fired in Morgan, burned deep, and permeated her every cell. "There is no 'that's all' with Thomas Kunz. He's showing me that there is no safe place. He can get to me no matter where I am. In my car, on the base, in my home, and even in my own bed."

"Morgan."

She stuffed her things into a bag. Shoved them down, her anger hot. "What?"

"Stop this." Jackson said.

She whipped around, glared at him. "Stop this?"

He held her furious gaze a long moment, then pulled her into his arms and held her close, burying his face at the curve of her neck and cupping her head in his hand. "Don't do this, baby," he whispered close to her ear. "If you get angry, you can't be effective. Then he wins." Jackson brushed her ear with the tip of his nose, pressed a kiss to her lobe, her temple. "He wins."

She turned her face to Jackson's, kissed him hungrily, passionately, redirecting all of her emotions to him, accepting all he was feeling into her, taking her time, sharing not exploring, giving her attraction to him full permission to expand and grow and fill her with desire.

He let out a low groan and parted their lips. "Better."

"Much better." She tipped her nose, rubbed it against his. "Let's get out of here."

The *Sunrise* was parked at the dock under a street lamp. Normally at this time of night, the fishermen and deckhands were done for the day and would have gone home. The slips would be full and the docks busy but calm, filled with tourists lazily strolling down the wooden planks, looking at the boats, discussing the unusual names on them, the towers and fishing rigs, dreaming of owning one, and just relaxing and enjoying the night breezes floating in off the gulf.

But with Hurricane Lil bearing down on Magnolia Beach, the entire chemistry of the marina had changed.

Tourists were asked to get off the docks and out of the way. Fishermen and deckhands worked frantically to clear the decks of anything strong winds could make flying projectiles. Anchors were checked, chains extended, mooring ropes loosened and drawn in, and the boats lined up, waiting to get out of the pass from the marina to the gulf so the boats could be taken into the bays where they'd be more protected from the storm surge and devastating winds.

"The only other time I've seen this place so crazy was for the blessing of the fleet." Jackson motioned to the stern. "Grab that rope, will you?"

Morgan pulled the rope into the boat and looked up. "Taylor Lee?"

She walked right past Morgan as if she hadn't heard her.

Impossible. Morgan signaled Jackson. "Something's wrong."

Taylor Lee paused a couple of boats farther down the dock. "Hey, where's that beer you promised me?"

A man came topside from the cabin on a forty-footer parked six slips down. Morgan dropped down low, peeked at him over the *Sunrise's* side. "Jackson," she shouted in a stage whisper, then pointed low just off the deck. "Stick."

Jackson slid down beside Morgan. "Any sign of the other two?"

"No. Just him."

Jackson looked around. "They can't be far," he told

her. "The bastards run in packs."

Morgan tapped her cell phone and speed-dialed Home Base. When Darcy answered, she whispered. "Stick is at the marina. Taylor Lee's roped him in. I can't believe she didn't call in backup or—" Morgan looked at the dock beside her, and her blood ran cold. Jazie was coming down the dock, arm in arm with Merk.

"Have they lost their minds?" Jackson asked. "What the hell are they doing?"

"I have no idea," Morgan said. "But I damn well don't like it." They were going to get the ass chewing of a lifetime for this . . . if any of them survived.

The next thing Morgan knew, Jazie had shoved Merk into the back of the *Sunrise* and then leapt in after him, coming down on his neck with the heel of her shoe. "Jackson," Jazie said, shooting him a frantic look, "I could use—"

Merk landed a right cross solidly on Jazie's jaw. Her head jerked back, and before Morgan could get to them, Jazie whipped out her Glock and shoved the barrel against Merk's nose. "Do not move," she warned in a tone Morgan had never before heard come from her throat. "If you do, I will shoot to kill." Her sweet, soulful tone sounded positively lethal. "I kid you not."

"Darcy," Morgan said into the phone. "Get a chopper down to the marina ASAP. We need someone to take out the trash."

"All three cans?"

"Not yet." Morgan said. "One in the can, one in hand, and one unaccounted for at this time." She shot a look back over at Taylor Lee, who had her back to Morgan.

Jackson bound and gagged Merk, then pulled him out of sight from the dock. Then the two of them and Jazie turned their attention to Taylor Lee, who was calmly sipping a beer, chatting with Stick a half dozen boats down the way as if she hadn't a worry in the world. If the dock hadn't been so busy, he surely would have noted the scuffle. "Jazie, what the hell are you two doing?" Morgan asked.

"It's the craziest damn thing," she said, perching on the seat with her back to Stick's boat. "You know Taylor Lee's been spending every spare dark moment trolling the bars down here for these jokers. She swore they had to be on a boat, and I had to half-agree because they weren't in any hotel. Anyway, she got a glimpse of them inside her head in a bar, and it just wouldn't let go, so we had to find the bar."

"The point, Jazie," Morgan said from between her teeth. "Now, please."

"She called and asked me to come with her. Rick had some kind of meeting tonight with the county commissioners."

Probably with Emergency Services about hurricane preparations. "So you came bar-trolling with Taylor Lee and you two ran into the assassins?" Morgan attempted to push the briefing along.

"We found the bar Taylor Lee saw; then there they

were—two of them, anyway." Jazie hiked her eyebrows. "We haven't seen Payton."

"And you felt totally comfortable putting yourself in their faces without requesting backup or uttering a single word to me?"

"It wasn't like that, Morgan," Jazie assured her, picking up on her anger. "The opportunity just kind of presented itself, and you were tied up with the photographs and the lab explosion, and then with getting your house burned down."

"Oh, hell," Jackson said. "Tell me she's not going to crack him in the head with her beer bottle." Disbelief etched Jackson's voice and turned to horror. "Morgan, she's going to crack him in the head with a beer bottle."

Morgan darted her gaze from him to Taylor Lee just as she sideswiped him in the back of the head. Morgan scrambled off the stern and onto the dock. "Jazie, stay put."

Jackson followed Morgan, who ran down the dock to Stick's boat and slid to a stop. Taylor Lee stood sipping her beer and watching all the activity going on in the surrounding boats. "Hey, guys."

"Unbelievable." Jackson dragged a hand through his hair. "Un-freaking-believable."

"Unorthodox," Morgan corrected him. "Which is probably why it worked."

A flash of movement caught Morgan's eye. Stick dove over the side of the deck. "Damn it." Taylor Lee drew her weapon.

"No, don't shoot!" Morgan shouted. The dock was slammed. They couldn't afford gunfire under these conditions.

Jackson glared at Taylor Lee. "You should have secured your prisoner before finishing your beer."

"He was secure," she said, her temper close to exploding. "I'm not incompetent, Jackson. I cuffed the bastard to the deck rail."

"Enough." Irritated, Morgan lifted a hand. "No sign of Payton?"

"Not firsthand. Stick was showing me his boat, but he said he had to get to his hotel within an hour." She cast Jackson a defiant look. "I suggested I go with him, but he turned me down." Her expression conveyed her feelings on that. "I intended to follow him, but saw Jazie take down Merk and figured Stick would get suspicious when he didn't show up to help secure the boat, so I went ahead and knocked him out."

"What hotel?" Jackson asked.

"I don't know."

"Let's get back to Jazie." The wind whipped Morgan's hair into her face. She shoved it back and returned to the dock.

"They're going to get killed doing things like this." He sighed his worry.

"They're trained professionals, Jackson," Morgan said. "We operate differently, but not mindlessly."

"For God's sake, Morgan, she whacked him with a beer bottle."

"Which didn't present any danger to anyone but him . . . and her." Morgan tapped her temple. "Think collateral damage."

"Okay, I'll give her that. But he's a freaking assassin. One of most proficient in the world or he wouldn't be working for Kunz."

"No buts, Jackson. It worked."

"Right up until the part where he got away."

Morgan gritted her teeth. She couldn't argue that point, and she could smack Taylor Lee herself for putting herself in that kind of position. "She handcuffed him. How was she to know he'd get out of the restraints?"

"He works for Kunz." Jackson's voice went flat. "She should have expected the unexpected—and the worst."

While they argued on the dock near the boat, Taylor Lee boarded. "Jazie's out." Taylor Lee's face showed blind panic. "She's out cold."

Morgan and Jackson rushed aboard the *Sunrise* and saw Jazie sprawled face down on the deck. Taylor Lee was on her knees beside her, checking Jazie's pulse. Relief washed over her face. "She's breathing."

Morgan dropped down and checked her pupils. "Jazie?"

Her eyelids fluttered open. "Payton . . ."

"Are you okay?" Morgan asked.

"Yeah." She rubbed the back of her head, then shook it to clear her mind, sending her long hair tumbling down her back.

Morgan checked her neck, her shoulders and arms. "I want you to go to the hospital and get checked out."

She nodded. "I'd be brave and refuse, but I think I'd better get the doc to take a look." She rubbed the back of her head with her fingertips. "I've got a hell of a goose egg back here."

"A chopper will be at the landing pad shortly." It was used often for medical evacuations from the beach and the marina.

"I'll walk her down." Taylor Lee moved around Jackson toward Jazie.

Morgan stood up, going toe to toe with her team. "Take fewer chances with your asses, okay?"

Taylor Lee's long black hair blew in the wind, and she hooked a resigned thumb in the belt loop on her hip-slung jeans. "Okay."

"And less alcohol, too."

"Morgan, how can one troll bars for men and not drink?"

"Get creative." Morgan smiled but kept the warning in her tone so Taylor Lee didn't miss it. This was a direct order, and she wanted the woman to know it.

Her cell phone rang. Cursing under her breath, Morgan answered.

"How's that garbage?"

"Spilled into the sea."

"All of it?"

"All we had. I'm afraid so." Embarrassed by that, Morgan frowned. "But don't cancel the chopper. Jazie appears to be all right, but she was knocked unconscious with third-party help." Darcy would get her meaning. They'd had two; a third assisted in the release. "I want her checked out."

"I'll notify Dr. Vargus. Chopper's ETA is three minutes."

"Thanks."

"I've got those phone numbers. Haven't yet reviewed them, but they're in."

"Can you fax them to the harbormaster's office?" The office was on the dock, and Morgan could get them right away.

"Sure."

"Thanks, Darcy." Morgan flipped her phone closed and dropped it into her purse. "Let's go."

Taylor Lee and Jazie walked down the dock to the shore. Jackson fell into step beside Morgan, and they went to the harbormaster's office. Neither of them said much, their irritation at fever pitch over losing not one but two G.R.I.D. operatives. They were in worse shape now than they were before. The assassins knew the entire S.A.T. team by sight.

Fifteen minutes later, Morgan and Jackson were sitting in a booth in Diane's coffee shop reviewing the listing of phone numbers that Darcy had faxed over.

Morgan was hot, worried, and irritated that she and her team stood on shaky ground. Not having a clear fix on their allies and enemies when they were dealing with G.R.I.D. had her scared half out of her wits.

Jackson reached across the table and covered her hand. "Don't do it, Morgan."

Puzzled, she asked, "What?"

"Beat yourself up." He softened his voice so only she could hear.

It wasn't necessary because the coffee shop was crowded and noisy. Everyone was speculating on the storm. When Jim, meteorologist and reporter from the Weather Channel walked in, a loud wail of a groan rang out that literally shook the walls. Jim was the most respected and appreciated man everyone hated to see—for obvious reasons in hurricane country. Where Jim was sent, the storm followed.

Jackson added a packet of sugar to his coffee, then ran his fingertip down the page of phone numbers. When he reached the bottom, he flipped the page. "You guys are mental . . . I mean, other than shooting me, you use your minds in your work, not physical tactics. Be grateful Taylor Lee or Jazie wasn't killed."

"I am grateful." Their training was light in physical combat. They were Special Abilities and didn't have the combat training Amanda, Kate, Darcy, and Maggie Holt had gone through. The S.A.T. missions required the team members to use mainly their special skills, their minds. Jackson was right about that.

He finished reviewing the list of phone numbers.

"None of these look familiar to me." He frowned. "Do you have a calendar?"

She pulled one up on her organizer. "What date do you want to check?"

"May 16."

"This year, right?" she asked. When he nodded, she checked. "Saturday."

"I need a pen."

Morgan passed one over. He ticked off dates, verifying each of them to be Saturday.

"Three of these calls are from the same number," he said. "One came through while Bruce was still in Iraq. Two were made after he left Iraq but before we know for a fact that he had returned home."

"What are you using as verification of his being here?" Morgan motioned the waitress for a refill on her tea.

The weary-looking woman poured it from an ice-filled pitcher and set the glass down, then returned to the counter. The place was buzzing, every seat was taken.

"His arrest." Jackson lifted a shoulder. "It's all we've got where we can prove Bruce was Bruce."

Morgan pulled out her phone. "What's the number you're seeing repeated?"

"Don't call it from your cell," Jackson warned her.

He didn't want her identity showing up on caller ID. "Darcy," Morgan said, informing him of her intentions.

Shooting her an apologetic look, he reeled off the

number. "It's foreign. No clue where, though I have my suspicions."

So did Morgan. She relayed the number to Darcy, and an image of Laura's emerald ring flashed through her mind. She'd had it on in the photos and in Morgan's office. A snapshot of her in the morgue—her finger broken, her skin scraped bloody raw and bruised—formed in Morgan's mind. She blinked to clear it.

"Stand by one." Darcy put her on hold for a second.

Morgan glanced out the foggy window. People were darting around, some standing under the coffee shop's overhang, trying to stay dry. The rain was coming down in torrents, and conditions would only continue to deteriorate. "We need to get that boat moved," she told Jackson. "Feeder bands are moving in."

"As soon as you get off the phone."

Darcy came back on the line. "I've got good news and bad news."

"Good first."

"It's a satellite phone," Darcy said.

Satellite was great. It could be anywhere on the planet, but it could also be traced. "Bad?"

"We know the calls were made from the South Pacific."

"That's good news."

"That's as close as we can get on a location right away."

As bad news went, having to wait for detailed information was better than expected. "Darcy, Laura Stern made those calls to Jackson."

"Did she?" Darcy asked.

Morgan met Jackson's gaze across the table. "What are you saying?"

"The calls came in to Jackson, but who says Laura made them?"

Morgan didn't answer, but a fissure of fear opened inside her at what the question implied. "Exactly what are you telling me?"

"We—Jazie and me—have been through every mode of transportation out of here, Morgan. There isn't a shred of evidence that Laura Stern took a trip anywhere. Not one."

"Her photos contradict that," Morgan said.

"Kate is reviewing them now to try to pin down the location. All joking aside about her and Nathan's island excursions, she's got the most experience with tropical locations. She loves to dive. But unless Laura Stern owned a plane or she drove her car halfway across the country before flying to wherever those photos were taken, she didn't go."

She'd seen the photos and she still had doubts? "I don't know how Laura traveled, but she did travel," Morgan insisted, her stomach knotting, suspicions rising in Morgan against Jackson that she didn't want to consider, much less feel. "I swear it."

"Because you don't like what this could mean about Jackson? Or because your abilities tell you it happened?"

Brutal, but when the stakes were this high, Darcy couldn't afford to be anything else. "Both." Morgan answered just as bluntly, and then a compelling thought hit her. "Does he have a private plane?"

"He who?" Darcy asked. "Bruce?"

Morgan didn't answer.

"Jackson's within earshot, right?"

"Yes." *Riddled with questions and staring me right in the eyes.* Morgan prayed this time his keen perception would be taking a break.

"Jackson?"

Again, she didn't answer.

"Kunz?" Darcy asked but it sounded more like a statement. "Never mind. I see where you're going. Judy and Laura are friends. Judy wants Laura to come to some island for the festival. Kunz sends a plane for her."

"Yes," Morgan said, relieved that she hadn't had to say any of it aloud.

"Of course he has planes—all kinds of aircraft, actually." She paused. "Mmm, private plane. That would work. Maybe his pilot filed a flight plan. The festival was . . ."

"May 21," Morgan said.

"Later." Darcy abruptly disconnected the call.

Morgan braced for Jackson's questions. What should she tell him? What should she not tell him? Oh, but she hated the thought of keeping more secrets from him.

Amazingly, he looked away and didn't ask her a thing.

"You should wait here—stay dry—while I take care of the boat."

"No." She slid out of the booth. "I'm going with you." G.R.I.D. knew where they were and would be watching the marina. They probably wouldn't attack here again. They'd assume a high-alert order had been issued and that the marina was under close observation. Ordinarily it would have been, but with the storm, the commander had deemed the likelihood of a second attack minimal. She was probably right, but Morgan wasn't willing to bet Jackson's life on it. "I'm going to watch your back."

An hour later, they had taken the *Sunrise* through the pass into the gulf and were heading into the bay. Dozens of boats lined both shorelines, some tied to trees, some anchored, some tied off to docks that backed up to homes built on the bay. Jackson kept heading inland, going in deep.

They were in a break between feeder bands. The air was heavy and thick, moist and clinging. Soaked and sweating profusely, Morgan finished moving the last of the loose items on deck down below.

Jackson started to drop anchor.

"Keep going," Morgan said. "Another few minutes and you'll be right behind my house. We can dock there."

They passed two boats. Both fishing rigs with high towers and angry captains, arguing over a spot they both claimed was theirs and where they always anchored during hurricanes.

Jackson shrugged at the wheel. "Storms bring out the

best and the worst in people."

They did. They really . . . Morgan stilled, let the intuitive inkling come into sharp focus. *Laura in a storm. Laura under fire. What would she do?*

What she always did, of course.

Of course.

Protect Bruce.

CHAPTER 12

"Colonel Drake would have a stroke if she knew we were here."

"Better here than in the Camry or on the boat," he said, walking to the living room windows to take a look outside. "Who drives a red Saab?" Jackson shouted to Morgan in the kitchen.

"Taylor Lee." Drying her hands on a dishcloth, Morgan walked to the window to double-check.

Jackson eased an arm around her waist in a way so familiar, natural, and comfortable that she slid into it and pecked a kiss to his neck, then opened the front door.

Taylor Lee scrambled up the steps, bent against the howling wind and heavy rain. When she reached the porch, she stopped and pulled off her raincoat. "Hey."

"Come in." Morgan stepped aside so Taylor Lee could pass her.

"Whew!" She stepped inside. "Hi, Jackson."

He nodded.

"I figured you'd be here—process of elimination," Taylor Lee said. "Cell tower is down, and I couldn't get you on the house phone."

"Must be yours. I was just on mine."

"Probably." She frowned. "That damn service has more dead zones than a cemetery has plots."

Jackson had been cool toward her since the conflict at the marina, but that comment warmed him into smiling. "Why are you out in this?"

She swiped at the rain on her cheeks. "Just letting Morgan know Jazie is fine."

Morgan gave her don't-feed-me-bull look. "The truth?"

"I figured you were here, and I didn't know if you were alone or Jackson was with you." Taylor Lee shrugged and needled him. "Figured you might need me to swing a mean beer bottle or something."

She was worried G.R.I.D. would come calling and find Morgan alone. Another two-for-one situation now. *Damn it.* "Are you hungry?" Morgan waved for her to come with her into the kitchen. At the stove, she stirred a pot of spaghetti sauce.

"No, thanks. I've been deskbound since we left the

hospital. I was going stir-crazy."

"Jazie called a few minutes ago to say she was home safe."

"Who's with her?"

"She mentioned someone named Eric."

"Eric Montgomery," Taylor Lee said. "He's been in love with her most of her life, and the blind girl can't see it."

Morgan hadn't realized that. "Is this the first time she's mentioned him?"

"Yes. See what I mean?" Taylor Lee plucked a couple of grapes out of a bowl on the bar and slid onto a barstool. "I went through all the Sterns' financial records. There's nothing there out of the ordinary." Taylor popped a plump grape into her mouth. "Laura didn't spend much on herself. Not even the usual indulgences."

Most homemakers didn't. Everyone and everything else usually came first. "No travel expenses, clothes for a trip, nothing like that?"

"Nothing." Taylor stared at a grape, ate it, and then asked, "What kind of woman doesn't splurge a little before a hotshot vacation to an island in the South Pacific?" She grunted. "I know no such women."

Jackson took the spoon from Morgan, who'd gotten caught up in the conversation and forgotten about stirring the sauce. "Bruce was always on Laura to buy herself things. It wasn't that she didn't like them; she hated to shop."

"Eeek, blasphemy!" Taylor Lee screeched.

He grinned. "Sorry, but it's true. She hated it. Even grocery stores bugged her, any kind of shopping." He smiled wistfully. "I used to bribe her. I'd go to the store if she'd make me a peach cobbler. I love it and, man, she made a wicked one."

As soon as he stopped speaking, his expression turned from amused to grief-stricken. He'd recalled that she wouldn't be making one again.

Morgan changed the subject, breaking the silence. "So no shopping, no abnormalities in spending, no large withdrawals anywhere around May 21, and, according to Jazie and Darcy, no travel. "We're missing something. The woman went to an island. We have the photos proving it. So why does nothing in her life back up our proof?"

Taylor Lee tilted her head. "Because someone wanted it wiped out. The proof, that is. Someone wanted the evidence to refute the proof she'd been anywhere at all."

Jackson dipped a teaspoon into the saucepot and tasted, then added a dash more salt. "Why would Judy Meyer give a damn if anyone knew Laura had come to visit her?"

"She wouldn't." Morgan's flesh crawled, and she instinctively rubbed her arms. "But Kunz might."

Jackson and Taylor stared at her, waiting.

"We've been looking at this from the perspective that Kunz wanted something from Bruce, and he killed Laura to get it. We've mentioned the possibility that Kunz did exactly what Joan Foster says he's always done: gone after his primary target, but we've been focusing on Bruce."

"Okay, let's consider all this from that perspective. Kunz went after Laura because she was his primary target." Jackson tapped the metal spoon on the side of the pot. "Sauce is done."

"Let's eat." Taylor Lee came around the bar into the kitchen and pulled out another plate, another set of silverware.

"She obviously does this a lot," Jackson whispered.

Morgan grinned, and Taylor Lee reached around him and snagged a glass out of the cabinet. "She does," Taylor Lee said of herself. "Every chance she gets. She hates to cook."

"Ah. That explains it." He bit back a smile.

When they were settled at the table eating, Morgan said, "What if Laura came to visit Judy for the festival and Kunz didn't find out until then who Laura's husband was or what he did for a living?"

Jackson passed the hot French bread to Taylor. "Do you think for a second that Kunz would bring in someone he hadn't checked out? No way," he answered himself. "And he wouldn't allow Judy or anyone else to, either."

Taylor Lee chewed, swallowed, and twirled another bite onto her fork with the aid of a spoon. "Darcy is pretty much betting the place is either a G.R.I.D. compound or Kunz's private hideaway."

Morgan digested that. "An otherwise uninhabited

island would be a good place to hide, you have to admit. And he has seemingly disappeared off the face of the earth every time the S.A.S.S. has gotten close to him."

Jackson took a long drink of water. "I don't believe it," he said flatly. "If it was a vacation in a place he never intended to return to, that'd be one thing, but a compound or his safe haven? No way would he let Laura come there."

"Unless he was seizing an unexpected opportunity," Morgan countered. "Judy wanted Laura to visit. Kunz checked her out and learned about Bruce. Kunz blessed his good fortune and seized the opportunity." This felt right. Really, really right. Morgan went on. "Hell, creating doubles takes time. Kunz could have pumped Judy for insights on Laura, created Bruce's double, come up with a plan to get to Bruce's classified information, and then waited until the double was ready to insert before encouraging Judy to have Laura come to the island for the festival. Even Judy wouldn't know what Kunz was doing."

Jackson thought that over through two bites. "That, I buy."

"Mmm, good spaghetti," Taylor Lee said. "I can buy into that, too." She glanced at Jackson. "And I agree there's no way in hell Kunz would bring anyone he didn't have the lowdown on—not to his hideaway, his G.R.I.D. compound, or even on his vacation. The man controls his environment." She grunted. "Damn. I guess that makes me disagree with you, too, Morgan. Well, it can't be helped.

That's my take."

Morgan's cell rang. She left the table to answer it. "Cabot."

"Darcy's had me viewing the base gate tapes," Jazie said. "Guess who entered Providence about twenty minutes before the bomb blew at the photo lab?"

Morgan didn't have to think. Jazie was broadcasting it as clearly as if she were hooked up to a microphone wired to a class-A sound system. "Bruce's double."

"Yes!" Jazie said, then grunted. "You do take some of the punch out of things by knowing them ahead of time, Morgan."

"Sorry." Morgan's mind whirled. "Anything else?"

"Not yet," she said. "Kate's going through Laura's pictures, trying to peg a location for us."

"Good." Morgan dabbed a napkin to her mouth. "Call me if she comes up with anything."

"Will do," she promised. "I'll be at Providence until the storm passes."

"I thought Eric was with you at your house."

"He's at the operations center. Emergency management. He just dropped by to make sure I was okay."

"I see."

"I didn't want to be by myself, so I drove out to Regret."

G.R.I.D. and the storm. She was broadcasting that, too. "Sounds smart to me. No unnecessary chances."

."I'd feel better if I could find Taylor Lee. Her cell's out."

"She's sitting at my table, eating spaghetti."

"Oh, good." Jazie sighed. "Now I can relax."

"Do you need to speak to her?"

"No, I just wanted to know where she was. G.R.I.D. goons being on the loose worries me, especially now that they can identify us."

It worried Morgan, too. "I understand."

"Later."

Morgan closed her phone, set it on the bar, and then returned to the table. "Bruce's double blew up the photo lab, and, Taylor Lee, your cell is definitely out. Jazie couldn't get through to you. She's at Regret."

"Regret?" Jackson asked.

"S.A.S.S.'s Home Base."

Jackson nodded, then said to himself more than to them, "The shack on the abandoned bombing range."

"We don't advertise that," Morgan told him.

"Right." His neck flushed, and it crept to his face. "Sorry. It's just . . . refreshing to be around women you can talk to without holding back most of what goes through your mind."

"Damn it." Taylor Lee frowned. "Kunz framed Bruce for the lab explosion, too?"

Morgan nodded.

"Now isn't that interesting?" Jackson said. "Considering

Bruce is still in jail for a Kunz-framed murder."

"Very," Morgan said, glad to finally hear Jackson say he didn't believe Bruce had committed Laura's murder. "He knows we have the DNA, and he or one of his henchmen— likely the latter, since Kunz doesn't assume spit and triple verifies everything—believed Bruce would be released and out of jail before the photo lab blew up." Thank God Commander Drake had held off on having him officially exonerated and released.

"Why?" Taylor Lee said, not making the leap.

Jackson and Morgan locked gazes across the table. "Because," she said, "he wants Bruce out of the way."

Jackson nodded his agreement.

"Laura was definitely the target."

He nodded again.

Something crackled, startling them all.

The lights went out.

"Transformer just took a hit." Taylor Lee pushed her chair back from the table. "Storm's here and the party's over."

Morgan lit a candle in the center of the table. Taylor was setting her dishes on the countertop next to the sink. "We're stuck until the storm runs its course, so I'm going to get home before it gets any worse out there."

"If wires are down, you'd be better off to stay put here," Jackson told her.

"It's not far." She moved through the house to the front door and retrieved her raincoat. "I'll be home in five minutes."

Morgan had a bad feeling. "Jackson's right, Taylor Lee. Stay here with us."

"No way." She shrugged into the coat, gave them her best sultry look. "When Rick's waiting for me at home? I love your company, guys, really. But I think not."

That bad feeling got worse. "Taylor . . ."

"Quit borrowing trouble, Morgan. It'll be fine." She tapped her head, signaling she'd seen something to back up her words, then opened the door and walked through to the porch. "Come lock up."

The heavy metal door closed before Morgan got to it. She locked the deadbolt and felt Jackson come up behind her and drop an amazingly sensual kiss to the back of her neck. "She's right," he whispered, his breath hot on her skin. "We're kind of stuck until the storm passes."

Morgan's chest hitched. Smiling, she turned to face him and leaned back against the door. "Whatever shall we do?"

He turned mischievous. "I have an idea."

Outside, something exploded.

Jackson hit the floor, pulled Morgan down with him, and crawled over her to the window to look out. "Oh, no. Son of a bitch," he said on a rush. "Son of a bitch."

Morgan looked through the edge of the glass.

Taylor Lee's car was ablaze.

CHAPTER 13

"No!" Jackson grabbed Morgan's hand, kept her from running out the door. "G.R.I.D."

Morgan broke loose, retrieved her weapon, and headed back toward the door. "We've got to get Taylor Lee out of there!"

"Back door. Back door." Jackson moved through the house. He opened the back door, looked out, and then motioned Morgan to go left, down the driveway. "Give me a twenty-second lead."

He took off to the opposite side of the house, taking the long way around.

Odds were good that if the G.R.I.D. assassins were still there, they were on that side of the house. It had the best protection vantage points. Morgan ticked off twenty seconds, the glare from the flames making her sick. There was no way Taylor Lee could have survived that fire. No way.

Tears filming her eyes, her throat tight, Morgan hugged her back to the brick wall, slid down it all the way to the edge of the front porch. The rain was so heavy, it was nearly impossible to see anything but the fire. She still scanned the yard, the neighbor's lot, and stepped away from the house long enough to check her own roof.

The rain was nearly horizontal. Morgan was hot and cold and angry and sad and shocked. Totally shocked.

She moved farther out, into the yard, bowed her head to protect her eyes. The rain pelted her, stung her skin, and the wind whistled in her ears, slicked back her clothes, tugged at her eyelids. It took all she had to keep herself upright.

Something moved to her right.

Recognizing Stick in her peripheral vision, she fired, turned toward him, and fired again.

He fell to the ground.

A shot rang out behind her. *Jackson!*

She dropped, rolled, and took cover behind a fat, spiny bush. A second shot sounded. She saw its flash and then heard another shot fired. A shadowy figure in black crumpled to the ground next to a magnolia. *Merk. That had to be Merk.*

Where was Payton?

Where was Jackson?

Morgan inched forward to see around the bush. Jackson

was standing under the old oak, his back to its trunk, his elbows bent, prepared to fire. He was waiting . . .

Morgan heard a click. Looked up onto her front porch and saw Payton, leaning over the railing looking down at her, his Glock pointed at her head. "Drop your weapon, Stern," Payton shouted.

Morgan was on all fours, one hand braced in the dirt holding her gun. She lifted the other hand into the air. "Okay. You've got me. Okay."

He ignored her, shouted to Jackson. "I'm not bluffing, Stern. Two seconds, and she dies."

Morgan tipped up the barrel of her gun and squeezed the trigger.

Payton dropped, thudding on the porch. A millisecond later, he fired at Jackson.

Jackson rolled around the trunk to the far side of the tree, drew down on Payton, and then fired.

Nearby, wounded but not down, Merk ran to a van parked at the curb across the street. Morgan aimed for its tires but missed. He sped down the street and then out of sight.

Payton fired another shot at Morgan. It raised mud that splattered, but missed her.

Where was Jackson? The wind blew the flames, set them to dancing, and Morgan used them to scan the yard but couldn't locate him. Suddenly, he appeared at the far end of the porch and squeezed off a shot.

Payton howled and crumpled, injured but not dead.

"Morgan?" Jackson called out.

"I'm fine." Fine? She was rattled to the bone.

"Come watch this bastard."

She crawled out from behind the bush and then stood up, muddy from the neck down. Payton was in a heap on her front porch, his leg bleeding profusely. Jackson had popped him just above the knee.

He retrieved Payton's gun, patted him down, and pulled a spare from his boot, then backed off and told Morgan, "If he moves, kill him."

"My pleasure." She nodded.

Jackson ran to Taylor Lee's car. The rain was dousing the flames, but the vehicle had burned so hot the paint had blistered. Intense heat radiated from it, far too hot to touch. Jackson got as close as he could and looked in through gaping holes where the windows had been. "She's not here!" he shouted back to Morgan. "She's not in the car."

Where the hell was she, then? Morgan looked down at Payton. "What were your orders?"

He glared at her.

"You're picking the wrong time to mess with me. Answer my question, or I'll make you believe Thomas Kunz is a rank amateur at torture. You have my word on that."

Horror flooded his eyes.

It was justified. Everyone knew Kunz loved to torture. It was a game to him. Sick, despicable bastard.

"We thought she was you," Payton said. "We were

supposed to grab you."

"And do what with me?" Morgan pushed.

He didn't want to answer. "I can't. He—"

"Is the least of your worries, buddy. He's on a freaking island. I'm right here."

Surprise raced over his face, tightened his jaw.

"I'm looking for a reason not to kill you." *The van. She was in the van.* Morgan picked up on that clearly, but insisted on verifying. "Where the hell did Merk take her?"

"I don't know. I swear. He didn't tell me."

Jackson came back to the porch. "Morgan."

She heard him but couldn't force herself to look away from Payton, couldn't stop herself from getting closer to him with the gun. "If I find out you're lying to me, you will regret it."

"Morgan," Jackson stepped between them, tipped the barrel of her gun away. "Go call this in and bring me some rope," he said. "Will you do that for me?"

The anger overtaking her cooled to a roiling boil, and she tamped it down, down, down until she felt more in control. "All right. Yes. Yes, I can do that for you."

"She lost it," Payton said. "That woman was out of her mind."

Jackson kicked Payton in the face. "She's mine, and you just tried to kill her. Say nothing, and you might just live. Another word about her, and I'll drop your ass right here. I swear to God, I will."

Vindicated, Morgan rushed inside and left the front door open. *Taylor Lee.* Guilt swamped and crushed Morgan. *It should have been me. They were trying to abduct me. It should have been me . . . Rope.*

Right. Jackson needed rope.

She got some from the garage and tossed it to him from the front door. "Do *not* bring that garbage into my house."

"I won't," Jackson promised.

"I want him off my porch," she said. "Tie him to the tree. Maybe lightning will strike his sorry ass and spare me the cost of a bullet."

Payton mumbled something, and Jackson said, "You're stupid, man. Telling a smart woman carrying a gun you meant to kidnap her—after you tried to shoot her—and you expected . . . what?" Jackson laughed, but there was no humor in it. "You'd better pray like hell the OSI gets here to pick you up before she has time to think on it much. Otherwise, she's really going to be pissed. Even if she doesn't kill you, she'll blow out your knees for pure spite."

She wanted to—*oh, how she wanted to*—but she wouldn't drag herself into his cold-blooded ditch. She'd take the high road, even if she cussed being on it every step of the way. Still, Payton didn't know what she would or wouldn't do, and believing she would blow holes in his kneecaps could make him more cooperative.

Phone. She had to get to the phone, notify the commander.

How the hell was she going to explain this? Ignoring a direct order to stay away from the house. Taylor Lee abducted . . .

G.R.I.D.—G.R.I.D.—had Taylor Lee!

"Morgan! Morgan!"

Taylor Lee!

Morgan slammed down the phone, ran through the dark house, and collided with a drenched Taylor Lee near the white leather sofa in the living room. "Oh, my God!" Morgan caught her in a hug. She was shaking. They both were. "I thought Merk had you!"

"He did." Her chest heaved; she was winded, and trying to talk was difficult. "He knocked the hell out of me right after I shut the front door. I came to tied up in the back of their van."

"Where is he now?"

Taylor Lee's dark eyes glinted pure hatred. "Somewhere between Magnolia and Hickory." She pulled away and went to the kitchen sink, turned on the water, and splashed her face. "Sorry bastard."

"What do you mean, somewhere between Magnolia and Hickory?" Was he dead? Alive? Still fleeing in the van?

"I kicked his sorry ass out on the street." Taylor Lee

cupped her hands, splashed her face again, and then reached out for a paper towel.

Morgan grabbed a clean cloth from the drawer and passed it to her. "You just left him there on the street?" Damn it, now he was loose again.

"He's dead, Morgan." Taylor Lee blotted her face. "We were going about eighty when I shoved him out, and he hit the pavement." She frowned. "Did you see my Saab? If the son of a bitch wasn't already dead, I'd kill him again."

Morgan picked up on Taylor Lee's furious thought, *Vintage. Vintage!*

"You're absolutely sure he's dead?" Morgan asked.

"If he wasn't when he hit the ground, he was after the truck coming at us hit him. He got caught by at least six tires." She finished drying her face and started on her arms. "I worked a long time for that car."

"I'm sorry about your Saab." Morgan reached for the phone. "Could you go tell Jackson you're okay?"

"Where is he?"

"Um, on the front porch." Morgan grabbed her arm. "Don't touch his prisoner."

"What prisoner?" Taylor Lee frowned, her expression turning as dark as the night. "Were the other two here, too?"

"Stick is dead," Morgan said with a nod. "Payton was shot, but he's still alive."

"We can fix that easy enough." Taylor Lee clamped

her jaw down tight enough to crack and started out.

Morgan grabbed her arm. "Do *not* kill the man. I need to know what he knows."

"Okay." She pursed her lips, her chin trembling with pure rage. "I'll wait."

She wasn't overstating or exaggerating. She intended to kill him. "Taylor Lee."

She glared at Morgan. "All right, damn it." Frustrated, she fought to control the anger shimmering through her entire body. Tough battle, but finally she won. "I'm not going to kill him, okay? I'm just going to see what's on his devious mind."

"Okay." Morgan watched her go and hoped she hadn't just made a mistake, cutting Taylor Lee semi-loose in her current frame of mind. "But don't disappoint me on this. I'm trusting you."

Seconds later, Taylor Lee's outraged voice carried back to Morgan from the porch. "Did you do that to my car, you sorry sack of shit?"

Something thudded.

Payton howled.

"Taylor Lee, ease up."

Only a dead man would miss the warning in Jackson's voice.

"Ease up? This asshole tried to barbeque me, Jackson."

He said something Morgan couldn't hear, but Taylor

Lee's response came through all too clearly. "You could just take a walk and let me interrogate him. It'd save us a lot of time and trouble. I guarantee you, it'll be productive."

"No," Payton said, sufficiently terrified. "Don't do that."

"I won't," Jackson said. "Not yet. Men get the job done, but women . . . You cross a woman, and she gets mean."

"Don't leave me with her," Payton said. Clearly, he was a believer. "Please."

"You want me here, then you start talking," Jackson told him. "The minute you stop, I'm gone and you can deal with her."

Morgan bit back a smile. Taylor Lee was plenty angry; she wasn't faking it. But she'd also promised Morgan she wouldn't kill him. She wouldn't, but she might make him wish he were dead. Jackson would rein her in if she got too close to the line.

Relieved, Morgan called Home Base and filed her report.

"I can verify Merk's death," Darcy said. "I heard the truck driver's 911 call. We've got an OSI agent on the way to the scene now." She paused and then went on. "Kate and Maggie will pick up Payton. They're about ten minutes out."

"All right." Morgan hoped she and Jackson could keep Taylor Lee leashed that long. The Saab had been her pride and joy, and she was going to have a wicked bruise on her face. Two offenses, and that didn't count her joyride in the van. "I expect the coroner will come pick up Stick's body?"

"It'll be a while, but yes."

"Should I pull him out of the yard and put him in the garage or something?"

"No. Don't move the body."

"Okay." Morgan was glad about that. She didn't want the men anywhere around her and certainly not in her house.

"About Laura's photos," Darcy said. "Kate is pretty sure she's pegged the island. The coin is from the Cook Island chain, but she thinks, and Nathan agrees, the skyline on that picture with the thatch-roofed building—do you know the photo I mean?"

Morgan recalled it perfectly. "Yes, I do."

"I've now verified it's Tavanipupu, a resort in the Solomon Island chain," Darcy said. "CIA counterparts tell us Kunz is not there, but a lot of the surrounding islands are remote and uninhabited. They're working to check them out and get a fix on him. Hopefully we will have an update by the time you arrive."

Uninhabited. Remote. He probably traveled directly to his own island and never set foot on anything around it. That was Thomas Kunz's way.

Morgan had expected it, but hearing it confirmed

still rattled her to the core. "Perfect location for Kunz and G.R.I.D." A flash went through her, and she relayed it to Darcy. "Look for a private airstrip."

"Will do," Darcy said. "Like I said, we're having field agents in the area try to pinpoint a more precise location. Commander Drake elevated the classification to a priority one, hoping we can get our hands on Kunz before he bugs out. She wants you on scene as soon as possible. Transportation is on standby, so be ready to fly out of here as soon as the storm passes. Weather office expects that will be in four hours, thirty-seven minutes, 4:32 A.M. And Jackson is cleared to go with you."

Morgan rolled her shoulders, working out some stiffness. "We'll be ready."

Sleep-deprived and storm weary, Morgan and Jackson flew to New Zealand, sleeping on and off through the twenty-five-hour flight—more on, than off—and then connected to a flight that would take them to Honiara in the Solomon Island chain. From there, a flight to Tavanipupu wasn't possible—flights ran only on Mondays and Fridays. However, Darcy had assured them that a CIA agent named Gaston would meet them and handle transport when they left the plane.

When not sleeping, Morgan and Jackson talked quietly about any and everything except the mission, and the more they talked, the more certain Morgan was that she'd finally found a man she wanted to be with as much as she wanted to *be* at all. Would that hold after the mission was over? She believed it would, but time would tell. For now, the possibility was enough. "I was beginning to think you didn't exist, Jackson."

He gave her a soft smile that crinkled the skin near his eyes, clasped her hands, and squeezed. "I know what you mean."

"Have you thought about what happens to us when this is all over?" It had taken most of the travel time for her to work up the courage to ask a question she might not want answered, but in the last few hours, she had reached the point that not knowing what was on his mind ate at her. Possible responses had spun through her brain like a lump of clay on a potter's wheel, taking different shapes and forms, but in all of them—and there had been many— she hadn't anticipated the answer he would give her, which wasn't an answer at all, but a question:

"What do you want to happen, Morgan?"

Everything. Absolutely everything. I think we're right. I think this thing between us will work. I want you to be the one. But I also want time to know you are—time when we're not in a crisis with Kunz.

She felt all of that and more in every atom and cell of

her entire body, intuitively and emotionally. Yet while Jackson was perceptive, he wasn't functioning in that way at her level. He needed more time to discover what came to her instantly, through her gift, and it wouldn't hurt her to experience the practical side of a relationship with him, either.

"Don't think, honey," he said. "Just be honest with me. Tell me what you want."

She looked from the buttons on his shirt back into his eyes and saw a gentleness in them she'd never seen him share with anyone else, and though she was inspired to be blunt, she couldn't be—not without first explaining her gift to him. Unfortunately, history had proven repeatedly that the cost of honesty might be their relationship. It was a price she wasn't willing to pay. Not with him. Not yet. "I want . . . more," she finally said.

"You want . . . all," he amended without heat. "You want everything."

She blinked and forced herself not to look away, though she was terrified he'd see the truth in her eyes. "I want not to be wrong, too, Jackson. We've both been hurt, and we don't want to do that to each other. I don't know about your track record with women, but mine with men has been abysmal. Two serious attempts, two serious failures, and I don't want you to be a third."

"Because . . ."

She shrugged. "For all the obvious reasons."

"I meant, what made the two attempts fail?"

"The usual."

"Quit talking around it and get specific, Morgan."

"The job, the secrets, the crazy hours, the unexplained, short-notice and long-lasting absences."

"But we don't have those problems."

They didn't. His clearance was higher than hers. "There were other reasons, too," she said, treading lightly. How did she tell him the one reason that dwarfed all the others?

He rubbed her thumb with his, their hands still clasped on his thigh. "This is the first time since we've been together that I've felt you weren't being completely honest with me," he said. "I don't like it. What are you afraid of?"

Not at all surprised that he had picked up on her fear, she looked away, terrified of being pushed into a corner with only one way out: telling him the truth about her intuitive skills.

Don't do it. You'll lose him. You know you will.

She would, just as she had lost everyone else in her life who had mattered to her. Her parents had considered her odd, one of her sisters thought she was a nutcase, and the other was scared of her. No one until Jazie and Taylor Lee had simply accepted her as she was—and they did because they were odd, nutcases, and scary to others, too. No doubt that's what had caused Taylor Lee's multiple engagements. She hadn't admitted it, but Morgan knew.

"Morgan." Jackson paused, then nudged her. "Honey,

look at me."

She steeled herself and then met his gaze.

"You have your reasons, and it's okay," he said, sounding tender and empathetic. "I'll tell you what I want."

It was okay? Just like that? Without shoving her, without insisting? Without condemning her for not revealing everything she could and more? Relief had tears choking her throat. Unable to talk, she settled for a nod.

"I want you," he said simply. "I want us. All of it." He brought their hands to his lips and kissed her knuckles. "I want everything."

The cry in her throat rose, tears filmed her eyes, and a little mewl escaped from her throat. "Really?" She didn't dare to believe it.

He nodded. "It's right with us, Morgan. I know it down to my soul." An attendant walked past, and he waited until she had moved out of earshot. "What I don't want is a lengthy long-distance relationship."

"Me, either." She'd finally found him and she wanted them to be together, sharing their lives. "But my practice and my work with Sally. I can't—"

"I can," he said. "There's a reserve wing at Providence. As soon as this is over, I'm going to talk with Secretary Reynolds and try to get him to assign me to it."

"Jackson, are you sure that's what you want?"

"I'm sure I want you, and that's where you are," he said. "Listen, honey, I'm not a kid. I've had relationships that I hoped would eventually grow to a glimmer of what we've got. They never did." He wrapped her hand in both of his. "This is it, Morgan. Sometimes you get one shot. Only one. This is ours, and I'm taking it."

"I feel the same way, but there are things about me you don't know . . ."

"Same here," he said. "But we'll learn. We've got time."

"But, wait—"

He held up his free hand. "I know you need more time to feel comfortable with this. That's prudent, and I don't have a problem with it. So we'll take it slow and see where it goes. Sound fair?"

"More than fair." But she couldn't let him make drastic changes in his life without being totally honest with him. She couldn't do it. "It isn't just us and timing and the absence of crises, Jackson. We need time together for another reason, too, and it's a big one that has a lot of impact on my life. If you're with me, it'll have a big impact on yours, too."

"What is it?"

No signals, no signs of whether he was dreading this or glad that whatever it was had now been brought out in the open. That didn't do a thing to settle her fears or calm her nerves. She thought about keeping her mouth shut about it, but that was definitely the wrong thing to do. He deserved the truth. "I'm intuitive, Jackson."

He laughed. "Yeah, you are."

Confused, she blinked, and then blinked again. "No, I mean . . ." She paused, looked around, then lowered her voice to a whisper. "I'm *really* intuitive."

"I know, honey."

He looked as if he expected her to say more, but she had no idea what else to say. She settled for, "It's my special ability." Surely he'd get her meaning now.

He smiled and stroked her face. "Is this your big secret? The one that's had you in knots?"

She nodded.

"Ah, Morgan." He sighed, pulled back to see her face more clearly. "Honey, even a man only semi-conscious couldn't be around you more than five minutes and not know that."

She stilled, frowned, blinked, then tilted her head. "Really?"

He nodded. "It's evident in everything you say and do."

She hadn't realized it. Hadn't thought of her gift in that way and certainly hadn't noticed it in her interactions with other men. He wasn't getting it. He couldn't be grasping the scope of it. "Jackson, I don't think you understand the realities of what I'm—"

"I get it." He nodded to add weight to his claim. "I swear, I do."

She thought about what he was telling her and reached

an inevitable conclusion that stunned her and had the bottom dropping out of her stomach. "You're not just perceptive, are you?"

No answer.

"Son of a bitch," she muttered softly. "You're intuitive, too."

His eyes twinkled. "Ah, the light dawns."

Morgan glared at him. "Well, you could have told me."

He rolled his eyes back in his head. "You knew."

She started to deny it, but the truth was she had indeed known. Again and again, she'd thought it. Hell, she'd even told the commander that Jackson was too perceptive to be anywhere but front and center on her need-to-know loop. "Yeah, I guess I did know, even if I didn't truly realize it until now."

"I have to say I'm not like you," he warned her. "I don't have your range."

Interesting. "What is your range?"

"Limited at best," he confessed. "Except when it comes to you."

"Me?" That surprised her.

"I think it's the chemistry. Something happens to me when I'm around you. It's like there's this whole new layer, a deeper level of insight."

Oh, yes. "There is that."

"It hones the focus," he said, a lilt in his voice. "Or

something like that."

Something like that. It was hormones, and he damn well knew it. The input of multiple layers of sensory impressions simultaneously rather than sequentially. He was teasing her. Teasing her, *about this*. She could barely believe it.

"Could be hormonal?" she suggested.

"Maybe." The devil glinted in his eye. "But it's probably gas."

Morgan laughed. She couldn't help herself. "Jackson, you're incorrigible."

"No, I'm not." He leaned over and kissed the tip of her nose. "But I am crazy . . . about you."

Happiness settled inside her. "I'm crazy about you, too." She turned her head and kissed his cheek, and an image formed in her mind of them spending that time together, getting to know each other without fires and bullets and death and destruction intruding. It was a nice image.

And she prayed they survived the mission and lived long enough to see it become reality.

Because, unfortunately, as much as she wanted that reality, G.R.I.D. and Thomas Kunz himself were equally intent on a different reality: one in which Morgan and Jackson were dead.

On the commander's one-to-ten scale, she had ranked the danger on this leg of the mission at ten. The best it got was an eight, and that was only if the CIA had failed to pinpoint the location of Kunz's hideaway compound by the time Morgan and Jackson arrived in Honoria.

If Kunz had bugged out, then the risks to everyone involved diminished. But if the CIA had been successful, then the danger spiked off the charts. The bean counters were so convinced of it that they'd expanded their thinking and tagged the entire island chain as the kill zone.

The plane landed, its tires squeaking on the landing strip.

Morgan swallowed hard. Eight or ten? Danger increased or decreased? Were they in or out of the Kunz-defined kill zone?

Soon, they'd know . . .

CHAPTER 14

Daniel Gaston had short and spiky blond hair, blue eyes, and a forgettable face, which was an asset in CIA circles generally, and in Gaston's covert assignments for the CIA specifically.

Privately, before boarding the first flight, Morgan had explained to Jackson that Gaston had worked with the S.A.S.S. on previous missions in the Middle East and on the U.S.-Mexico border case Darcy had handled last July. One never talked openly about business matters in public places, especially when anyone could be trying to intercept their every word for the purpose of information or intelligence gathering. With everyone being suspect, it was far too risky.

Morgan recognized Gaston on sight. Having seen his

photo on the "Active" wall in the S.A.S.S. headquarters bunker at Regret, she headed in his direction.

"Dr. Cabot," Gaston said. "Good to see you."

"You, too, Daniel," she said, then handled the introductions.

Gaston and Jackson shook hands.

"This way," Gaston said, motioning them through a throng of people, some reuniting with loved ones and others boarding the plane. Most were tourists, gauging by their well-rested looks.

Gaston led them to a white Land Rover and opened the door. Jackson crawled into the back, and Morgan slid onto the passenger's seat beside Gaston. Hands on the wheel, he started the engine and pulled out. There was no traffic, and one turn off the main thoroughfare took them on a bumpy, dusty dirt path heading toward the shore. "We'll have to take a boat from here," he said.

"How long will it take to get to Tavanipupu?" Morgan asked, rolling with the pitch on the rutted road.

"We aren't going there," he said. "We're heading farther out."

"Why?" Jackson asked, gripping the hand bar beside him.

"Late yesterday, we got a positive ID on Judy Meyer. Apparently, she likes to shop with the locals on Tavanipupu. One of the vendors there made a delivery for her. This morning, we got on it."

"Was he there?" No need to mention Kunz's name.

"No. He bugged out."

Difficulty odds just dropped from ten to eight. Commander Drake would have mixed emotions about that. She'd be glad Morgan and Jackson weren't facing Kunz, but she'd be upset as hell that Kunz was still on the loose, wreaking havoc and plotting terrorist attacks.

Gaston glanced over. "Looks like he departed within the last twenty-four hours, though it might have been thirty-six—we've gotten conflicting stories on that. But he left behind plenty you'll want to see," Gaston assured her. "We've got the area manned and secured."

"What was the area?" Morgan asked. "A G.R.I.D. compound or—"

"No, no compound," Gaston quickly glanced at her, then darted his gaze back to the road. "Though it appears as if he had an operations command center up and running there."

"So this place was just somewhere he went to hide when the heat got too hot."

"It's a little more than that." Gaston's eyes lighted, and he let out a low whistle. "A 15,000-square-foot resort built for one," Gaston said. "Amazing place."

"Oh, man. We found his . . . did we find Thomas Kunz's private home?" Jackson asked, incredulous.

"Looks like it was exactly that." Gaston's smile touched his eyes.

Morgan sensed it was so but remained totally perplexed. "And he just walked out and left everything?"

"No, he didn't do that," Gaston said, grimacing. "He made sure we wouldn't get much in the way of personal data on him. But the house itself tells us far more about him than we knew up to this point."

"So the place is empty?" Morgan attempted to clarify.

"Not exactly." Gaston hit a deep rut, rolled across it, tossing the Land Rover into a steep pitch.

Morgan grabbed the door and held on until they leveled out. "Then what exactly did he leave behind?"

"Something personal, Dr. Cabot. You'll get what I mean soon enough," Gaston assured her. "You have to see it yourself to understand . . ."

Morgan supposed she would have to see it for herself, considering Daniel Gaston was being about as clear as mud.

Gaston pulled the boat into a cove and putted alongside a long wooden pier. Near the shore, a man he hadn't introduced, seated at the bow of the boat, jumped out and tied off to the pier. Then Gaston cut the engine. "We're here," he said. "This is it."

Three other boats were anchored in the water inside the cove, and a speedboat was tied off on the other side of the pier opposite them. Jackson looked at them and then at Gaston. "I take it all of these are ours."

He nodded.

"The divers, too?"

That observation surprised Gaston. "Yeah."

"Where are they?"

Gaston stepped out of the boat and hopped onto the wooden planked pier. "Under us." He turned around and looked back at Jackson, who held Morgan's arm while she stepped ashore. "Kunz favors underwater compounds, and since we didn't find any signs of one on the island itself . . ."

Morgan grunted. Kunz had gone underground to build compounds in Iran, and Kate had the memories to prove it. He also had done that on the Texas border with Mexico. His going underground here was definitely possible.

They walked past four men stationed above them at various points along the shore, then took the stairs up the steep cliff from the beach. Gaston didn't speak to the men—obviously protecting their identities—so Morgan acknowledged them with nods. One appeared to be local from his tanned skin, clothing, and distinct facial features. The other three were decidedly American and not trying to hide it.

None of them nodded back, a signal that officially they weren't there, and a nonverbal directive to forget that she had seen them. She glanced at Jackson and sensed he knew the drill.

At the top of the steps, the house came into view. It was breathtaking and huge, its terraces landscaped beautifully with palms and tropical flowers. As they drew closer, Morgan saw the residence was made of brick. Shocking to see white bricks here. Really shocking, when everything had to be brought in by boat or . . . "Is there a landing strip on this island?"

"Oh, yeah, and a helicopter pad," Gaston said. "Kunz could depart the fix at a moment's notice by sea or air, fixed wing or rotor."

They walked past a viewing post and then onto a terrace. Not so much as a leaf littered it. White columns stretched up to the roof of the house, and Morgan moved under the overhang, blissfully grateful for the shady reprieve from the relentless sun. "I'd like to walk through."

"Sure," Gaston said. "The area you most want to see is at the dead center of the house, down a level. It's secured."

Morgan nodded to acknowledge she'd heard him and then walked through each room, opening her senses to whatever input might come. Yawning space. Soft colors, light pastels, luxurious lighting fixtures, and palm-leafed ceiling fans. It had all the promise of a very elegant, expensive, and surprisingly livable home. But not one stick of furniture remained in it. Not so much as a trash bag twist tie in the kitchen cabinets, or a smudge of toothpaste in the bowl of the bathroom sink.

"Professionally cleaned," Jackson said, walking up

beside her. "From all appearances, they did a very thorough job of it, too."

"I don't expect his men dared to disappoint him on this assignment." Kunz would have had their heads on platters.

"Oh, yeah. He'd definitely find that offensive and let them know it in no uncertain terms." Jackson looked out the window. "Great view."

They looked at the cove, with its aquamarine water, pristine white sandy beach, and quiet gentle breezes rippling through the lush green foliage and brightly colored flowers.

"It's beautiful," Morgan said, "and very soothing." She kept walking, but there was little to learn of the man in his empty house, and she couldn't pick up anything of note in the way of residual imprints because there'd been too many others through it before her. She had sensed Kunz here, but he had been at ease then and not tense.

He'd known that he had plenty of time to leave before they found his home.

"Okay, I'm ready," she told Gaston. "Take me to the hub."

She followed him to the center of the house and through a guarded doorway that she had assumed on her walk-through was a closet. It wasn't. It opened into a round room with a five-foot border of walkway. Inside the border, a wide, ornate spiral staircase led down to the floor below. "His remote operations center." she speculated.

Gaston nodded.

Two armed men stood at the foot of the stairs.

Morgan looked around. It was a large underground area, at least eighty by eighty. Bare floors, bare white walls, no windows . . . and no support beams. In every visible corner, something had been removed from the walls near the ceiling. Morgan paused, focused. *Security cameras.* She stepped off the stairs and into the room.

A twenty-foot-long, stark white, curved desk that had been hidden by the stairs came into view. Surprise flickered through her. "He left a desk?"

"It's built into the wall," Gaston said.

They walked over to the desk. Two more guards manned it, one at each end, and with each step closer, Morgan felt her dread grow stronger and stronger—so strong it nearly stole her breath. "Jackson." She looked over at him. "Prepare."

He nodded, letting her know that he'd picked up on whatever was coming, too. His expression stiffened, grew more guarded and closed.

Morgan moved around to face the desk. Shock pumped through her, and she understood the sensation of dread completely.

At her side, Jackson gasped. "Bruce."

"It's not him." Morgan clasped his arm. "Bruce is at Providence," she reminded Jackson. "He's safe."

Gaston darted a gaze from the dead man to Jackson, then to Morgan. "Holy shit, he's his brother?"

"His brother's double," she whispered.

"I should have picked up on the resemblance," Gaston said, looking truly repentant. "I'm sorry, man." He backed off to give them space and a moment to recover.

Jackson rubbed at his neck, blew out a shaky breath. "It's not him. It's not Bruce." Jackson worked through the shock of seeing what appeared to be his brother, dead, propped into a sitting position on the floor against the wall of the desk with his throat slashed wide open and a photograph pinned to his chest.

Morgan moved closer to get a better look at the photograph. Kunz, Judy Meyer, and Laura at the festival, standing side by side and smiling. "Look at his hand," she told Jackson.

Kunz was wearing the commemorative coin ring.

"There's another photograph, Dr. Cabot," Gaston said, rejoining them near the body.

Morgan looked back at Gaston. "Where is it?"

He nodded and gripped the double's shoulder, leaned his body forward. "Nailed between his shoulder blades."

Squelching a bolt of revulsion, Morgan moved to the side of the body and then closer to the desk for a better view of the picture.

Kunz was standing alone in the exact spot he'd stood with Judy Meyer and Laura in the previous photograph.

"Meyer must have taken this one," Jackson said from the other side of the body. "Kunz is still smiling."

More interested in his hand, Morgan glanced at it. The commemorative coin ring was still on his finger.

And next to it, on his pinky, was Laura's emerald.

Jackson noticed. Outrage radiated from him and flooded her, and Morgan met his gaze.

His voice vibrated with tumultuous emotions—*anger, regret, outrage, remorse*—that didn't show on his face. "I need your cell phone, Morgan."

Raw-nerved, Jackson needed to talk to Bruce. To hear his voice and be reassured to the marrow of his bones that his brother really was alive and well—and safe. Understanding completely, she fished the phone from her purse and passed it to him. "Go through Darcy," she said softly. "It'll be quicker."

He nodded, glanced at Gaston, and then went upstairs and, she assumed, outside.

"Rough business," Gaston said, his hands in his pockets. "Seeing your brother dead like that."

Morgan thought he'd heard her earlier, but obviously he hadn't. "It's not his brother."

Gaston frowned and then realized what was going on. "Another body double?"

She didn't confirm or deny it, but she didn't have to; he'd worked with the S.A.S.S. on previous missions and had run into this situation before.

"I'm done here," she said. "I expect you're having forensics run a thorough check of the premises and surrounding grounds, just in case his cleaners missed anything."

"Every square inch," he assured her. "But it's an exercise in futility. Kunz is into redundancy. If the first one missed, the five who cleaned after the first didn't."

"Maybe we'll get lucky on something." She turned away from the body. There were no marks. He had been caught off guard, taken totally by surprise. "Did Judy Meyer leave with Kunz?"

Gaston nodded. "He hired a couple of locals to help empty the house. They reported that she was on the plane."

"Maybe she wasn't as careful," Morgan said, holding out a little hope for clues to where they'd gone from here.

"He'd cover for her," Gaston said, resigned to finding nothing at all. "He doesn't leave his back open to anyone else, not even to the woman sharing his bed."

She hoped Gaston was wrong about that, but her intuition warned her he was right on target. Kunz was even more anal about covering his tracks than Colonel Gray was about monitoring events at Providence.

Gaston followed her up the stairs. "Are you ready to go back to the airport?"

"As soon as Jackson gets off the phone," she said, not at all eager to get back on a jet for the next twenty-five-plus hours. She was still vibrating from the last flight. "Unless there's something else we need to see . . ."

Gaston denied it. "We've videoed Homeland Security and Home Base," he said. "The rest is just housekeeping."

"What about interviewing household staff?"

"If there was any, he took them with him. This place is all that's on the island. Most of the folks around thought it was uninhabited like all the others around it."

"They had no idea he was here, or how long he'd been coming here?"

"None," Gaston confirmed. "He and Judy had been spotted island-hopping, but no one knew where they landed except for the one local who delivered some items Judy had bought in Honoria."

That didn't fit. "I'm shocked Kunz let him come here and leave alive."

"Kunz wasn't here. Just Judy, and she blindfolded the man as soon as the boat departed shore at Honoria, so he couldn't track their route and come back. But he has a thing about checking his watch, and he knew when they'd left and arrived. He also had a keen sense of the direction he was going."

"How did he track that?"

"By the angle of the sun on him." Gaston smiled.

"Simple still works." Morgan smiled back.

"Works well, too. He was scared to come back here on his own, so he avoided it, and whenever Judy came into his shop, he stayed out of sight. She scared him, and he had the feeling that if she saw him again, she'd kill him."

"He was probably right about that."

"I'd bet on it," Gaston said. "Especially if she was foolish enough to tell Kunz she'd brought the man here."

"Definitely." Morgan totally agreed. "But he got you here."

"Directed us straight to it," he said. "Not a single false turn."

"Mmm," she murmured. "Since there's nothing else on the island, Kunz is going to play hell trying to sell."

"He won't sell it," Gaston said. "We'll post some folks here for a while because the honchos will consider it prudent, but I'm telling you, Dr. Cabot, there's no way in hell Kunz will ever return to this place."

All this and it'd be empty until it crumbled and the island reclaimed it. Maybe they could make a mental hospital or something out of it. "I wonder where he will be?"

"Don't we all?" Gaston grunted. "Wherever it is, I'm sure it'll be far, far away . . ."

CHAPTER 15

Forty-six hours later, Morgan and Jackson sat at the Providence base hospital, across the conference room table from Jazie and Taylor Lee. Commander Drake occupied her usual place at the helm, and Dr. Joan Foster sat at the foot.

"So, as it turns out," Sally Drake said, "Laura was Kunz's target all along and Bruce was incidental to everything that happened, a target of opportunity that presented itself along the way."

"Yes," a weary Morgan told the commander. "There's only one thing that I can't figure out, and that's where Bruce went on the side trip he made after leaving Iraq and before showing up at home. Three days are totally unaccounted for."

"I've accounted for Bruce's whereabouts during that

time," the commander said. "He was on a side trip, as you suspected."

"Where?" Jackson asked, tense yet again.

"The Pentagon," Drake said. "He went to meet with General Shaw and Secretary Reynolds."

Surprise rifled through Jackson, and it was apparent in his voice. "He reported it?"

When Commander Drake nodded, relief washed through Jackson like a flood.

"He recognized Kunz from a photo Laura had emailed to his cell phone. One of her, Judy, and Kunz at the festival." A tender look settled in Sally Drake's eyes, proving that she knew what she next said would mean to him. "Knowing he could lose his job, Bruce reported it, Jackson."

Morgan's throat thickened; her chest went tight. Bruce had taken responsibility and done the right thing, knowing that he could lose his career as a result. He had tried to protect the U.S. and his wife by reporting it, aware that he'd probably lose his security clearance and that without one he couldn't serve in his position.

Jackson sat stunned, jaw slightly agape. Morgan understood why. A lifelong cycle of protecting Bruce, and Bruce letting him do it, had been broken.

Bruce had stood alone, and he'd protected his brother, keeping him out of harm's way and off Kunz's radar, too. It didn't take an intuitive to know that would mean the world to Jackson, who had known so little nurturing in his life.

"We can't know the official reason for that side trip, of course," the commander said, though everyone at the table knew exactly why he had made it. "But his time and actions are accounted for, and the Secretary and General Shaw consider that aspect of the case unremarkable."

They'd spared Bruce. Secretary Reynolds and General Shaw had pulled him out of the ashes like a phoenix.

Taylor Lee pursed her lips. "So Laura went to this festival to visit her high school friend, Judy Meyer, who happened to turn out to be Kunz's significant other, and they took this photo that Laura emailed Bruce on her cell phone, likely from the island."

"According to Bruce via Darcy," the commander said, "Laura emailed the photo to him from the island on Judy's cell because her phone had no service in that area."

Morgan felt a little ripple of pleasure. "So we have Judy's cell phone, picked up from Bruce's phone."

"Don't get excited," the commander said. "Judy dumped the phone right after Laura used it."

"Before Bruce returned from Iraq." Jazie joined the dialogue. "Bruce recognized Kunz and told Laura who Kunz was—the mastermind of G.R.I.D.—and then he left Iraq and went to the Pentagon to inform the powers that be."

"Which means Laura already knew the man living with her as Bruce wasn't Bruce," Joan piped in. "Otherwise, she wouldn't have emailed Bruce at all."

"How did she do that?" Taylor Lee asked. "Email to

Bruce gets picked up by the double."

Commander Drake answered. "Bruce and Laura had unused accounts that they routinely checked but never from home or work or their own computers. Those wouldn't have registered on Kunz's henchmen's radar."

Jackson stepped in. "So realizing Bruce wasn't Bruce, Laura e-mailed using that secret account to see what was going on and what she should do. Kunz's henchmen caught on because they were already monitoring her every move."

"Yes. Laura knew the man in her home wasn't Bruce," the commander confirmed. "She and the real Bruce were trying to figure out what to do to neutralize the body double when the real Bruce received the photo and recognized Kunz."

"Makes sense," Morgan agreed. "Neutralize the double without costing Bruce his job—"

"And his ass." Jackson cut in. "Laura would have been terrified Kunz would kill Bruce. I'm surprised she didn't kill the double herself and bury the body in her backyard."

"She actually considered that," the commander said. "Bruce nixed it, thank God, or they might both be dead."

"Laura figured Kunz would kill both of them," Taylor Lee added. "You know the bastard had to try to blackmail her into getting information from Bruce. He was too rich a target to blow off. Even if he was just one of opportunity."

"No, Taylor Lee. I don't think so," Morgan said. "Kunz could get bio information in other ways. What he feared most from Laura was that she would reveal his island hideaway. He put a lot into that place, and my guess is that every time we've gotten close, that's where he's gone aground until things cooled off. Without a map and a lot of luck, we never would have located him there."

"True," she conceded.

"So Bruce served a double's purpose, which was . . ." Jazie led, looking at Morgan to fill in for her.

Joan did it instead. "To encourage Laura to do whatever Kunz wanted, and to make her keep her mouth shut about his retreat."

Morgan held up a fingertip. "And to see if Laura would keep her mouth shut about it. That's why Kunz inserted Bruce's double with her. To determine whether or not she realized what she knew, and then if she did, what she'd do about it."

"Only Bruce's double didn't pass the wife test," the commander said. "Laura noted differences in the men, in ways a wife would notice. That's when she discovered the real Bruce was in Iraq and in Kunz's crosshairs."

Jackson stepped in again. "She knew if she went to the authorities, Bruce and his job would be jeopardy. And she didn't come to me because she didn't want to pull me into the kill zone."

He was right about that, though Morgan suspected that had been a point argued between Laura and Bruce. Laura had wanted to tell Jackson, and Bruce hadn't.

"So Laura did what she did best," Joan Foster said,

realization lighting in her eyes. "She protected Bruce."

Morgan nodded. "She left the coin in my shoe so I would find it and put it together with the coin she left on her camera so I'd pick up on the importance of the film."

Jazie let out a near wail. "She didn't dare risk having the film developed. Kunz would get it, and you wouldn't have been able to connect the dots. Oh, my God. Laura knew Thomas Kunz was going to kill her."

"I'm sure she did," Morgan said, feeling it to the marrow of her bones. "Though I believe she thought Kunz was after Bruce and his classified information. I don't think she realized that what she knew was even more valuable to Kunz."

"His location," Taylor Lee said.

"Right." Morgan looked at Joan. "You got us thinking in that direction, when you said Kunz never went for a secondary target. He hit his primary target every time."

"It's still true," she said. "I've never known him to do anything else."

"But why did he take her emerald ring?" Jazie said. "Why is he showing it to us even now in the photo he left on the body double's back?"

Morgan looked at Jackson who nodded, and then told them, "It was a warning to Bruce. Kunz knew from the body double that Laura was behaving strangely and expressing worry, and that cued Kunz that she'd likely discovered the real Bruce was in Iraq and not in her home."

"Intercepted phone calls, email, any of a thousand ways to pick up information that basic," the commander said.

"Exactly. So Kunz pressed Bruce, who'd always been protected by someone else, knowing he'd do the same thing again because that's his normal reaction. People stick to habit and do what comes naturally. Except that Bruce didn't react normally: he left Iraq."

Taylor Lee grunted. "Which made it necessary for Kunz to immediately kill Laura to keep her from talking."

Jackson nodded. "But Kunz knew, even if we didn't, that Bruce had broken a lifelong habit and gone to the Pentagon and told the honchos the truth. Then he put Laura, thus the double, on notice that he was coming home. Kunz steps in, orders the double to leave the house and lie low until Kunz issues further orders. Bruce returns home, and Kunz's assassins move in, kill Laura, and frame Bruce for her murder, which negates his credibility in everything he's said and done and gets them both out of Kunz's way."

Sally Drake sat with her head propped on her hand, following the conversation. "Bruce had to be under direct orders from General Shaw and the Secretary of Defense to not say anything to anyone, including Laura. There were forty-six doubles unaccounted for still out there in high-level, sensitive positions, including his own."

"I agree that they ordered him to keep silent, Commander," Jackson said. "The assassins expected you to cut Bruce loose when his DNA didn't match the murderers.

You didn't, but obviously Kunz didn't know it. He ordered the double to get the film—he would be taken as Bruce, with every right to enter the property—but the film was gone. So Kunz had the double destroy the photo lab to keep us from getting the photos, and also to frame Bruce for another crime, to wreck his credibility and get him out of Kunz's way."

"Then Kunz retrieves the double, brings him to the island and kills him," Taylor Lee said, "because, well, what good is an exposed double when his counterpart is going to be sitting in jail for blowing up a government facility?"

"True," Morgan said. "And this probably would have ended there except Kunz learned the photos were safe, his haven retreat had been exposed, and we were very close to proving Bruce hadn't killed Laura. So he cut loose the G.R.I.D. assassins on all of us."

"And we killed two of them," Jackson said.

"Could have been three," Taylor Lee told the commander. "And it should have been after what the bastards did to my Saab, but Jackson wouldn't let me shoot him." She paused and frowned. "Has that jerk said anything worth hearing, anyway?"

"Payton," the commander said, "has been extremely cooperative. The problem is that he doesn't know much. No one under Kunz beyond his operation commander and his second-in-command ever knows anything more than the essentials required to fulfill their specific duties."

"Well, I hope he'll at least be in jail a while."

"Twenty-five years," the commander said. "Maybe longer."

"I guess that'll have to do."

Taylor Lee's frown proved she didn't think the sentence was sufficient, but then she was still pissed off about her car. Morgan bit back a smile. "File a claim on the Saab, Taylor Lee. It's covered."

"It is?" She looked stunned. "My insurance guy said it wasn't."

"It's covered." Morgan smiled at her, and the commander nodded to verify it.

Someone tapped at the door.

"Enter," the commander called out, a smile in her voice.

Bruce walked in.

"Welcome, Captain Stern." Commander Drake stood up and extended her hand.

Bruce shook it, his gaze on Jackson, who stood and embraced him and clapped his shoulder with such force it would have knocked Morgan off her feet. She watched, her eyes tearing up.

Bruce pulled away from Jackson and looked at the group seated around the table. "I wanted to thank all of you," Bruce said, his voice catching. "For what you did for Laura and me."

Jackson looked at his brother. "I'm sorry I doubted

you, bro."

"I depended on it, and it was justified," Bruce said, then looked at Morgan. "I won't ever forget what you did." His eyes filmed over, and he blinked hard. "Laura trusted you completely. I wish I'd been as wise." He cleared his throat. "I didn't think Kunz would kill her. She and Judy were such close friends, you know?"

Kunz would have killed his mother, anyone, to keep his sanctuary intact, but telling Bruce that would serve no constructive purpose, so Morgan kept it to herself.

"Well." The commander stood up. "I'd say that puts this one to bed." She looked at Bruce. "I'm glad you're out of jail, Bruce, and I am so sorry for your loss. Laura was a brave woman and totally devoted to you. I hope there's some small solace in knowing that."

"Thank you, Commander," he said. "Maybe in time."

She nodded and repeated, "Maybe in time."

Jackson, Bruce, and the commander shared a few words.

Morgan sniffed, and Joan passed her a damp tissue. "Sorry, it's the only one I've got."

Her eyes were red-rimmed, too. "At least you can blame your pregnancy. Raging hormones and all that."

"Honey, look around the table. Even Dr. Vargus is misty eyed. It's called being human."

Morgan glanced around and gave Joan a teary-eyed smile. Tears streamed down Jazie's face. Taylor Lee was dry-eyed and actually smiling, though whether it was because of the tender moment or because her Saab would be replaced, Morgan didn't hazard a guess. "Human. Sometimes it's too easy to forget."

"Don't worry." Joan clasped her arm. "We'll remind each other."

"Yeah, we will." Morgan smiled at her.

"Did the commander warn you that Kate is giving Amanda's bridal shower?"

Laughing, Morgan nodded.

"Let me walk you out, Bruce," the commander told him.

"When will I be able to bury Laura?" he asked. "Do you know yet?" He blinked rapidly. "I can hardly stand to think of her being in the morgue."

"I know." She patted his arm. "The ME just released her body, so you're free to proceed. Just let him know what funeral home you want to use after you've made the arrangements."

Bruce looked back at Jackson. "Will you be here a while, Jax?"

Jackson nodded. "For as long as you need me."

He sent Jackson a bittersweet smile etched with relief.

"Well, I'm going car shopping," Taylor Lee said.

"I'll go with you." Jazie grabbed her purse. "They're having a scratch-and-dent sale at Toyota. We could see—"

Taylor guffawed. "You've got to be kidding me. A

scratch-and-dent sale? Have you lost your mind?"

"From the storm," Jazie said, clearly at a loss for the cause of Taylor Lee's objections.

"I will *not* buy a car from a scratch-and-dent sale, Jazie Craig. Not in this life or the next. Forget it."

They walked past Morgan and Jackson and into the hall. "Oh, you're such a snob, Taylor Lee . . ."

Joan rolled her gaze, paused beside Jackson. "It was a pleasure, Captain."

He shook her hand. "Thank you, Joan. I'm grateful for everything you've done."

"Yes." She patted their clasped hands. "I know you are. I've been there, too." She had relied on the S.A.S.S. to spare her and her family two years ago, just as Jackson had in this situation. "It gets better . . . easier to swallow." She rubbed her stomach. "Oh, geez. You'll have to excuse me."

"What's wrong, Joan?"

She winced. "My water just broke."

"The baby's coming?" Jackson sounded mortified.

Joan nodded. "Commander, could you help me waddle over to Admitting."

"It's not time yet."

"I know," she said. "The baby, however, doesn't. He's coming."

"You!" Commander Drake barked at an orderly coming down the hall. "Wheelchair. Here. Now."

The guy looked shell-shocked, until his gaze lighted

on Joan.

"The baby?"

She nodded, and he smiled.

"Move your ass, soldier!" Commander Drake shouted. "If she has this baby in the hall, you're going to be pulling extra duty until the boy graduates from college."

He took off running.

Less than two minutes later, he returned with a wheelchair and two nurses. They loaded Joan in the chair and then rolled her down the hallway. The commander went with her, barking orders, and dialing her cell phone. "Simon? Simon, get over to the hospital . . . *stat*. Joan's in labor . . ."

Morgan smiled, watching them go, and when they disappeared around the corner, she looked up at Jackson and smiled. "You okay?"

"Yeah. Just remind me never to piss her off." He lifted Morgan's hand and brought it to his lips.

She chuckled. "Commander Drake gets a little excited about family matters."

"I noticed with her reaction to Bruce." He lowered their hands and they started walking out of the hospital. "A new record," he glanced at his watch. "We've been together, and it's been at least forty hours since anyone's taken a shot at me . . . including you."

"Are you going to hold that over my head for the rest of my life?"

"Absolutely not," he said emphatically. "Just for forty or fifty years—you know, until it wears thin."

She exaggerated a frown and held it so he wouldn't miss it. "You're putting your forty-first hour in serious jeopardy," she warned him. "We'll see how it goes, then take a longer-term look."

"Fine." He grinned. "But we should hurry and celebrate this success before something else happens and we have to start a new countdown."

"Stop it, you." Morgan elbowed him in the ribs. "Let's go clear our heads."

"Anything you say," he told her, clasping their hands. "I never argue with a smart, armed woman."

"That's a sound policy." Morgan gripped his hand, and they walked outside. "I strongly suggest you hang onto it." And finally she gave him the words. "And me."

He stopped right outside the door. "You've decided what you want, then?"

Morgan summoned her courage and looked him right in the eye. "For now."

"Now's good." He nodded. "Now works."

And hand in hand, they walked out of the kill zone.

EPILOGUE

Two months later

"Morgan!" Jackson came in through the back door, shouting for her. "Where are you, honey?"

"Right here." She walked into the kitchen, dropped the cell phone on the counter, and let herself be swept up in Jackson's arms. He nuzzled her neck, and she giggled. "Whatever's happened, I like it."

"I got it," he told her, his eyes shining. "The transfer to Providence."

"Oh, Jackson!" She squealed her delight, squeezed his neck in a heartfelt hug. "When do you come?"

"Three weeks." He untangled her hair from the button on his collar. "And I'm on leave until then."

"Awesome, honey," she said. It was fabulous news. "No more commuting between Magnolia Beach and Biloxi for either of us."

He whirled in a circle, holding her up off the floor. "They created a slot for me. I'm working directly under Colonel Gray."

Commander Drake's nemesis. "Oh, boy." The pissing contest would remain on for the foreseeable future. But to have Jackson here with her, Morgan would gladly endure it. "We should do something special to celebrate."

He nipped at her neck, snuggled her suggestively. "I'm ready when you are."

She laughed again. "Great idea, but lousy timing."

"Why?" He let her down on the kitchen floor.

"Bruce is coming over for dinner." She reached into the fridge for a soda.

Jackson snatched it, put it back, and then passed her a bottle of water. "Drink this instead."

Morgan gave in gracefully. "My kidneys love you."

"I love them, too," he said, peeking into the pots on the stove. "Mmm, looks good."

"It's starch," she said in a droll tone. "You'll love it." She plucked a grape from the fruit bowl. "Check the fridge door. We have other news, too."

He walked over, looked, and paused on the wedding invitation. "Amanda and Mark. Well, they're all set, eh?"

"It's to us," Morgan said, beaming. "Our first official joint invitation." *They were a couple in the eyes of their friends and coworkers.*

"We should frame it, hang it on the wall, or something."

He was trying to support the significance. Morgan smiled. "I think we're good without the frame, but I'll keep it in mind."

He looked to something stuck up on the fridge door beside it. "*Kate* is giving Amanda's shower." He guffawed. "You've got to be kidding me."

Morgan slipped on an oven mitt, fully appreciating his reaction. "I thought I told you."

"I don't think so, but you might have during the ordeal and I just forgot it."

The ordeal. It was a safe way to refer to the time of Laura's death, Bruce's arrest, and all the trouble with Thomas Kunz without reliving every event all over all again. "I might not have," she said, really unsure herself.

He rubbed his neck. "I think you better be armed for that wedding shower," he said. "Maybe wear my bomb-squad gear."

"Jackson," she admonished.

"Hey, you know as well as I do that Kate likes nothing better than to blow up stuff."

Morgan couldn't deny it and chuckled. "Commander Drake warned me a couple days ago. The cake is shaped like a brick of C-4." He grunted and grabbed a grape. "Be grateful she didn't use the real thing."

Morgan laughed, but his point was valid. Kate did

love to blow things up. "She is planning fireworks."

"For a bridal shower?" He arched an eyebrow. "Even I know that's not . . . done. But it should make it memorable." He walked toward the door.

"She's trying so hard to make it special," Morgan said. "No one has the heart to say anything."

"They'd damn well better not," he said. "If Kate's doing it and it isn't her way, Amanda and Mark won't like it a bit." He opened the back door. "Objecting and dealing with Kate is bad. But dealing with her and Mark and Amanda? Who's that crazy?"

Interesting take. One Morgan hadn't considered. But he was right. "Where are you going?"

"To stick an extra fire extinguisher in the back of the Jeep while I'm thinking about it." He shrugged. "Just in case Kate's a little *too* enthusiastic."

Morgan started to tell him that wouldn't be necessary and then thought better of it. "Couldn't hurt."

He walked back and pecked a kiss on her lips. "You're awesome, you know."

Morgan smiled, her heart full. "Damn right."

Her cell phone rang.

Jackson lifted it from the counter and answered. "Cabot's phone."

"Jackson?"

"Hi, Commander Drake," he said, recognizing her voice. "How are you?"

They chatted for a moment, and then Jackson said, "She's right here. No, no problem. I'm on my way out." He passed the phone.

"Hello." Morgan watched him duck into the garage and shut the door.

"I was hoping we'd get a bit more of a break," Sally Drake told her. "But I guess Kunz is settled into his new crib, wherever it might be."

Kunz. Making trouble again. "What's up, Commander?"

"I just got a call from our friend Gaston," she said. "He thinks double number forty-five has just shown up. I need to activate the S.A.T. report ASAP."

She wanted the team at Regret as soon as possible. Morgan shot a wistful look over at the stove. So much for a quiet family dinner. Jackson and Bruce would have to enjoy it without her.

"Darcy will contact Taylor Lee and Jazie. I need you here right away."

Morgan grabbed her purse and headed for the garage. "Yes, ma'am."

The line went dead. She folded her phone and looked for Jackson. He was straightening up at the back of the Jeep. "Activated. I've got to go right away. Ten more minutes and the stuff in the oven is done. Watch the pots. Don't let anything burn."

He opened her car door. "I'll manage."

"Yeah, you'll burn everything and tell Bruce I did it."

"I swear I won't—unless it's absolutely necessary. He's bringing Laura's recipe for peach cobbler. If I have to lie to get it, you're toast."

"Well, considering how much you love her cobbler, I'll make the sacrifice, but only if I have to—and, Jackson, it will cost you."

"I'll pay. Anywhere. Anytime."

"Oh, yes. You surely will." She smiled and planted a quick kiss on his lips. "I'll be careful, and if I have to deploy, I'll call."

He closed the door, stepped back, and gave her a smart salute. "Be careful, and tell Taylor Lee no cracking anyone in the head with beer bottles—use the gun."

Morgan winked. "I will." She depressed the garage door button, and it opened. Backing out, she called, "Jackson?"

Heading into the house, he stopped and turned back. "You're awesome," she yelled out to him.

He smiled. "Damn straight."

She smiled back, pulled out of the driveway, and headed down the street, her cell phone ringing. She answered it. "Cabot."

"Morgan, did you get the call?" Taylor Lee asked. "He's at it again."

"I heard." Morgan sped up. "I'm on my way . . ."

LORI G. ARMSTRONG
SNOW BLIND

The frigid winter months are mighty slow in the PI biz for Julie Collins and her partner, Kevin Wells—until the duo is hired by a young woman to investigate problems at her grandfather's assisted living facility, where they encounter lax security, unqualified healthcare personnel, and a shady senior volunteer organization.

Julie barely has time to delve deeper into the puzzling case before she reluctantly finds herself in an isolated cattle shelter on the Collins ranch with her father during a raging blizzard. There is no escape from her father or from the biting cold and bitter memories.

A missing hired ranch hand found dead on the ranch only complicates matters further. In trying to uncover the truth about the man's death, Julie is forced to wrestle with issues that make her question old wounds and new family loyalties.

Kevin's reckless involvement with their new client tests the bounds of professionalism, and Julie's relationship with Tony Martinez is strained, as he deals with power struggles within the Hombres organization, putting them both in jeopardy.

When the bodies and the snow piles up, Julie seems at odds with everyone, leaving her to wonder if she's being blinded to the cold, hard truths in her life by love . . . or by hate.

ISBN#9781933836591

US $7.95 / CDN $8.95

Mass Market Paperback / Mystery

Available Now

www.loriarmstrong.com

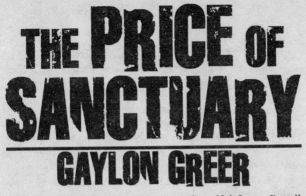

THE PRICE OF SANCTUARY

GAYLON GREER

Shelby Cervosier murdered three men in self-defense. Brutally beaten and raped by her captors, she does what any woman would do: kill or die. To avoid manslaughter charges, one involving a sadistic immigration officer, Shelby cooperates with the Caribbean Basin Task Force, a sleazy undercover government agency. In exchange for legal amnesty and political asylum in the United States, she completes a treacherous mission in Haiti. Now the agent who hired her wants her dead. Facing a contract on her life, Shelby flees with her younger sister, Carmen, to find safe haven in America with two assassins in close pursuit.

Hank Pekins accepts the contract. Like any competent killer-for-hire, he captures Shelby and escorts her . . . to his farm in a remote part of Colorado? That wasn't part of the deal. A killer kills. A paid assassin doesn't protect an illegal immigrant and turn her into his lover.

In a coldhearted profession where ruthlessness rules and emotions obscure an annihilator's judgment, passion has no clout at the critical moment the job must be executed. But Hank knows that his own days are numbered. Money cannot buy human life. Especially not the life of the woman he adores beyond reason.

The second assassin loves no one. Vlad, known as The Impaler, intends to complete his assignment. First, he will torture Shelby in his trademark style, and then he will kill her. No one, not even Hank, will stand in this psychopath's way. For Shelby Cervosier, what will be *The Price Of Sanctuary?*

ISBN#9781605420585

US $24.95 / CDN $27.95

Thriller / Hardcover

JUNE 2009

R. GARLAND GRAY
DARKSCAPE
THE REBEL LORD

Lord Lachlan de Douglas, a noble warrior lord, is heir to a Clan of Ancient Earth. Bold, rebellious, possessing strength and passion, he defends his clan from annihilation against a wretched war of masked vengeance and treacherous shadows. Until one day, a sudden horror alters his being, condemning him to a world of private anguish and torment.

Kimberly Kinsale, a diplomat's daughter, is a rare beauty motivated by honesty and integrity. Serving as a lieutenant in an elite combat fighter group aboard a war ship, she governs her life by the intrigue and lies of her commanding officer. A moment of lunacy and folly, a secret revealed, and Kimberly stumbles upon an unspeakable deception.

Now she must decide. Maintain her loyalty, or betray her Clan and ship for a Douglas enemy lord who can prove the truth--never knowing the battle for justice will take her through Lachlan's nightmare, a rage so deep, a suffering grounded in shame and pride, even when peace shines in sight.

For theirs is an unexpected passion, born in the fires of a shared need and desperate struggle. Kimberly must fight the sinister legacy of the matrix robots and trust the handsome enemy lord with her life, her heart, and her very soul. But as time slowly runs out, even an exquisite love may not be enough for salvation.

ISBN# 9781933836485
Mass Market Paperback / Sci-Fi Romance
US $7.95 / CDN $8.95
Available Now
www.rgarlandgray.com

KURS
PHIL BOWIE

Hotshot pilot John Hardin has a dark history.

He and his beautiful Cherokee girlfriend, Kitty Birdsong, are enjoying life in the Great Smoky Mountains when Nolan Rader, a former BATF agent, emerges from John's violent past and demands help to save his younger brother, Clint Rader, from the vengeance of an outlaw motorcycle gang known as the Satan's Ghosts.

A warped genius called Brain controls the Satan's Wraiths, an elite cadre of trained hitters within the worldwide gang, and Brain is privately conducting psychological research on Clint prior to killing him.

John must agree to help Nolan Rader or face exposure about his past—and the only way to find out what he must know to save Clint Rader is to infiltrate the biker gang. This leads him down a lethally dangerous path between the law and the outlaws, ranging from Canada to the Bahamas.

As events close in and the execution draws near, can John find some way to save Clint Rader before time runs out?

ISBN# 9781605420608
Mass Market Paperback / Suspense
US $7.95 / CDN $8.95
Available Now
www.philbowie.com

ANN MACELA
YOUR MAGIC OR MINE?

A battle over the "correct" way to cast spells is brewing in the magic practitioner community. Theoretical mathematician Marcus Forscher has created an equation, a formula to bring the science of casting into the twenty-first century. Botanist Gloriana Morgan, however, maintains spell casting is an art, as individual as each caster, and warns against throwing out old casting methods and forcing use of the new. A series of heated debates across the country ensues.

Enter the soulmate phenomenon, an ancient compulsion that brings practitioners together and has persuasive techniques and powers—the soulmate imperative—to convince the selected couple they belong together. Marcus and Gloriana, prospective soulmates, want nothing to do with each other, however. To make matters worse, their factions have turned to violence. One adherent in particular, blaming Marcus and Gloriana for the mess, wants to destroy the soulmates.

Something's got to give, or there will be dire consequences. The magic will work for them…or against them. But with two powerful practitioners bent on having their own way, which will it be—Your Magic Or Mine?—and if they don't unite, will either survive?

ISBN# 9781933836324
Mass Market Paperback / Paranormal Romance
US $7.95 / CDN $8.95
Available Now

TRAFFYCK

THE THRILLING SEQUEL TO CHERNOBYL MURDERS
MICHAEL BERES

In the underground of contemporary Eastern Europe lies a treacherous world contaminated by more than Chernobyl radiation and industrial waste. As communism collapsed, the foothold of social order tolerated a lurking subculture of child pornography and human trafficking. Traffyck, as they say.

A former runaway and Kiev nightclub stripper, Mariya Nemeth pulls herself from the dredges of wretchedness to attend school and marries a man she believes has abandoned his shady past. But Mariya learns her husband's past is still his present. He is murdered, a consequence of sex trade operations.

When she convinces Kiev private investigator Janos Nagy to take the case, Mariya discovers the real passion of her life, a lover immersed in the romance of Gypsy culture. Meanwhile, a world away in Chicago, Lazlo Horvath, having solved the Chernobyl Murders decades earlier, senses trouble brewing for his protégé and is drawn back to his homeland.

From Chicago's Humboldt Park to the Romanian Carpathian Mountains to the bleak abandonment of Ukraine, a frightening chain of events threatens countless lives when perversion, unacceptable to civilized society, is revealed.

Savvy, outraged, and linked by ancestry, Mariya, Janos, and Lazlo pierce the underbelly of Ukraine's sex trade where power is more important than human lives.

ISBN# 9781605421056
Hardcover / Thriller
US $24.95 / CDN $27.95
NOVEMBER 2009
www.michaelberes.com

michelle perry

The Three Motives for Murder

The small town of Coalmont, Tennessee is shattered when a car crash on graduation night leaves three of its teenagers dead and another three fighting for their lives. Four years later, the aftershocks still ripple through the town, and no one feels them more than Natasha Hawthorne, the young driver.

When someone targets the survivors of the horrific crash for murder, the obvious motive is revenge. But things aren't always what they seem, and the notion of revenge served cold doesn't ring true with Brady Simms, newly appointed police chief. To make things even more difficult, Brady ultimately finds himself standing squarely between the killer and his next victim, the woman who broke his heart four years ago.

As the killer escalates his attacks, Brady's only hope of saving the intended victims is to get into the mind of a sociopath. When the relative of the first victim makes a startling revelation, Brady reopens the investigation and what he finds will change all of their lives forever.

ISBN#9781932815801
Jewel Imprint: Emerald
US $6.99 / CDN $8.99
Available Now
www.michelleperry.com

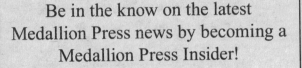

Be in the know on the latest Medallion Press news by becoming a Medallion Press Insider!

<u>As an Insider you'll receive:</u>

• Our FREE expanded monthly newsletter, giving you more insight into Medallion Press

• Advanced press releases and breaking news

• Greater access to all of your favorite Medallion authors

Joining is easy, just visit our Web site at <u>www.medallionpress.com</u> and click on the Medallion Press Insider tab.

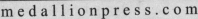

Want to know what's going on with
your favorite author or what new releases
are coming from Medallion Press?

Now you can receive breaking news,
updates, and more from Medallion Press
straight to your cell phone, e-mail, instant
messenger, or Facebook!

Sign up now at <u>www.twitter.com/MedallionPress</u>
to stay on top of all the happenings in and
around Medallion Press.

For more information
about other great titles from
Medallion Press, visit